Florida Boy

William Culyer Hall

FLORIDA BOY

Cover by Jon White

ISBN: 9781886104815

The Florida Historical Society Press
435 Brevard Avenue
Cocoa, FL 32922
http://myfloridahistory.org/fhspress

P·R·E·S·S

For Cheryl

Also by William Culyer Hall

September's Fawn

The Trouble with Panthers

Table of Contents

Author's Note and Acknowledgements

Florida Boy is entirely a work of fiction. Certain historical names are used for the sake of realism, but no character is based on or intended to depict an actual person. All episodes and dialogues between characters are products of the author's imagination.

The author would like to thank Mr. Andy Tucker for his graciously offered insight on cattle ranching in Florida. Thanks also to the people of the Florida Historical Society for deeming this novel worthy of publication.

Prologue

When she wakes her world entire is there with but a gentle cast of her eyes . . . eyes whose pupils are black pearls of melancholy innocence, depthless beauty. She sits upright reaching out her arms, stretching her youthful nakedness to life, her skin glowing alabaster in the meager light offered by the great room's lone window. A plethora of birds caged along the far wall stir with her, a sudden murmur of peeps and chirps, every beady eye fixed on her radiant self as if she is the sun to dawn their day. She stretches, eyeing the many species stepping and bobbing along their perches, opening and closing wings useless save for balance. When finally she lowers her arms, she sweeps covers from her legs and swings her feet to the wood floor. She stands and gently rocks her head from side to side, her dark mane swaying and brushing the small of her back, her figure still boyish but budding breasts portending the future. She turns slightly, noticing for the first time what roused her from sleep. "Good morning," she says, making no move to cover her nakedness from the gnome-like figure standing fixated on her person.

A hint of a smile flares briefly on the old man's face as he studies her with bleeding eyes. "And to you, my sweet Sarah," he says. He steps forward, leaving the double doors through which he's entered only to halt again directly beneath the pair of oil lamps that, save for the small window overlooking Joplin's main street, is the room's sole source of light. He raises his right hand to adjust wire-rimmed glasses on his hawkish nose, a hand whose nails are inordinately long and hooked sharply like claws of reptilian kind. A tailored tweed suit, gray and charcoal. Surgical shears clasped in his left hand. "I trust you slept well," he says, gliding past the girl and on to a cage housing a pair of fledgling robins.

"Yes," the girl answers. "I always sleep well." She moves soundlessly to the man's side and stands watching the young birds.

"Clear conscience," he says, consulting his coat pocket and extracting a single kid glove which he slips onto his right hand. He raises the gloved hand toward the cage door, turning the hand this way and that in the air as if admiring the fine leather now covering it. "The human touch can be lethal," he says. "One can never be too careful when handling new recruits."

"I know," the girl says.

The man looks at her. "Because I've told you so."

"Many times."

With the gloved hand he opens the cage door and reaches inside and captures one of the robins. He cups the bird, spreading its left wing with a finger, then brings the shiny scissors to bear, and with them, clips the tips of the gray feathers, saying, "The primaries. You clip them, and the creature is yours forever. It will never know flight."

The girl nods. "A bird that has flown is incorrigible."

The old man smiles. "Yes," he says. "It pleases me to know that you listen."

The girl grins. "Knowledge is good," she says, "but it may also be dangerous."

He nods. "Your memory is flawless."

"Flawless?"

He smiles. "Perfect."

She nods. "I will remember."

"I know you will." He flares the other wing and clips it and returns the bird to its cage. As he reaches to capture the other robin, there comes a knock at the double doors. "Miss Etta," he says. "Will you see her in?"

The girl Sarah turns and skips toward the doors, her bare feet fostering no audible record of her passage. At journey's end she reaches and pulls the leftmost door inward, stepping aside with a little bow and a wave of her free arm as though greeting royalty. "Won't you please come in," she says, her speech formal, almost mechanical, but her eyes betraying the sheer joy she feels within.

Beyond the door stands a woman whose skin is the color of strong coffee, a lady with smiling eyes and whose pale blue, ankle-

length dress is stretched taut over various regions of her moun-
tainous frame. In her right hand she holds a sheaf of hangered
clothes which she extends toward Sarah, saying: "Step your naked
self back, child. So I can show you what Mista King done bought
you."

Sarah backs away, opening the door wide. Miss Etta glides into
the room, her eyes cut to the old man who is just now returning the
second robin to its cage. "Mista King, you want to come see what
we picked out—fore she tries em on and all?"

King shuffles toward the pair while removing the glove from his
hand and pocketing it in his coat. He scarcely glances at the
dresses in passing, saying: "I'm sure they will be sufficient for our
little trip. Just instruct her in the particulars needed to avoid
embarrassment out there." He pauses at the door with his hand on
the knob. "I've got to check on business downstairs, but I'll return
shortly to see how you've done."

When Miss Etta nods her understanding, King opens the door
and steps out onto the landing at the head of the stairwell, allowing
faint piano music to waft into the room from somewhere below,
music abruptly silenced when he clicks the door shut and bolts it
from the outside.

Miss Etta rolls her eyes upon hearing the dull clank of the deadbolt. "Huh," she huffs. "Old man don't trust nobody." She flashes a
sharp look at Sarah. "Now don't you go repeatin nothin Etta say.
You do that, and old Etta be gone from here."

Sarah nods and reaches and pats Etta's great brown arm reassuringly. She then sidles close to the woman, captures the arm holding
the clothes with both hands and presses her cheek to its warmth.

Etta reaches with her other hand and caresses the girl's hair,
strokes it gently for a good many seconds. "I know," she says. "Old
Etta loves you, too." Etta then taps the girl's bare shoulder. "Now
get your naked self over to the bed. We got to see can we civilize
you. You cain't be takin no train ride naked as a jaybird."

Sarah cocks her head quizzically. "Civilize," she says.

Miss Etta pulls free of the girl's grasp and prods her toward the bed. "I know you don't know that word," she says, walking with the girl. "That's plain as the big nose on my face. Ain't your fault, though—your heathen ways. Mista King be anybody else, he be locked up for raisin you the way he done." Reaching the bedside, she lays the clothes down and turns to look Sarah in the eyes. "He ever touch you, child?"

Sarah shakes her head. "The human touch can be lethal."

Etta frowned. "He tell you that?"

Sarah nods.

"Well, he must of been speakin bout his own wrinkled self. Humans got to touch, elsewise they wouldn't be none." Miss Etta pauses and grasps Sarah by the shoulders. "Listen," she says, "I don't care what he say. You most twelve, now, and I promise you he thinkin bout touchin you. I spect he been plannin it for years. Only reason he took you in and keep you like a prisoner." Etta then nods vigorously, as if suffering an epiphany. "You just like one of his birds," she continued. "You just don't know no better, but that bout to change. He take you all the way to Florida, you goan see how other folks behave. You goan see they don't live locked up never seein the light of day. You goan . . ."

"Florida?" Sarah interrupts.

"It a place way down south, a place where the sun always shinin, and it don't never get cold."

"You've been there?"

Etta shakes her head. "Ain't never left Joplin, but I seen pictures and all."

Sarah frowns. She clutches Etta's arm with both hands and huddles close to her side. "Well, I don't want to go there. I don't want to go anywhere."

Etta breaks free of Sarah's grasp. She gathers her up and hugs her. "My poor, sweet child," she says. "God don't want you stay in this old place. He want you free to do and go as you please. I thinks maybe God done touched Mista King, and him don't even know

4

it—that why he all of a sudden want to take you out in the world. I don't know, but I hopes and prays that be the reason. I surely do."

To this Sarah says nothing. She stares blankly then turns and glides across the room to the narrow window overlooking the street. She stands with the window's sill pressed against her navel, gazing fixedly at the bustling drama some fifty feet below, at the comings and goings of the nameless, untouchable characters that have entertained her for as long as she can remember. Her eyes are wide and hold a look of terror. "I'll go," she says. "I'm afraid, but I'll go."

1

A Sad Song in St. Lucie

His journey between the great unknowns began one moonless night in the spring of 1898. No trumpets nor tolling bells, no fanfare of any sort, only the palpable fear of first-time parents, themselves not far beyond the selfsame wonder they now dared to produce. Fear lasting hours as he came in a feet-first drudgery rife with tears and sweat and blood, with piercing screams and urgent words of encouragement. . . . And beyond the clapboard walls housing this ordeal, the profound silence of a Florida where the height of pine and palm and oak and cypress yet exceeded any ambition of man, where an ancient night sky's stellar beauty yet existed in crystal clarity. A world very still. Not a whisper of wind, only the earth turning and the night passing with indifference until an unpracticed cry within the home announced the first breath of John Morgan Rawlerson.

James Arthur Rawlerson, a cowman by birthright, brought his pregnant wife to Fort Pierce shortly after construction for the Florida East Coast Railroad passed the tiny hamlet bound for the southernmost reaches of the state. Having quit working cows for others in Osceola County, he came south to begin a cattle operation of his own. The land he leased was raw and wild, a few hundred acres west of Fort Pierce belonging to a winter resident of

Palm Beach, a Yankee named Vogler who had no use for land other than its propensity to increase in value. On the property was a four-room cypress dwelling, a clapboard affair with a tin roof that scarcely leaked at all. A decent house, James Arthur and his wife Raylene thought, and one that quickly became a home as time passed and memories seeped into its every nook and cranny. Good and bad memories: the birth of John Morgan followed by brother Archie fourteen months later; celebrating the new century's arrival; a series of miscarriages spaced over five years; then the miraculous birth of twin girls after all hope was abandoned; mourning the passing of friends both old and new, distant relatives. Days, months, and years passing and their cattle and horses propagating until prosperity surely loomed in the not-so-distant future. And surrounding their insular existence the rest of the world also thriving.

In 1901 the sixty-six inhabitants of Fort Pierce incorporated. Four years later county lines were redrawn, designating Fort Pierce as county seat of the newly shaped St. Lucie County. Regular train traffic began to arrive and depart the town's depot, prompting an explosion of citrus production, of people. By the end of the new century's first decade the town held more than a thousand souls, nearly fifty businesses, a smattering of motor cars, and a burgeoning school. Tourists coming and going. And at the fringe of things, people like the Rawlersons, hard people working a hard land, fueling the engine of life that progress might indeed continue, might hurtle headlong down the slope of time to an ultimate destination known only to God.

*

In the fall of his fifteenth year, John Morgan—though he'd not know it for years to come—met his future in a most improbable way, on a day beginning like most others yet destined to evolve like no other in his then short life.

When the rooster's second proclamation registered in his mind that morning, he opened his eyes and bolted upright. He swung his feet to the cool wood floor and sat waiting for conscious thought to seep back in from wherever it goes during deep sleep. His first realization was his brother's rhythmic breathing emanating from the darkness above. Another plea by the rooster, followed by a barely audible barred owl's "Good morning to you all." Grasping the edge of his bed, he rocked forward sufficiently to clear the bunk above and rose to a standing position. He stretched then turned and called to the darkness: "Archie," he said.

A muffled groan issued from the upper bunk, then, "What?"

"Day's breakin."

Another groan and a rustle of sheets. "I don't care. Shit, John Morgan, leave me alone."

Turning away from his brother, John Morgan cautiously stepped forward, hands extended and groping the darkness for the dresser pictured in his mind. Locating the chest-high top with his fingers, he tracked the smooth pine to a box of matches and plucked one and struck it alight with a flick of his thumbnail. When the darkness retreated he reached and raised the soot-blackened globe of a lamp standing next to the matchbox. After lighting the wick and lowering the globe, he turned back to address his brother. "If you're late for school agin, you'll care. Mrs. Hardin'll see to that."

"I ain't scared of her."

John Morgan leaned to capture breeches draped over the end of his bunk. When he shook the denim jeans straight, the buckle of the leather belt they held tinkled a tune familiar to any morning he could recall, and continued to do so as he stepped into first one leg then the other and pulled them up and commenced to button the fly. "You ought to be terrified," he said, reaching for a long-sleeved shirt hanging from a bedpost. "After she's done wearin your tail out, Daddy'll show you his whip."

When Archie offered no reply, John Morgan exhaled one of his own. "All right," he said. "Suit yourself." He donned the pullover shirt, tucked it in, and buckled his belt. He stepped to the dresser and fingered another match from the box before exiting the room into a hallway dark save for a dim light at one end.

9

He moved toward the light until coming to a closed door on his right where he paused and knocked softly with a knuckle before opening the door and entering the darkened room beyond. "Hey, you two sleepyheads," he said, "time to get up."

Silence.

He stood until his eyes solved the puzzle of darkness within the room, then he sidled between two single beds to a cable spool situated against the wall. After locating and lighting a lamp on the makeshift nightstand, he confirmed left and right the motionless forms of his two little sisters, his eyes instantly brighter, the characteristic intensity gone from his face. "Come on, you two. You've got chickens to feed and books to read."

Marcy stirred first; rolling to her back the blond seven-year-old opened her blue eyes and smiled up at him. "Hey, John Morgan," she said. "Guess what I was dreamin?"

John Morgan cupped his chin pensively. "Let me see," he said. "Was you all grown up and married to Billy Barlow?"

Marcy fashioned a mean face. "Heck no," she said. "I mean Billy's okay and all—a really fast runner—but I wasn't dreamin bout him. I dreamed you took Maggie and me fishin—took us out to Okeechobee and I caught the biggest bass in all of Florida. It was so big we had to fetch the wagon to get it home."

John Morgan said nothing. He simply smiled, while wagging his head from side to side.

Marcy, studying his face, squinted her eyes in puzzlement. "It was a good dream," she said.

"I reckon it was. It's just that I ain't never seen a girl so crazy bout fishin is all. You're supposed to . . ."

"Tomboy," Maggie injected, still wrapped tightly in her top sheet and facing the wall. She rolled toward the light, revealing a face almost the mirror image of her sister's. "And she talks in her sleep."

"Do not."

"Do, too."

John Morgan suddenly bent over and reached a hand to each girl's sheet-swaddled side and commenced to tickle. When they squirmed and kicked and giggled for him to stop he immediately did but then threatened that if they didn't get up he'd tickle them senseless. "I got work to do," he said, then left the room, a hushed laughter swirling in his wake.

In the kitchen he found the lamps suspended over the oak table casting the room in amber, a thin ribbon of steam curling silently from the mouth of a speckled pot atop the wood-burning cook stove. A new smell of coffee all but drowning out what he'd long associated with the word "kitchen," a blend of wood smoke and culinary aromas comforting to his psyche, the sweet breath of sustenance itself. He crossed the room to the door where he paused and captured a hat from a wallpeg, a ratty gray Stetson sweatbespoke by not only himself but his father before him. After donning the hat and squaring it, he stooped and gathered in turn a pair of boots and a galvanized pail from the floor. He then thought to open the door and the heavy rough-hewn cypress gate obligingly swung inward as if having surely read his mind.

When Raylene Rawlerson—a clutch of speckled eggs nested in her apron—stepped through the door, John Morgan moved aside to let her pass. "Mornin, Mama," he said.

Raylene smiled up at him and echoed his salutation as she strode past and headed toward the cookstove. There she carefully transferred nine eggs from her apron to a handled woven basket on the counter next to the cast iron stove. A pinewood counter top worn smooth by years of service. "I don't know why I can't never remember the basket," she said.

John Morgan had started out the door. He stopped and looked back at his mother. "Ma'am?"

Raylene looked. She waved a hand at the basket. "At least twice a week I forget it—when I go to collect the eggs."

"Oh," said John Morgan, shifting the pail's handle to the hand already holding his boots. "Reckon you need to tie a string around your finger."

11

Raylene reached and got a heavy skillet from a nail on the wall. "I might just do that," she said. She set the pan on the nearest burner and reached and got the grease can from the stove's rear corner. She shot John Morgan a glance over her shoulder. "Your shadow ain't up yet?"

John Morgan shook his head. "He's movin kinda slow this mornin."

"Well, I spose that's a good thing. Bout time he leave you to work without his pesterin."

"Arch ain't no bother to me."

Raylene spooned grease into the pan. She shook her head. "Well, you best get to Queenie. That calf's bawlin like it ain't et in a week."

John Morgan stepped through the door and pulled it closed behind him. Dark. No moon and the coming sun only a rumor below the eastern horizon. A soft light emanated from the pole barn to the north, a yellow glow casting in silhouette the structure's skeleton and a man and several horses milling about within it like characters in some backlighted performance. As he sat the two-step stoop to dress his feet, a shadow-form moved to his right: the cur dog Roy rising from its wallowed-sand bed in the drip-line of the house, stretching and shaking and then sauntering to the boy's side to sniff his person before returning to its bed to circle and settle again in a tight curl of apparent satisfaction. After witnessing the dog's ritual, John Morgan pulled his final boot on and briefly sat looking and listening. An owl called in the creek swamp east of the house, and the rooster immediately answered from its pacing limb in the great oak lording over the home's backyard. The calf bawled as he rose to his feet and began striding the sandy yard toward it and the rest of the activity in the barn.

When he walked beneath the tin roof his father looked up from saddling a bay gelding, casting him a glance before resuming his labor, and saying: "Queenie's already in the stall. Figured it might shut that calf up—if it was to smell her and all." James Arthur grunted to pull the cinch-strap tight then half-hitched it secure through the saddle ring before turning back to his oldest son.

"Didn't work, though. Milk's the only thing goin to shut that scamp up."

John Morgan gave a little grin and nodded and continued on past his father and the standing horses. He entered the first of six stalls where a Jersey heifer stood devouring a mixture of cracked corn and cottonseed meal, one-eyeing his approach and swishing her tail. He sidled in beside her and set the pail beneath her udder while stroking her shoulder with his free hand. "Mornin, Sweetheart," he said. He straightened and lifted a three-legged stool from the topmost board of the stall and positioned it adjacent to the pail. He removed his hat and set it on a post. As he settled on the stool, the calf two stalls over bawled and paced. Pressing his forehead to the heifer's flank, he briefly massaged her bag then grasped the two nearest teats and began to rhythmically strip them top to bottom, producing twin jets of ivory liquid that alternately drummed the pail's bottom. "We gonna build that new hog trap today?" he said.

James Arthur had left the gelding and was in the process of saddling a sorrel filly. "We are," he said. "But I want you to ride in to town first. Post a letter for me, pick up some things your mama's needin."

A mosquito buzzed John Morgan's ear but the cow's incessantly swishing tail shooed it away before it chanced to light and draw blood. "I heard there's sickness in town."

James Arthur paused to turn and look. "Where'd you hear that?"

"Archie. He said half the kids laid out yesterday. Said Mrs. Hardin was feelin bad her own self."

"He present that as reason to lay out himself?"

"Yessir. I reckon he did. But I don't think he was cryin wolf this time. He seemed serious."

James Arthur walked to the stall and stopped. He bumped back his hat and commenced to watch the milking, his arms lounging on the top fence board, his right boot propped on the bottom one. "Serious," he said. "It ain't often I hear that word and your brother paired up."

John Morgan shot his father a quick glance but said nothing. He milked.

"Seems like somebody'd send word, if it was anything to worry about."

John Morgan paused and looked up. "I could stop on my way in," he said, "ask Mrs. Hardin about it."

James Arthur stepped back from the stall boards. He reached and gave the top board a rap with his hand. "Sounds like a plan," he said. "If Arch is tellin the truth, him and the girls can come on back to the house."

"He's tellin the truth."

"Better be. I get no joy out of punishin you boys, but I'll not tolerate a shirker. Never could. Never will."

John Morgan switched to the other two teats without a break in rhythm. "Yessir," he said. "I can vouch for that."

James Arthur nodded and reached and adjusted his hat. He turned and began walking toward the house. "Hurry and finish on up there so we can have some breakfast. It'll be daylight fore you know it."

John Morgan quickened his pace, the rising tide of milk in the pail now a continuous clash of concentric circles. "You ain't got to hurry me," he said to no discerning ear save his own. "My belly's way ahead of you on that one."

*

When he led his bay gelding from the barn his brother and sisters were already walking the sandy ruts angling just right of the now-risen sun, the family drive that would ultimately lead them to the Okeechobee Road. His father, after having bid the three farewell, turned and walked from the stoop to intercept him and his lead.

"Go on ahead of your brother and sisters and check with Mrs. Hardin," James Arthur said, reaching out a hand and catching hold of Shorty's hackamore. "If there's sure enough somethin goin round, double back and send em on home." James Arthur's eyes narrowed. "And when Arch begs to go with ya, you tell him no. I want him back here."

John Morgan nodded and handed the right rein to his father. Then, still holding the left rein, he turned and grabbed the pommel horn with both hands and swung up and into the saddle. He toed the stirrups and took the right rein from his father when it was offered. He squared his hat and sat looking down, awaiting further instructions.

"Mama give you the money for her supplies?"

"Yessir."

James Arthur withdrew an envelope from his breast pocket. He held it up to his son. "She give you enough to cover postage?"

He took the letter, gleaning his mother's printing and the address at a glance. "Yessir. She did." He slipped the envelope into his breast pocket. "You still tryin to get Mr. Vogler to sell us the place?"

James Arthur's eyes narrowed. "Had I wanted you to know what was in that letter, I'd of told you."

John Morgan turned and looked up the drive at his shrinking siblings. He looked at his father. "Yessir," he said. "I reckon you would have."

His father stepped forward and reached to withdraw a slender pump rifle from its boot scabbard beneath John Morgan's right leg. Pointing the twenty-two's muzzle skyward, he pulled back the forearm slide enough to confirm an empty chamber then closed the bolt and lowered the rifle to trail by his leg. He gestured toward the barn. "I think this'll be better off in the tack closet till you get back. No sense temptin fate by totin a gun to town."

John Morgan nodded his agreement.

"You know where to find me when you get back?" James Arthur asked, raising his free hand to shield against the sun, to witness his son's response.

"Out on the palmetto flats? That lone oak between the two cypress heads?"

James Arthur scuffed the sand with his boot. "Well, I'll be," he said. "Somebody does listen round here. Well, get movin. Lord willin, I'd like to be done buildin that trap by noon."

John Morgan nodded and turned the horse. Touching its flanks with his heels, he urged it first to a trot, then an easy canter which quickly overtook first his brother and then his sisters. He rode a short distance beyond them, then halted and turned the horse to face their approach. Maggie and Marcy dressed in identical pale yellow dresses, white socks and brown laced-up shoes, the two of them tiny for their age and smiling and veritably skipping along and swinging their lunch pails in a most carefree manner, as though surely venturing forth on a long-anticipated adventure of some sort. While a good distance behind, Archie shuffled barefoot with his brogans yoked about his neck, his head down and his hands repeatedly trading the small weight of his lunch pail as if a burden not worthy of either, his demeanor blatantly that of one taking medicine. John Morgan briefly watched them come, his horse standing and stepping, swinging its head first one way then the other in an attempt to turn, as if anxious to continue following the twin ruts girded by pine and palmetto. "If I don't come back," John Morgan called to the girls, "go on to the schoolhouse as usual." Then he raised a hand goodbye and let the horse have its head.

He let the horse run the several hundred yards to the Okeechobee Road then reined it to a fast walk as they turned northeast on the more heavily traveled thoroughfare. Almost immediately upon entering the broad trail, pine and palmetto flat woods gave way to oak and palm and sweet gum marking the north-to-south run of Fivemile Creek, the ground on both sides of the road falling gently away but the road itself staying level to the wooden bridge spanning the narrow channel of aquatic ambiguity. At the bridge the horse briefly protested crossing the uncertainty of the rough-hewn planks and their gapped spacing, but ultimately surged forward in a loud clatter of frantic jumps to reach the sure footing on the far side.

He rode beyond the creek with its escort of hardwoods and the growth transitioned to great expanses of broom sage dotted with islands of palmetto and gallberry, pine and sable palm. Then a huge live oak loomed ahead on his right and beneath the tree a cypress shack stood deeply shaded and scarcely visible amongst outstretched limbs of enormous girth and length, an unadorned structure equally congruous to its surroundings as the tree sheltering it. But in the sandy yard a crop of eyesores loudly announcing the presence of man: a single-horse coach missing a wheel and its frame and outstretched traces contorted and bowing to that loss, the decaying conveyance seemingly executing a slow descent into the sugar sand supporting it; several wooden turpentine barrels whose tin bands had long since rusted to failure; garbage, cans and bottles, and rotting paper. Then, as if to complete the scene of degradation, a pair of emaciated dogs of a breed defying all taxonomy launched from beneath the house with hackles raised, came forward in an odd sideways trajectory to yap and circle horse and rider until some boundary had been exceeded and whereupon the pair suddenly fell silent, turned as one to strut high-headed and high-tailed back into the dark obscurity from whence they'd come, back into irrelevance, the certain home of creatures such as they.

Beyond the home place an outbuilding overlooked a plowed field and a small holding pen in which stood a brace of mules with heads stretched high and eyes intently watching John Morgan's passage. On the opposite side of the road the haphazard diversity of natural woods succumbed to the orderly rows of an orange grove. In the distance, on both sides of the road, peaked tin roofs glinted in the early morning sun, the unmistakable sharp angles of man sawtoothing the horizon and marking the western advance of ever-expanding Ft. Pierce.

Nearing the first of the homes, he began to see children here and there, some approaching from the east but the largest contingent milling about where Delaware intersected the Okeechobee Road. At the schoolhouse a few hundred yards north up Delaware, two adults stood before the still-closed front doors. Seeing this, John Morgan knew the answer to the question he carried in his mind.

Still, he rode on to a group of older boys that stood gawking at his approach. Halting the horse, he looked squarely at the tallest boy, saying: "Ain't no school today, Henry?"

Henry Weeks fashioned a little grin and shook his head. "Heck, no, John Morgan. Half the town's sick." He jerked a thumb eastward over his shoulder. "They say even old Doc Clark has got it."

"Got what?"

"Spanish Fever," said Henry. "The grippe or somethin. Real high temperature and all."

John Morgan looked down at Henry and looked again at the distant schoolhouse. His horse stepped and stood and shook its head. A stocky, freckle-faced boy with a square head and deep-set green eyes had moved close to John Morgan's left boot, was reaching and fingering a braided whip coiled about the pommel horn. "You get any closer," John Morgan said, "that snake's apt to bite."

The boy withdrew his hand, grinning broadly and revealing a large gap where his top front teeth had once resided. Henry Weeks and the other boys chuckled and scuffed the ground with their mostly unshod feet. At this John Morgan turned his horse westward and put it forward with only a lift of a hand to signal his goodbye.

He rode, coming upon his sisters just past the old oak-sheltered house. After instructing the twins to return home, he rode on, curious as to why Archie was nowhere to be seen. He found his brother sitting on the wooden bridge spanning Fivemile Creek, his bare feet dangling in the air and him peering out over his knees to study the slow progression of water ten feet below. Halting his horse at the foot of the bridge, John Morgan sat shaking his head. He bumped back his hat, saying: "You're done lollygagging, you need to escort your sisters back to the house." He leaned and spat. "If you start now, y'all might get there together."

Archie cut his brother a quick glance. "Ha, ha," he said, slapping his leg. "That's almost as funny as you look. I'm comin with you." He sprang to his feet and reached to grasp the saddle's comb.

"You cain't, Arch. Daddy wants you to the house."

Archie dropped his lunch pail and reached with both hands to climb aboard the horse.

At this John Morgan shook his head but said nothing. He simply turned his horse eastward and put it forward at a trot, leaving Archie alone on the bridge nursing a frown of abandonment.

*

The children were gone from the streets near the schoolhouse, not a soul to be seen. Several workmen in bib overhauls were busy at the new brick building destined to house the town's first power plant, but save for them the outskirts of Ft. Pierce now seemed deserted. He rode on and when he reached the business district there was some activity. Doc Clark's Model T sat parked in front of the pharmacy, a few people coming and going, a few more across the street at the hardware. At the butcher shop a couple of elderly men straddling orange crates, and formerly engrossed in conversation, suddenly fell silent when John Morgan rode before them. They sat seemingly frozen in time until the boy reached and tipped his hat, upon which each man raised a finger in greeting, their eyes sparkling with recognition. He rode on toward the morning sun, his horse's hooves clopping smartly on the packed shell and lime-rock forming the street, ancient sealife dredged in to bolster the all-too-soft native sand. A gentle breeze from the east carried the briny scent of the Indian River, along with a sound not unlike the persistent cough of some great beast of the imagination. As he passed the town's lone boarding house the general store loomed ahead and beyond it, at the road's end, the train depot. A north-bound steam locomotive sat parked on the tracks adjacent to the loading dock, its coupled load consisting of two sleeper coaches and a dining car. Crates of pineapple and citrus stacked on the dock. White clouds of steam jetted from beneath the great locomotive with each pressure-releasing huff of its idling engine. Three crewmen stood next to the engine, smoking cigarettes and talking amid the iron beast's fast-evaporating breath. A uniformed conductor paced near the rear of the last coach, swinging his arms and reaching to consult a pocket watch just as John Morgan halted his horse in front of the general store.

Stepping down from his horse, he noticed for the first time the people seated on a bench next to the store's open double doors, a large colored woman and a pale young lady dressed in white lace and holding before her a matching parasol open and resting edgewise on the porch floor so that she was visible only from the shoulders up. Piercing dark eyes watching his every move and instantly setting him uneasy. For a moment he stood like a man having gazed into the eyes of Medusa. Then he gathered himself sufficiently to step forward and cinch the reins to a support post, his hands suddenly afflicted with palsy, his mind tumbling with sensations both foreign and frightening. He diverted his eyes to the crushed oyster shells beneath his boots. He searched the mob of sable palms standing beyond the train depot, the wide-open expanse beyond them where sky and earth convened in an ambiguous haze. *Don't look at her* roared in his mind, but he had no choice. As he ascended the three steps to the porch, the girl's gaze again captured his and when she smiled his legs nearly buckled. "Hey," he heard someone say, oblivious to the fact he himself was the one who had spoken.

The girl turned to the colored woman. When the large lady nodded, she again looked to the boy. She smiled and said: "Hello."

John Morgan stood at the top of the steps, his hands searching for a pants pocket. He stepped and stood, reached with his right hand to confirm the letter protruding from his breast pocket. He was suddenly aware of voices coming from within the store, an amalgam of male and female voices too numerous to be intelligible. He gestured with a hand toward the doorway. "I've got to go inside."

The colored woman's right hand shot to cover her mouth, as if trying to stifle a cough. "Well, get yourself on," she chuckled. "We's just tourists, is all. We don't own the place."

John Morgan stood, the monotonous huff of the locomotive to his left and his horse shaking its head and blowing behind him. He looked through the doorway at people mingling inside, in the aisles and along the counter ranging deep into the great old building that had once been a canning plant. He looked back to the girl and when he looked at her she suddenly let go of the parasol and stood and stepped close to him. She held out a closed hand as if making an offering of some sort. "I live in Joplin," she said, casting a glance back at the colored woman whose face instantly clouded with a look of concern.

John Morgan looked at the delicate hand hovering before him, raising his own reflexively to accept whatever was being offered. A sweet scent filled his head, made him feel dizzy as the fist opened and a coin-like disk dropped into his palm. He studied the nonmetallic, gold-colored wafer, the raised crown in its center and the words imprinted around its circumference, the words "House of Kings." He gazed once again into the girl's eyes. He shook his head. "What is it?" he said.

"It is where I live."

John Morgan looked at the disk and looked at the girl. "Kind of small, ain't it?"

The girl shook her head. "Oh, no," she said, wagging her head from side to side, her face the picture of seriousness. It is a very large building, much larger than anything here." She gazed into his eyes, her hand rising and gesturing to the disk in his hand. "I am told it is very valuable and it must be kept from sight for men have killed for far less and . . . "

"Child . . ." the colored woman interrupted.

The girl hushed but did not turn to look at the lady. She leaned close to John Morgan as if to embrace him but stopped short of touching him and only whispered: "It is so you don't forget me."

As if to punctuate the girl's statement, the locomotive's steam whistle suddenly issued a short blast, followed in quick succession by two more.

The colored woman, with a great exhalation of breath, unseated herself from the bench, capturing the parasol from the floor before stepping to the girl's side and gathering in her pale arm. "Oh, Lord," she gasped. "We gots to get back on the train, child."

People began filing out of the store, causing John Morgan to step left in order to clear a path to the steps. He stood close to the colored lady but his eyes fixed on the girl's. "What's your name?" he said.

At this the colored woman swung the parasol into position over the girl's head and gave a tug to her arm. She fired a quick glance over her shoulder then focused on the boy. "She called Sarah," she whispered, "but you ain't heard me say that. You ain't heard me say nothin." With that she pulled the girl forward into the flow of people descending the steps, her actions executed with a poverty of movement belying her massive size.

John Morgan stood with mouth agape watching the pair stride arm-in-arm to the waiting train, watching the girl repeatedly look back at him before finally disappearing into the bowels of the coach last in line. And when she was gone from sight he said "Sarah" aloud, then looked down at the disk in his hand and said "Joplin." Then, slipping the disk into his pants pocket, he turned to enter the store and almost collided with a pair of men exiting side by side, a short man, sixtyish, sporting bifocals and flesh-toned gloves and next to him a younger, swarthy man, muscular, dark linen suit, and whose expression virtually shouted "Step aside." John Morgan obliged, and the pair swept past without hesitation or acknowledgment of his concession. He moved on into the store, pausing just beyond the threshold and standing like a man suddenly realizing he's lost, like one trying to wrench himself from dream to reality. He continued to stand until the sole person left in the store looked up from behind the counter to acknowledge his existence. Then he came to. "Mornin, Mr. Cobb," he said. "I got a letter to post."

*

It was mid-morning when he rode up to the house. The twins—sitting Indian-fashion on the lone patch of carpet grass surviving in the yard, their readers open in their laps—looked up and smiled a hello as he stepped down from the horse and reached for a pair of paper-wrapped bundles secured behind the saddle's comb. With the bundles stacked under his right arm, he briefly stood watching his sisters, just looking around. No clouds in the sky. The

October sun hot on his shoulders as Marcy looked up at him beseechingly.

"Let's go fishin, John Morgan," she said.

"Cain't, Sweetheart. I got to help Daddy."

"Awww," Marcy sighed.

He started to walk, but then stopped and turned back to his sister. "Maybe if we get done early enough, I'll take you this evenin."

"Promise?"

"Cross my heart and hope to die," he said.

*

When he entered the house his mother sat mending a pair of his father's socks in the good light offered by the south-facing kitchen window. "Hey," he said, striding to the kitchen table where he set the two bundles along with fifty-six cents in change he fished from his pants pocket.

Raylene Rawlerson laid her work on the floor and rocked forward sufficiently to exit the rocker. She came to the table and reached and touched the larger of the two packages. "Mr. Cobb have everything?"

"Yes, ma'am. That's your denim. Said you got the last he had."

Raylene nodded. She reached and plucked the change from the table. "He say anything about the sickness? He doin okay?" Not waiting for his reply, she turned and carried the coins across the room to a shelf above the stove where she reached and deposited them into a lidless mason jar.

John Morgan shrugged. "He seemed fine. He had a store full of customers when I got there."

His mother cocked her head to one side, her eyes squinting. "Really?"

"Nobody we know. There was a train at the station, bunch of tourists stoppin by on their way back north."

"Oh," she said. "So you didn't ask him. That's a shame, cause he'd know if there's reason to worry. A person can't draw a breath in town, he don't hear about it."

John Morgan smiled and nodded. He stuffed his hands in his pants pockets and turned toward the door. "Daddy say I needed to bring anything out there?"

Raylene shook her head. "He took Arch with him, so I'm sure he'll be happy to see you."

John Morgan looked at his mother without comment. He walked for the door, saying: "Reckon I'll see you this evening, then." He pulled the door open but paused before stepping outside. He looked at his mother. "Where's Joplin at?" he said.

"What?"

"You ever hear of a place called Joplin?"

Raylene looked at the floor. She looked at her son. "Joplin, Missouri, is the only one I know of. Why do you want to know?"

John Morgan looked at his horse standing three-legged in the yard. He looked at his mother. "The most beautiful girl in the whole world lives there," he said, "the girl I aim to marry one day."

Raylene dropped her work to her lap. She stared quizzically at her son, cocking her head and smiling nervously. "What in the world are you talkin about, John Morgan? What girl?"

John Morgan dipped his head, smiling sheepishly. "I don't know," he said. He hesitated briefly in the doorway before simply stepping into the yard and saying "Bye" as he swung the door closed behind him.

Raylene momentarily studied the space vacated by her son, then merely shook her head and muttered, "Boys."

*

After procuring his rifle from the tack closet, he mounted up and guided the horse westward past a hogwire dog pen where four Walker and Bluetick mixes rose from their sand beds to howl and plead that he take them with him. Ignoring the dogs' plea, he continued on to a cattle trail deep set in the sand and snaking northwestward across pine and palmetto flatwoods. He rode at a brisk walk, his horse stepping smartly, its head sawing from side to side and bobbing a rhythm familiar, a beat born in ancient times when first the souls of man and horse chanced to entwine. He passed through wiregrass and palmettos cropped closely by cattle; poor rations, yet by far the most abundant offered by the native, unimproved land. Crossing a shallow drain feeding Fivemile Creek, he wove his way through an oak and palm hammock where a number of rangy cows, obviously wild as the land sustaining them, scattered before him like a flushed covey of quail. Giving the startled cattle little thought, he rode on until exiting the shade of the hammock where he halted his horse and sat studying the far-reaching flatwoods ahead.

Two cypress heads loomed in the distance, stands dome-shaped and gray amid the pale-green ocean of palmettos and gallberry, a great live oak standing dark and umbrella-like midway between the two mobs of cypress. Beneath the oak, silhouettes of horses and men drifted like animated offspring of the huge tree's shadow. John Morgan briefly watched the activity before putting the horse forward with a touch of his heels.

As he drew near the tree his father's sorrel and Archie's paint stood with heads erect and watching him come. Beyond the horses but still beneath the oak's canopy, a shirtless James Arthur knelt next to a pairing of lighter posts rising vertically from the ground, his left hand grasping one of the posts for balance while with his right he used the handles of a post hole digger to tamp the earth down around the post's base. A few feet away Archie stood flipping an antler-handled hunting knife at some imaginary target on the leaf-strewn ground. When the gelded paint whinnied, both boy and man turned an eye to witness their blood relation's arrival.

Once beneath the tree's canopy, John Morgan dismounted, dropped his reins, and circled his horse, his eyes surveying the work already accomplished, the four double-posted corners of the trap, the taller post pairs centered on the east-facing mouth of the rectangular structure, cross-barred at the top to accommodate a sheet of eighth-inch steel destined to be the drop gate. He stopped next to his brother and bumped back his hat with a thumb. "Looks like I might as well of gone fishin. Y'all ain't left much for me to do."

Archie waved the knife at his brother, parrying like some medieval swordsman issuing a challenge.

John Morgan raised his hands high. "Don't stick me," he said, feigning fear, "I surrender."

Archie grinned broadly and scuffed the ground with his shoe. "Hey," he said.

James Arthur got to his feet and righted the inverted digger before jabbing its twin-bladed business end into the ground. Releasing the twin-handled tool to stand alone, he then reached and pulled a rag from his hip pocket and began mopping sweat from his glistening face and neck and shoulders. "There's plenty left to be done," he said, eyeing fat-lighter poles on the ground beyond the standing corner posts. "Need you to ride to the old trap—fetch the slide gate and cable." He paused and made a sweeping gesture with the hand holding the rag, indicating what appeared to be plowed patches of ground within the oak's area of influence. "Just look at the rootin round here," he said. "I believe this old oak's akerns done pulled all the hogs out of the creek swamp." He stuffed the rag back in his pants pocket. "When the akerns play out here, it'll be easy to put the old trap back in workin order. Just slip the gate back in and bait her up."

"Too bad we don't have two gates," John Morgan said.

"Yeah, well," James Arthur said, swinging his arms and suddenly popping his sweat-soaked rag in the air as if venting some pent-up anger, as if surely having interpreted his son's comment as an insult.

Seeing this, John Morgan immediately turned and gathered in his horse's reins. He grabbed the pommel horn and swung into the saddle. He looked down at his father. "Spose they's hogs in the trap," he said.

James Arthur looked east, toward the distant creek swamp. He looked at his son, shrugged his shoulders, and said: "Handle it." He turned and stooped to retrieve a bow saw from the ground. Righting himself, he continued with: "I wouldn't worry, though.

When I checked it yesterday, that week-old corn hadn't been touched."

John Morgan nodded and turned his horse eastward. As he rode from beneath the tree, Archie hurled an acorn that stung him squarely in the back, to which John Morgan slumped forward as though dealt a fatal blow.

Archie laughed aloud. He slapped his thighs and did a little dance in the leaves while his brother resurrected himself and continued on his way.

*

John Morgan rode through a quarter mile of stunted palmettos in the flatwoods and a few minutes on he could make out the crude trap in the apron of the creek swamp some distance away, a rectangle whose four walls of stacked lighter logs were chest high and shaded by the three sable palms amongst which it stood. A moment later he recognized the drop gate was down, that something was likely in the trap. He rode to the palm farthest from the trap where he stepped down from the horse and half-hitched the reins around the tree's smooth trunk in such a manner that the horse had little room to maneuver. When finished with the small task, he stroked the bay's neck reassuringly and stood studying his surroundings.

The sun had begun its slow descent toward Okeechobee on a day possessing few clouds to veil its passage. An impotent, variable breeze was just perceptible in the hardwood leaves defining the creek swamp, the palms and myrtles and broomsage following its edge. He listened. A pileated woodpecker called long and shrilly in the swamp behind him while a slow, deep respiration emanated from within the trap. He turned to his horse and patted its neck reassuringly. He slid the small pump gun from its boot scabbard and swung the rifle to trail by his leg then turned and stepped toward the crude enclosure, weaving amongst the many cabbage fans strewn over the sandy soil.

A few paces from the pen, a foul stench hit him with news of what he could not yet see. "Boar," his nose said, an assertion that

27

was quickly confirmed by his eyes a few seconds later when he reached the pen and peered over its top rail. He sidled up to the stacked lighter logs for a better look, resting his left arm along the topmost, his chin on the back of his hand. He watched the hog backed into the far corner, a boar black as coal with its stance wide and braced, its long snout hovering just above the ground, eyes deep-set and blinking nervously.

He stood studying the hog for several minutes, its unpleasant, musky scent threatening to nauseate him. "Damn," he eventually said, "ain't you a rank son of a sow."

The hog stood focusing its narrow gaze on the boy, its beady brown eyes seemingly about to combust. It began to pop its jaws, producing a yellowish-white froth of saliva that oozed forth to shape a hideous smile, to coat its curved tushes and long snout hairs. It issued a couple of mock charges, woofing and slashing the air with its long cutters.

John Morgan turned and walked back to his horse. After stowing the rifle in its scabbard, he untied his catch rope and got pigging string and what looked like a cold cream jar from his saddlebag. He carried these back to the pen where the boar was once again backed into a corner and watching his every move.

Setting the jar on the ground, he threaded the pigging string through a belt loop and then unfurled the catch rope and began building his loop. Holding reserve rope in his left hand and the loop in his right, he eased around the pen's perimeter, changing direction periodically and all the while studying how the boar reacted. When finally the animal stopped reacting and simply stood huffing and popping its teeth, John Morgan swung the loop once overhead then lobbed it neatly over the animal's head. The boar shot forward, managing to get its right foreleg through the loop before John Morgan snatched it closed.

The caught hog launched into a frenzied series of flips and runs, squealing and crashing repeatedly into the fat-lighter rails, the boy two-handing the rope and stepping quickly to the nearest corner posts where he hitched a loop around the pair and leaned back against the posts and the pandemonium beyond.

The boar fought for several minutes, the boy harvesting slack at every opportunity until he had the one-hundred-pound animal pulled back against the double corner posts, standing on its two hind legs and too exhausted to do much more than breathe and paw feebly at the air with its front hooves. At this point, John Morgan took several turns of the rope around the posts and tied it off and stood back to catch his own breath.

He removed his hat and briefly used it to fan his face then put it back on his head and turned to retrieve the jar from the ground. He circled to the trap's far end, to the only entrance short of climbing the rails. He set the jar on the ground and reached and grasped the braided wire cable clamped to the drop-gate's top. Hauling up on the cable, he raised the rusty steel sheet sufficiently to get a hand under its bottom edge. He then slid the gate up and out of its runs and turned and set it on the ground. He dragged the braided cable and its still-attached trip stake over the crude doorway's high cross-member and coiled it and laid it on top of the gate. Stooping, he gathered in the jar and duck-walked through the narrow opening and into the pen. He stood tall, eyeing the disabled hog while brushing sand and leaves from his jeans.

The boar struggled a bit when he stepped close to it, but with its hind hooves barely touching the ground there was little it could do save paw and growl and pop its jaws.

Kneeling before the animal, John Morgan unscrewed the lid from the jar and set them on the ground next to his knee. He fished his knife from his pants pocket, a three-bladed Barlow once belonging to his grandfather. He extended the principal blade, tested its edge with his thumb before laying it on the ground next to the jar. He then pulled the pigging string from his belt and lofted it before him, a bitter end in each hand and his eyes tracing its two-foot length before blurring the braided twine in focusing on the sizable testicles a few feet beyond. "You ain't gonna like this," he said to the hog. And with that he leaned forward and positioned the string behind the two orange-sized testes, encircling them and quickly tying off the circle and drawing the string tight about the upper reaches of the animal's scrotum. The boar kicked and squirmed and squealed, but for naught. Within a few seconds the boy was finished, the string triple-knotted and the future spread of one hog's genes forever stemmed.

Once the boar settled John Morgan again leaned in and knotted the string's two loose ends then pared them short with his knife. He reached up and caught the hog's left ear and with the knife cut two notches in its trailing edge. He folded the knife closed and slipped it in his pants pocket and reached and got the cold cream jar. With two fingers he excavated a glob of the dark sticky contents and used it to first paint the ear notches and then the boar's scrotum, the concoction smelling of creosote, petroleum, and alcohol, and having the consistency of tar. When done, he wiped his fingers somewhat clean on the boar's stiff back hair. He screwed the lid on the jar and stood to admire his work.

"Now don't try to lick that off," he said aloud. "It'll keep the screwworm flies off when your nuts get to rottin." He looked at his horse, which was looking at him, and then again at the hog which was one-eyeing him and breathing heavily through its frothy, open mouth. He reached and patted the hog's rump. "That's it," he said. "Behave while I get the rope off, and I'll let you go become somethin useful."

*

By the time he got back to his father and brother, the trap was finished save for the gate and they sat waiting for him at the base of the old oak. When Archie greeted him with, "I thought you ain't never goan get back," he merely flashed him a smile then stepped down from his horse and opened his right hand, letting the gate and cable slide from beneath his armpit to the ground. He briefly stood flexing his hand and the muscles of his arm, trying to restore feeling sapped by the awkward burden the gate had been. He then quickly explained to his father the reason for his delay, after which James Arthur simply nodded his approval and said: "A barr hog's some mighty good eatin." To which John Morgan smiled his own agreement and then squatted and gathered in the rusty steel sheet

30

and coiled cable. Rising with the hardware, he looked at his father. "You ready?" he said.

While he and his father installed the gate and set and baited the trap with corn brought for that purpose, Archie cavorted in the shade of the oak, chunking acorns at an imaginary foe and proclaiming to deaf ears the extent of his hunger. And when the work was done the three collected their tools and caught their horses and mounted them. They ducked their heads to clear the oak's low-hanging limbs and filed one after the other from deep shade and into full view of a sun whose position elicited the sole conversation of the ride home.

"Damn," James Arthur said, the post hole digger yoked across the bow of his saddle and rocking to the horse's gait. "It's near bout four o'clock."

"Pretty near," said John Morgan.

"Oh, well, least she's built. I think it'll prove out to be a day well spent. What do you all think?"

"I think so," John Morgan said.

"Think about what?" said Archie.

*

The hounds in their pen howled the riders' arrival while the cur dog Roy drifted silently among the horses' legs, sniffing with an air of absorption for the tale his nose alone would tell. They'd halted at the pole barn and were just stepping down from the horses when Marcy came running from the house.

"Maggie's sick," she blurted, stopping before her father, wide-eyed and trying to catch her breath.

James Arthur jabbed the post hole digger in the ground and reached and grasped his daughter's shoulders. He looked at her. Then he released her and turned to his sons. "Put the tools away before you see to the horses," he said. "I'll be right back."

With that James Arthur reached and caught his daughter's petite hand and together they hurried to the house. Marcy led him to her shared room where he found Maggie on her back in bed with covers pulled to her chin, Raylene sitting by her side. Maggie's face flushed, her eyes open but glazed and listless. A basin of water and a pitcher on the cable spool nightstand. Raylene turned to acknowledge his presence, her forehead deeply furrowed by concern.

"She's burnin up," she said.

Maggie's eyes drifted to her father. "Hey, Daddy," she said, her voice scarcely a whisper. A dry cough followed the salutation, a short staccato briefly lifting her head from the pillow.

He moved to the opposite side of the bed from his wife and reached and felt Maggie's brow. He withdrew his hand and looked at Raylene. "How long she been this way?"

Raylene's fingers worried the folded washcloth in her grasp. "About noontime she come in and said she didn't feel too good. Said her throat was sore. That's when I noticed she felt warm, but nothing like now. Fever's much worse now. I been bathing her with cool water but it don't seem to be helping."

"You give her anything?"

Raylene nodded. "At two o'clock I gave her cinnamon in milk. That always seems to work, but not this time. So at three-thirty I gave her an aspirin. I'm scared to give her another one, no bigger than she is."

James Arthur cupped his chin pensively. He sighed. "I'll send John Morgan to fetch the doctor." He reached and felt Maggie's forehead again then straightened and stepped first one way then another, like a man suddenly lost his bearings. "Keep moppin her with that water," he said. "We got to bring that fever down." He started for the door but noticed Marcy and stopped abruptly. "You need to stay out of this room, Punkin. Least till we know your sister's on the mend."

Marcy looked at him and looked at her sister in the bed. "Yessir," she said, then followed him from the room and on into the kitchen. "Daddy," she said, stopping him before he could exit the house.

James Arthur turned at the threshold and looked down at her. He reached and patted her blond hair. "Maggie's gonna be all right, Punkin."

"Promise?"

James Arthur turned and looked toward the barn then turned back to face his daughter. "I promise," he said. "Now let me get your brother movin. I ain't doin nobody any good standin here."

*

The sun was setting as John Morgan rode to town. Sensing the urgency in his father's voice he held his horse to a canter most of the way, his and the horse's conjoined shadow loping long over the road ahead, a dark and silent guide-on perfectly suited for a journey such as his. He rode like a dreamer, passing landmarks and people he scarcely noticed until suddenly his destination materialized ahead in stark clarity, as if the pharmacy was all he could perceive in the surreal world spawned by stress.

He halted his horse next to the doctor's parked Model T and stepped down and dropped the reins. He leapt onto the sidewalk and stepped to the door with its "Closed" sign leering through the glass like a cruel jokester. He rapped several times on the wood frame and then paused to listen. His heartbeat and the breathing of his horse behind him. He pounded again and a voice sounded from deep within the two-story structure, a female shouting: "Just a minute!" In a moment a woman wearing a gauze mask and a housecoat appeared beyond the glass, her auburn hair frazzled and her staring incredulously while gesturing to the sign and its statement of the obvious.

"I need the doctor," John Morgan called to her. "My little sister is bad sick."

The stern look broadcast by the woman's eyes softened. She stopped pointing to the sign and simply stood for a few seconds. She reached and unlocked the door and pulled it open, raising a soft jingle from a cluster of bells affixed to the overhead framing. "Dr. Clark is sick himself," she said, "too sick to help anybody."

The boy looked at his boots and looked at the lady, his mouth opening and closing but him uttering not a sound.

"What are her symptoms?"

"Ma'am?"

"Your sister—has she got the influenza?"

John Morgan gave a feeble nod. "I reckon so," he said, "if that's what's goin round. She's got a high fever and all—a sore throat."

"How old is she?"

"Seven," John Morgan said. "But she looks about five. She's real small for her age."

The lady nodded then turned and stepped back into the building. She went to the counter and gathered in a pencil and small notepad and began writing. After a moment she tore the top sheet from the pad and circled the end of the counter to a glass display case. Sliding the door open, she reached inside and got a small tin then slid the door closed and turned and came to John Morgan.

"Take these aspirin to your folks and tell them to follow these instructions. It's all I can do, all my husband could have done for you if he were well. It's all anyone can do for influenza cases."

Accepting the tin and the instructions, he glanced at them in his hand and looked at the woman. "I ain't brought any money," he said.

She gave a little wave of her hand as if shooing his statement. "Don't worry about it," she said. "Aspirin's cheap, and a woman's advice even cheaper."

John Morgan smiled and reached and touched the brim of his hat. "Thanks, Mrs. Clark. I hope the doc's better soon."

She nodded, above the mask her eyes telling a smile as she eased the door through a jingle to a sudden stop, a thunk reverberating in wood and glass until stifled by the deadbolt's click.

*

It was full dark before he reached home, the night so potent but for the bare sand of the road he might well have lost his way. Light from the house's two east-facing windows ultimately confirmed his course when winking into view one after the other, when glowing ahead like the yellow eyes of comfort itself. He rode into a lighted swath of yard conjured from the dark by radiance from the left-most window and dismounted and hurried for the door. His father and brother, sitting like solemn bookends at the kitchen table, jolted to life when he stepped inside.

"You ain't brought the doctor?" James Arthur said, rising from his seat and listing right and left to see past his son.

John Morgan shook his head. "He ain't comin. His wife said he's really sick—too sick to get out of bed, I reckon." He reached and got the tin and note from his breast pocket. "She gave me these aspirin and instructions to follow. Said it was all that could be done." He stepped forward and handed the note and tin to his father.

James Arthur unfolded the paper and stood staring blankly at it. He looked beseechingly to his son.

"It says to give her two aspirins every four hours," John Morgan offered, "to make sure she drinks lots of water and gets lots of rest—to bathe her in cool water iffen her temperature don't come down."

"We already doin all that," James Arthur said. He looked again at the note, his eyes darting from side to side in their sockets. "Givin her two aspirins place of one is the only thing different."

John Morgan removed his hat and stood turning it in his hands. He looked at his brother who seemed about to fall asleep at the table. He listened: coughing down the hall in the twins' bedroom, overlapping sessions of distinctly different timbres. Frowning, he looked to his father. "Where's Marcy?" he said.

James Arthur cast him a glazed look. "In bed," he said. "She's got it too."

*

For six days, while his mother tended to his sisters, John Morgan, along with his father and brother, busied themselves hunting strays and doctoring the navels of newborn calves against the threat of screwworm, butchering and curing the meat from three hogs caught in the new trap. They avoided the house save to eat meals of their own making and to sleep the fitful sleep of the chronically worried. John Morgan listened each evening as he lay in bed to his mother's dire reports to his father; listened and then prayed that her analysis was wrong, that his precious sisters would soon be well and his world again set right. But each passing day his mother's words did not waver, did not forecast that his prayers would be answered. He felt increasingly helpless, enraged by the mysterious malady befallen the two people he loved most in the world. Why? He wondered. Why would God create such a thing as influenza? Night after night he weighed thoughts such as these, searching for some solace, some explanation for this visit paid him by misery. But as in all lives, in his there would be no answer in the offing, not for this his first visit, nor for the many to come. What was going to happen, he ultimately concluded, was going to happen. All he could do was watch and wait.

Initially, the aspirin regimen reduced the girls' fever for brief periods but eventually seemed not to influence it at all. Their coughs progressed from dry to wet, producing thick sputum of a greenish-yellow hue, a vile matter portending the unthinkable horror to come, horror that rose to a crescendo early on the seventh day when Maggie simply stopped breathing—when Marcy passed a short while later, trailing her sister closely into death as she had into life.

The day following, the entire family transported the two blanket-shrouded bodies by wagon to the mortuary in town, a trip made in silence save for the occasional jangle of harness and the incessant grate of trundling wheels. The last day of October oddly beautiful for such a morbid task and the fact that it was Halloween kept from them by the numbing fog of loss through which they traveled.

Two days later the burial was held at the Methodist cemetery, the graveside observance immediately following the church's normal Sunday services yet sparsely attended due to the ongoing threat of flu. All in attendance save the family wore inept gauze masks and a standoffish air that portrayed perfectly their fear of the lurking danger. Raylene Rawlerson wailed softly throughout the short ceremony, her demeanor in sharp contrast to the stolid menfolk by her side, her two sons and husband whose cries were masked by mores not of their making yet so ingrained as to be worn without question or conscious thought. And when the pastor uttered his final amen a hush fell like a pall over the departing participants, a silence sudden and profound and perhaps the only escort appropriate for an ending so final, for the living as well as the dead.

At their wagon James Arthur steadied his wife as she attempted to step up and into the seat box, a step she now seemed incapable of making, or at the very least reluctant to take. While James Arthur climbed into the seat and Archie hopped into the bed, John Morgan stood in his ill-fitting suit at the wagon's rear, his eyes swimming and his hands fidgeting as if searching for a hat to hold. When his father turned and gave him a questioning look, the boy said: "I think I'd like to walk."

James Arthur looked at the reins in his hands and looked at his oldest son. He nodded once then reached and released the brake and gave the reins a shake, putting the horses forward.

When the wagon shot forward Archie briefly stiffened as if about to hop down and join his brother but ultimately settled back and merely raised a hand as if suddenly sensing that company was the last thing his brother wanted.

John Morgan gave a little halfhearted wave to acknowledge his brother then stood watching the remains of his family roll away and grow smaller and smaller until swinging in a wide arc onto the Okeechobee road. When an orange grove erased his kin from view he began to walk, to shuffle like a man with no particular place to go, to be.

The sand in the road was deeply rutted and so loosely packed that momentum was a thing not easily purchased. John Morgan subconsciously sauntered from side to side, the larger dunes and troughs dictating a wonky course like that of drunkards or the extremely feeble. His right-slanted shadow always slightly behind and mimicking perfectly his every weave and wobble. A slight breeze at his back and the sun pummeling his hatless head, he soon began to sweat and curse the brushed wool the day had demanded he wear. There'd been no rain for weeks so the sand held tracks dating back a good while and he fixated on them as he walked, his eyes tirelessly searching the ground like one having lost something precious, something without which he could not live. And when finally he came upon a matched set of windswept prints he stopped and sank to his knees. He extended an open hand to hover just above the small, ghostly shapes as though every fiber of his being wanted to touch them, to possess them. But thinking them far too fragile, he remained thus for several minutes, his hand hovering, his fingers tracing the dim lines repeatedly in the air. Then suddenly he stopped tracing and, with a wave of his hand, erased the small shoe prints forever. "Why?" he said, then bowed his head and wept.

*

By the second week of November some semblance of normalcy returned to the Rawlerson household, a masquerade initially, yet one the family would promote thereafter. In the days since the funeral John Morgan had not once mentioned his sisters, had not bared his thoughts on the matter at all. And the closest he'd ever come to doing so was one morning when his father cornered him in the barn.

He sat the stool with his head pressed to the Jersey's flank, stripping milk from the long teats while lost in thought, when suddenly his father's voice startled him.

"I want you and Arch to get us a deer for the smokehouse."

John Morgan jerked his head around to locate his father. "Jesus," he said.

"No. Just me," James Arthur quipped.

John Morgan turned back to his milking. "I ain't been seein a whole lot of sign."

James Arthur lifted a boot to rest on the stall's bottom board. He nodded. "Market hunters and screwworm," he said. "We're comin up on the new moon, though. You all concentrate your efforts around southmoon under, you'll get one."

38

John Morgan milked, producing alternating streams steady as a ticking clock. "You want us to go tonight?"

"I do. And I won't mind if it takes you a few days. Scarce as deer is, you may have to work them hammocks down along Tenmile Creek. They're still plentiful out there. Least that's what Henry says."

"You see Mr. Adams?"

"I did. He rode up on me when I was takin my lunch yesterday. We had us a good visit. Invited me to come run a fox or two tonight, so y'all best not bother huntin up his way. Deer'll be huggin the ground up there, with hounds in the woods and all."

"What about school?"

"School?"

"Archie's done missed a bunch."

"Yeah, well. I've decided Arch is done with school. The end of the year's almost here, and I need all the help I can get now that Vogler's raised the rent on us. Sides, 'cordin to Mrs. Hardin, Arch ain't reached the school half the days he set out for it."

John Morgan craned his neck to look at his father. "He raised the rent?"

"Yes, he did."

"The bastard."

"Watch your mouth."

"Yessir, but it seems like he always does it just when we're bout to make a profit, bout to start puttin a little aside for a place of our own."

James Arthur kicked the stall's bottom board. "He won't stop us. We'll have a place of our own if it kills me. A man's not a man . . ."

". . . till he owns land," John Morgan injected, completing a mantra he learned early in life.

He milked, neither him nor his father speaking again until he broke the silence with: "What about Mama?"

"What about her?"

"You reckon she's ready to handle bein left alone?"

James Arthur unleaned himself from the stall boards. He removed his hat and ran fingers through his hair and then set the hat back on his head. "I reckon she's already handlin it," he said. "Has to be. I expect she'll feel alone the rest of her life—whether we're around or not. I expect you all will."

John Morgan stopped stripping the cow's teats and sat staring at its blurred side. "You all?" he questioned. "What about you?"

James Arthur did not answer. He simply turned and walked away.

*

Mid-afternoon James Arthur saddled his horse and rode into town. He went directly to a "Tiger Den" in the colored quarters off Fifth Street and stepped down from his horse before addressing a cotton-haired man perched on a bench next to the shanty's only door, a man still as death but for his collapsed lower jaw ruminating in a slow circle of contentment.

"Afternoon, Bogator."

The old man squinted toward the voice, cataract-afflicted eyes like milky moons partially eclipsed by lids of wet mud. Khaki pants and shirt. Legs crossed with arms crossed atop them. With no shift in attitude, he executed a slow lean to one side and spat a brown stream closely resembling his own leathery skin. Righting himself, he said, "Yessir, Mistah Rawlerson. What kin I do for ye?"

"Need a quart of your finest."

Bogator's face formed a smile. "You be huntin the fox tonight."

"I am."

The old man's smile bled away. "Old fox ain't hurt you, but you goan chase him tryin to forget that what has."

James Arthur looked right and left at the homes crowding the old man's establishment, dwellings haphazardly fashioned from any and all things ever discarded by society. He looked at Bogator. "You know me pretty well."

Bogator leaned and spat and shook his head. "Nosir," he said. "I only know the man you be at times like this. I know that man cause I been that man my ownself."

"I reckon you have."

Bogator nodded. He chewed. "You bring cash money?"

James Arthur fished a folded dollar from his pants pocket and stepped to the old man. He tapped the back of a brown hand with the bill. "One Washington," he said.

The old man felt for the dollar and took it and raised the folded paper to his nose. After sniffing it, he uncrossed his legs and rocked forward to rise. When James Arthur took hold of him and steadied him to his feet, Bogator directed his blind stare at the cowman and told him he was much obliged and that he was sorry God had called his daughters home at such a young age, but for him not to worry for He surely had good reason and that reason would one day be obvious even to mortals like themselves. And he told him that he knew that catching the fox was of no importance to him but the chase all important and surely the first dose of medicine to ease the sorrow infecting him. But then he warned against banishing the painful memory of his daughters from his heart completely, for it in him was the only life left to them, and so should be guarded till the end of his days.

*

They rode out an hour before dark, two horsemen leading a pack mule, the cur dog Roy trying to follow but halting at the yard edge when admonished by John Morgan. Their course generally west-southwest but dictated more by the lay of the land than any intent of their own. It had been warm for days but now swirling winds and a dark reef of clouds along the horizon spoke of change.

"You reckon we goan get wet?" said Archie, him slouched in the saddle and studying the weather building beyond his ramrod straight brother with mule in tow.

"Looks like it," said John Morgan.

"We won't if we're back at the house."

"Ain't no deer back at the house."

"Shit," said Archie.

In the last light they made camp in a small palm and oak head about three miles from home, in a tiny island of diversity amid the seemingly endless pine barren north of Tenmile Creek. John Morgan quickly stretched his catch rope taut between two palms, over which he draped the canvas tarp he'd carried rolled behind his saddle. Together he and Archie staked the tarp's west end low to the ground. They then circled to the east corners where they threaded pigging string through the grommets and then stretched these lines taut and tied them off to two more palms so that end of their crude shelter opened waist-high and was sloped sufficiently to shed water. Next they spread Archie's smaller tarp as a floor and then tossed in upon it their respective wool blankets. They unsaddled and hobbled the horses and hobbled the mule once its yoked burden of canvas sacks had been set to ground.

A southwesterly breeze already evident suddenly began to torment the palm fronds overhead, raising but a whispered warning of what was surely to come. John Morgan glanced up at the rustling overhead, the starless void beyond, then squatted next to the canvas sacks and began sorting through their contents. He removed a kerosene lamp and a quart jar of extra fuel and set them beneath the tarp. The lamp fitted with a loop of wire for a handle and a piece of tin shaped around its globe to effect a somewhat focused beam of light. "Rain gets to our light, we'll play hell killin a deer," he muttered before returning to the sacks. He fished out a wool sock holding a half dozen shotgun shells and a box of twenty-two long rifle cartridges and tossed it next to the lamp.

"Gotta get the sugar," said Archie, stepping to the sack nearest him and pulling from it a paper bag half full and rolled closed. "I got to have sugar for my coffee."

"You ain't got to have it."

"Hell I don't."

"Well, set it in your saddlebag; it'll stay dry there. Get it and the flour and the coffee and the salt. Rain won't hurt the rest of that stuff in there. "

Last, they positioned their saddles and tack at the head of the ground tarp, along with the rifle and single-barrel shotgun, a twelve gauge longtom whose fractured forearm was held snug against the barrel by several turns of tightly wrapped pigging string.

Their perishables stowed, they hurried to gather wood ahead of the fast-growing darkness, lighter knots so fat with resin that only the heaviest of rains would hinder its burning. Once they had wood to last the night sheltered by the tarp, the camp they'd fashioned was lost in darkness until John Morgan set a match to kindling shaved from one of the knots. The flame, though tiny at first, soon eased the night back a few feet in all directions; the dome of light produced resurrecting proof of their labor and cloaked them with a comfort perhaps the oldest relished by man. Several more knots and the flames grew and the boys stood back to stare fixedly at the wonder inherent to their creation.

They stood silently watching the writhing flames for several minutes. At the dome of light's outer limits, the hobbled horses and mule also watching. Archie eventually sagged to his knees, unsheathed his belt knife and began to turn it this way and that in the fluctuating light, a replica of the fire there in the cold steel, then gone, then there again, his eyes and features ultimately morphing into those of a madman as he fixated on the crude lightshow of his own making.

John Morgan, his look morphing from puzzlement to concern as he watched his brother, finally said: "Put that dang pig-sticker away. Wish I'd never give you the damn thing. Hunt us up some oak wood so I can warm up Mama's supper."

*

By the time they'd eaten sweet potato, cornbread, and salt pork, the wind was gusting stronger. A dull roar rising in the southwest and growing louder was now upon them, the leading edge of the front raising a shout of clashing limbs and fronds and falling debris. The fire licking long over the ground like a thing tethered but bent on making an escape, its smoke and glowing embers shuttling away through the hammock as if the earth were suddenly spinning faster and carrying camp and boys into a night they'd long remember. And then it began to rain.

"Damn," said Archie, ducking beneath the tarp, his eyes wide with awe.

John Morgan, a hand holding his flapping hat in place, grinned at his brother. "You scared?"

"Hell, yeah," said Archie. "Ain't you?"

John Morgan nodded. "But we'll be all right, long as a tree don't fall on us."

John Morgan heaped more lighter knots on the fire then joined Archie beneath the tarp. They sat Indian-fashion facing the writhing fire, watching the rain slant across their tiny aberration of light in the otherwise seamless night, listening to the big drops pelt the billowing tarp, to the hiss they raised when conflicting with the fire. While the horses and mule stood with their rumps to the onslaught, their heads hung in an attitude of resignation, the boys huddled and watched and listened and soon the strong wind ramped down to a breeze and the downpour slackened to a steady drizzle.

Archie had his knife out. He sat with elbows pressed to knees, monotonously probing the dirt beyond the ground tarp. "Reckon why you and me didn't ketch the sickness?" he suddenly asked.

John Morgan shrugged. "I don't know. Just lucky, I reckon, long with a lot of other folks." He reached a hand up and pushed against the sagging tarp, causing a stream of water to briefly run off one corner.

Archie cleaned dirt from the knife's blade by dragging it across his knee. He then fetched a small whet rock from his pocket and began to hone the cutting edge with a circular motion. "Well, I'm glad you ain't dead," he said. "If you was dead, I'd just as well be too."

John Morgan looked sideways at his brother. "Don't talk like that, Arch. You got to live your own life. I may not always be around, you know."

Archie grew still, the knife in one hand and the whet rock in the other. "Yeah, you will. We get our own place, it'll be just the two of us. That's what you always say. You said it a thousand times. Ever time I get scared over somethin. 'Don't worry, Arch,' you say, 'I'm here. I'll always be here.'" He reached the knife forward sufficiently to wet the five-inch blade at the tarp's drip line before resuming his sharpening ritual. "Now ain't that what you said?"

John Morgan looked at his brother then refocused on the fire. "I said it and I meant it every time. But once you're a grown man, you can't keep holdin me to that *always* stuff. I expect we'll meet gals we want to marry and all. That happens, you goan be on your own."

"Ain't no gal goan keep me from bein your brother."

John Morgan laughed. He removed his hat and looked in its bowl then set it back on his head. "You almost thirteen and still talkin like that?"

Archie cocked his head in puzzlement.

"Well, you're bout to get throwed by that horse. Won't be long fore *anything* in a dress can make you forget you even got a brother."

Archie shook his head. "No, I won't."

John Morgan smiled. "I hear ya," he said. He reached to his side and captured a large chunk of the fatwood and turned back and laid it on the fire. He began removing his boots. "Let's get some sleep," he said. "This rain quits, the deer'll be stirrin like crazy."

*

Sometime in the night cold air kissed John Morgan awake and he sat upright to look and listen. A gentle westerly breeze eddying through the hammock. An occasional patter on the tarp overhead as moving air and gravity conspired to evict the last trace of rain from the canopy above. The fire was now just glowing embers. He scooted forward in his blanket and fed it a small piece of lighter then reached and shook his fetal-positioned brother.

Archie groaned.

"Come on. Get your shoes on. The rain's done quit and it's good and cold."

Archie stirred beneath his blanket, but quickly grew still once again.

"All right, suit yourself. Reckon I can hold a light and shoot too."

"It's my turn to shoot."

After dressing his feet, John Morgan lit the kerosene lamp while Archie slipped on his brogans and staggered a few yards into the darkness to relieve himself. John Morgan set the lamp on the ground and turned and ducked back beneath the tarp to fetch the rifle. Returning to the fire, he worked the weapon's slide to load a cartridge in the chamber then eased the hammer down to half cock.

Archie reappeared from the darkness. "How many bullets you got in it?"

John Morgan handed the rifle to his brother. "More than enough," he said. "One's enough if you shoot straight."

Archie shouldered the rifle and sighted it through a hole in the canopy, a ragged opening to the sky told by myriad twinkling stars. Lowering the rifle, he swung it to rest in the crook of his left arm. He stood tall, eyeing his brother. "Well," he said, "what are you waitin for? I'm ready to kill my first deer."

John Morgan frowned and shook his head. "Yeah?" he said. "Well, see that you mind that muzzle while we're walkin, so you don't kill me."

After checking the hobbled stock, John Morgan cut a near-straight sweet gum sapling and limbed its four-foot trunk save for a fork at the top sufficient to hold the lamp's wire handle. The stick in one hand and the lamp swinging from the other, he led Archie from the hammock into the more open pine woods where he set the lamp in the low palmettos then straightened and cocked his head back to study the heavens.

"Near bout three o'clock," he said in a low voice.

"How you know that?"

"Old Orion," John Morgan said. "He's done in the southwest quadrant, headed for the horizon. We got bout three hours till the moon shows itself, what moon there'll be with it bein new and all."

"Oh," said Archie.

They set a due-south course through the sparse pines and low palmettos, John Morgan carrying the lofted lamp like a flag bearer and Archie following his lead. When the ground began to slope downward, the light revealed a strand of hardwoods and palms ahead, whereupon they turned westward into a moderate breeze carrying the crisp, clean news of cooler weather to come. They moved slowly: a few deliberate steps before long pauses during which John Morgan's eyes incessantly panned the limits of the meager light. Stepping and standing, the wet undergrowth affording them silent passage. At a point where the low palmettos and gallberries abruptly gave way to a grassy opening—a chain of narrow, shallow ponds linked by a well-worn cow trail—John Morgan stopped mid-stride. "Deer," he breathed.

Archie eased right to see around his stock-still brother. Once clear, a veritable galaxy of tiny lights stretched along the far pond edge not fifty yards distant. "Shit," he whispered. "They's a passel of em."

"Six," John Morgan hissed. "The last one in line's a buck. Put it right behind his shoulder."

Archie shouldered the rifle and swung it to his right, to the last set of eyes. He strained to make out the body that carried them but could see nothing save the two tiny white lights. "Cain't see his body," he whispered.

"Look to one side," John Morgan instructed. "Use your side vision."

Archie tried not to stare directly at the bobbing eyes and like magic a dim form was there. He did this several times in rapid succession then sighted the rifle where he remembered the front third of the animal's body to be. He was shaking, but squeezed the trigger nevertheless.

At the crack of the little rifle the muzzle flash blinded Archie for a fraction of a second. When he regained his sight, the shining eyes were gone and the grassy opening seemed to him unbearably empty. His legs were suddenly palsied to the point where he could scarcely stand. "Did I get him?" he blurted.

"He hunched up when you shot," said John Morgan. "Think you hit him too far back."

"But I did hit him?"

"I'm afraid you did," he said, his tone joyless, one of concern. He stepped toward the spot where the deer had been, moving deliberately across the dry pond with his eyes searching the amber grass ahead. Upon nearing the wall of palmettos defining the far side of the grassy opening, he halted, signaling with an outstretched hand for Archie to do likewise. "Go easy," he said. "If he's gut-shot, blood's goan be hard to find."

They stood in place for several minutes, John Morgan's eyes panning left and right along the dim game trail that followed the pond edge. Eventually, he unhooked the lamp from the forked stick and lowered it to cast the meager light ever so slowly over the ground, searching for a beginning to the story they humans and the deer had just written, a first clue to a riddle he feared would not be easily solved. He stepped and stood, not proceeding until he'd inspected every inch of ground below the lamp. After moving right a few feet, he pointed to a whorl of freshly turned dirt with the forked stick. "Here we go," he said. "This is where he was standin."

Archie looked. "Looks like he spun and went that-a-way," he said, gesturing northward into the darkness.

John Morgan was silent. He skirted the fresh sign, studying the ground until locating the next set of splayed tracks where the deer had landed its first leap. He searched further, then stopped and pointed the stick at a glistening palmetto frond where the dim trail exited the open pond, at a tiny crimson smear running counter to the natural growth lines of the frond. "He's hit," he said, dropping the stick and reaching to touch the found evidence.

"I knew it," said Archie. "I done got me my first buck."

48

John Morgan moved his hand close to the light, studying the dark blood his touch had gleaned from the frond. He raised his hand to his nose. "You ain't got anything yet," he said. "This ain't lung blood. Liver, maybe, but it sure ain't lung."

"Will a liver shot kill one?"

John Morgan wiped his fingers on his pants leg. "Yeah, it will. But it'll take a while." He turned and looked out into the darkness. He looked at the eastern sky. "We best head back to camp," he said, "ketch us a little nap until it gets light, give that little buck time to stiffen up. He probably ain't gone a hundred yards or so. We go to trailin him now, we're apt to just jump him, run him clear out of the country."

Archie scuffed the ground with his shoe. "Shoot," he said, "I don't want to take no nap. I want to keep huntin." He raised the rifle and aimed it at the darkness. "I want to shoot me another buck. I'll shoot the next one right in the heart. Won't be no need to track the next one."

John Morgan reached down and plucked the forked stick from the ground. He stood tall and turned and began retracing the path they'd taken across the dry pond. "We ain't huntin another deer till we do right by this one," he said.

*

They added wood to the dying fire back at camp before ducking beneath the tarp to remove their footwear. It was much colder now. Their breath plumed before them as they wrapped in their blankets and sat watching the fire leap to the new wood like a thing alive, like an entity knowing that just such an offering was, for it, life itself.

John Morgan sat with his knees drawn up, his arms embracing his legs tightly in search of body heat. When first assuming this position something in his pants pocket captured his attention by gouging his groin area. He lay back and slipped a hand into the pocket and withdrew the tormenting culprit. Rocking forward to sit tailorwise, he snaked a hand free of his blanket to study the wooden disk in the firelight.

"What's that you got there?" asked Archie. "That a checker piece?"

"I ain't sure what it is. It ain't no checker, though—too big for a checker."

"Where'd you get it?"

"A girl give it to me."

"What girl?"

"A girl I met at Mr. Cobb's store, a few weeks back when I posted that letter for Daddy."

"Well, why'd you keep it? It ain't good for nothin."

John Morgan looked at his brother. "The hell it ain't," he said. "She said it was valuable. Sides, she's about the prettiest thing I ever seen, and I aim to give it back to her someday."

Archie looked at the disk then looked at the fire. "Well, how long we got till the sun comes up?"

"What?"

"I'm hungry. Let's fix us some breakfast."

*

As they set forth leading the mule into the thinning darkness, the covey calls of quail, along with the raspy cries of brown thrashers and the whistling passage of wood ducks and merganzers, sang to them with certainty that the godmade sun was about to rise. And when they'd retraced their steps of the night before and stood dew-soaked and expectant in the grassy pond, their shadows grew long before them as the dawn-song concluded and the new day was born.

After hobbling the mule in the pond, they found the blood smear of the night before and began a slow advance through the low palmettos, stepping and standing, searching with their eyes for any clue to the path taken by the wounded deer. It was tedious work, labor of a sort to which Archie was ill-suited.

"That deer ain't dead," he said after they'd searched for a half hour and found only one additional drop of blood, ten feet beyond the first. "I must of just nicked him."

John Morgan ignored his brother.

"Come on," he whined. "There'd be more blood if I'd hit him good."

"There ain't no blood cause the bullet didn't pass through. Little twenty-two hardly ever goes all the way through a deer."

"You don't know that."

"Hell I don't. I've seen it a bunch of times."

John Morgan continued to search. The next time he thought to check on his brother, Archie had retreated to the grassy pond and was sitting cross-legged with his head hung. John Morgan shook his own head as if to rid his mind of the sight then turned back to study the terrain ahead. Just beyond the last blood sign, he noticed a subtle opening threading its way northward through the palmettos and gallberries. He briefly studied this path of least resistance then began to walk at a right angle to the dim trail. He walked eastward about fifty yards then turned back west; no longer looking for blood, he now simply searched for the deer itself, zigzagging back and forth across the path he judged the deer had taken. He repeated this pattern for almost an hour, inching steadily northward until literally stumbling over the object of his search.

The young spike buck had died curled in a ball, having traveled less than a hundred yards before lying down. Rigor mortis had set in. When John Morgan grabbed hold of an antler to begin dragging the animal back to the pond, it was as if he dragged a statue of a bedded deer.

Archie leaped to his feet when he saw John Morgan stooped low and coming hard through the palmettos. He ran to his brother with eyes wide and mouth agape. "I knew it," he said. "I knew I shot straight."

"You beat all, Arch," said John Morgan, dragging the deer on into the open before releasing his grip and standing tall to catch his breath. He looked at the mule which stood cropping grass a few feet away then looked at his brother who was kneeling at the deer's head, admiring the six-inch antlers. "That knife of yours sharp?"

"Sharp enough to shave," said Archie, standing and reaching to slip the knife from its sheath.

"Well, give it here, and I'll walk you through how to gut this little feller."

"We goan butcher it right here?"

"No. We're just gonna gut him here. Then we'll break camp and take him on home. We'll butcher there, where we can wash the meat and all."

Archie extended the knife but then pulled it back. "I can gut him," he said.

"You can do some of it, but we done worked too hard to go and mess up the meat now. There's a couple of steps to this job I need to do, steps you need to just watch and learn." John Morgan paused and reached and grabbed the deer's hind legs. "Grab hold of his front legs and let's stretch him out. He's done got stiff as a board."

When they had stretched the deer long, John Morgan rolled it onto its back and straddled its ribcage, holding it in position with his legs. With his left hand he pinched white hair and hide at the sternum while reaching out to Archie with the other. "Give me the knife," he said. "I'll get you started."

He slit an opening in the hide as he pulled up on it, revealing the membrane encasing the internal organs. He slipped two fingers in the hole in the hide and pulled up and began a cut longitudinally toward the rear of the animal. "All right," he said. "Straddle him like this and you can open him up."

Archie did as told and John Morgan handed him the knife.

"Get your two fingers in there and spread em. Slip your blade in between em there and push forward. Pull up on the hide as you go so's you don't cut into the guts and all. You cut into the guts we'll have us a mess."

Archie did as directed and began inching forward.

"That's it. Go right on ahead. Carry your cut all the way down alongside his nut sack. That's it. Good job. Now come on back up to his sternum and make you a little hole in that membrane. Slip your fingers in there and do just like you did with the hide. Slit it all the way down, bein careful not to nick the stomach or an intestine. That's it. That's far enough. Now step off and let me get the liver and heart. We go home without them, Mama's apt to skin us."

Before straddling the deer, John Morgan gestured to the mule. "Fetch me that flour sack from the pack." Not waiting for Archie's return, he bent at the waist and went to work. "To get that old liver you got to first cut away the diaphragm, this tough joker here that separates the innards from the lungs and heart. Just take your knife and work along the inside of the ribs here. Follow the curve of the ribs, cuttin loose the diaphragm as you go. There. Then you just move over and do the other side. Follow the ribs and cut her loose. Your last cut is right here against the backbone. And then she's free. Then you just grab hold of the diaphragm and drag near bout everything out. Just like that, stomach, liver, intestines and all. "He paused and looked at Archie who had returned with the flour sack. "Reckon you can do it the next time?"

"Do what?" said Archie.

*

The ride home was pleasant, with the air cool and the late morning sun warming them about the neck and shoulders like a comforting hand. They rode side by side with the mule following obligingly, its yoked packs and the young buck sawing gently to the hybrid's stiff gait. They talked of the hunt and of how proud their father would be that they'd brought meat for the table without waste of time or ammunition. John Morgan's eyes panned right and left, marking their way while Archie occasionally glanced back at the deer, each occasion causing him to sit a little taller, to feel giddy with pride. They rode and soon home loomed through the pines ahead, the sight of which caused them to rein to a halt, to sit craning their necks in an attempt to understand the odd activity in their yard: a buckboard wagon with its brace of mules standing stock still in their harness while several men and a woman milled about solemnly at its rear, a Model T automobile parked beyond the wagon.

"That's Doc Clark's automobile," said John Morgan.

"That's Mama, ain't it?"

"Yeah, but I don't see Daddy."

"Wonder what's goin on?"

"I ain't got the foggiest notion, but I'm bout to find out."

They urged the horses forward at a trot, the hounds in the pens standing strangely silent as they rode past them and on into the yard. The faces of four men and their mother swung in unison to their approach, the men's stoic, displaying no emotion of any sort, their mother's drawn, streaked with tears. Raylene hurried to them as they dismounted, daubing her face with a wadded handkerchief as she came.

"Boys," she said, gathering them in a wide embrace.

"What's happened, Mama?" John Morgan pleaded. "Where's Daddy?" He noted the faces of Doctor Clark, Sheriff Carlton, Henry Adams, and an employee of Adams whose name escaped him. "Where's Daddy?" he repeated.

Archie stood holding his horse's reins, his eyes wide and focused blankly on the buckboard wagon.

Raylene grasped John Morgan's shoulder with one hand while waving the handkerchief at the wagon with the other. "He's gone, John Morgan. He's with your sisters now." She squeezed his shoulder hard. "His body's over in that wagon, but don't you go over there. It's a pitiful sight. I don't want you should remember him like this." She looked at Archie. "You neither, Arch. You stay away from that wagon."

Archie stepped and stood. He flung an arm back in the direction of the mule. "I got me a buck," he said.

John Morgan heard nothing past the reference to his sisters. Numb, he pulled away from his mother and started for the wagon, floated toward the wagon like a figure in a dream.

Sheriff Carlton, still wearing his soiled butcher's apron, stepped forward and tried to intercept him, but John Morgan brushed the shorter man aside and moved on to the wagon's side where he leaned in to look without hesitation.

A sheet of canvas covered the still form that lay lengthwise in the wagon's bed, an innocuous mound had there not been worn boots exposed at one end, familiar boots toed skyward and virtually shouting the truth. John Morgan reached a shaking hand in and pulled back a corner of the cover, revealing the head of a man turned at an impossible angle, a grotesque bulge in the neck below the base of the skull. John Morgan looked but briefly at the foreign features before laying the canvas back as it had been. Yet the horror etched in his father's face remained starkly clear, as it would for the rest of his life. He turned and looked to the men grouped at the wagon's rear, all standing with hat in hand and watching him intently. "What happened?" he said.

The men stepped and stood, casting glances at one another as if to elect a proper spokesperson. Then Henry Adams stepped forward and skirted the wagon to stand facing John Morgan. He looked at the ground and looked into the boy's eyes. "His horse stepped in a gopher hole," Adams began. He turned his grey felt hat in his hands. "I don't know what got into him. Honest to God, I don't."

John Morgan's eyebrows arched. "The horse?"

"No," said Adams. "Your daddy."

"I don't understand."

Adams scuffed the ground with a boot. "Well, reckon that makes two of us." He took a deep breath. "Let me start at the beginnin. Maybe we can make some sense out of it."

"Yessir," John Morgan said.

The cur dog Roy suddenly appeared from beneath the wagon and settled on its haunches next to the boy's leg, its canine eyes focused intently on the man Adams, as though it, too, awaited an explanation. Raylene remained standing with Archie before the milling horses and mule, her eyes glassy and her swaying slowly from side to side in the manner of the truly bereaved.

Henry Adams set his hat on his head. He looked at the ground and looked at John Morgan. "He got to my place bout dark," he said, "just had that big black and tan and that Bluetick bitch with him. I asked why he only brought the two and he said they was the only two worth a damn. Said the others had done got too old to be of much good."

"Yessir."

"Anyways, we seen weather was makin up, so we decided to wait it out in the barn. We built us a little fire in the open bay and set there sippin corn liquor—just talkin bout this and that till the rain quit. Don't know what time it finally did quit, but it had to of been pretty late. Round midnight, I reckon. Neither one of us had a watch, so that's just a guess."

"So y'all had been drinkin a good while."

Adams visibly stiffened, his eyes narrowing as he studied the boy. "Yeah," he said, "reckon we had, but wasn't neither of us too drunk to ride, if that's what you're thinkin."

John Morgan said nothing. He cast a quick glance at his mother then simply continued to look Adams in the eye, waiting for the man to continue.

"We wasn't drunk," Adams said. "Just a little tipsy is all."

"Tipsy," John Morgan echoed. "So what happened then?"

"Well, I turned out four of my dogs and we set out headin north. We hadn't gone but a little ways when the dogs struck and lit out due west. They must of got close enough to shake hands with that old fox fore he jumped, cause they was all six of them hounds in full cry. Sweetest music I've heard in a long time." Adams paused and turned to look at the three men behind him. "And like I told you all, this is when me and Jimmy always find us a spot to build a little fire and just sit and listen to the race." He turned back to John Morgan. "We done it a hundred times, him and me." He paused and stood shaking his head. "But not this time. No, sir. This time, for Lord knows what reason, old Jimmy just all of a sudden up and whips his horse to a gallop, takes out after them dogs and it dark as a blind man's night out there. Hell, I couldn't see the horse under me, so I wasn't bout to try and foller him. I wasn't sure what to do, so I went ahead and built a fire so he'd know where I was. Set there by it listenin to the race, waitin for old Jimmy to come on back. A couple hours after I ain't heard the dogs no more, my four come tricklin in, one after the other they come. But not Jimmy's pair, nor him either. So soon as it got light enough to see, I mounted up and went lookin. Found him almost a half mile from where it all started." Adams paused again and stood looking at the ground. "I found him pretty quick cause I remembered the way the race first took shape. I rode that way and wasn't long fore I seen his horse. Old horse was standin even though its right foreleg was snapped clean through." He turned and looked at the sheriff. "I put the thing down fore I come to get you, Dan. I disremember whether I told you that earlier."

The sheriff nodded. "You told me."

Adams likewise nodded then turned back to John Morgan. "Your daddy's two dogs was a-layin there next to him, like they was protectin him and all."

"He didn't say nothin?" John Morgan said.

Henry Adams' eyes squinted tightly in puzzlement. "Course not," he said.

John Morgan sighed and kicked at the ground. "I mean before, when he lit out after the dogs."

"Oh," said Adams. "Didn't say a word, just took off."

"That don't sound like Daddy. I ain't known him to be reckless, day or night."

"Me neither," agreed Adams. "Like I said, I don't know what made him do it. I surely don't."

John Morgan looked up at the cloudless sky, down at the dog squatted next to his leg. He looked at Henry Adams. "What'd y'all talk about? There in the barn, when you was waitin for the rain to stop."

Adams reached and removed his hat and briefly scratched his head before setting the hat back in place and squaring it. "Well," he said. "Now that you mention it, I reckon I done most of the talkin. Thinkin back on it, I reckon he did seem a bit peculiar and all, like as if he had the blues. Reckon I didn't think much of it at the time. Probably that good corn liquor he brung. It tends to have that effect on me, I know, only lettin me see the good side of a situation."

John Morgan nodded. He looked around as if calculating the sum total of all that rendered the scene in which he stood possible. He sighed and then he stepped around the dog still sitting by his leg to again look in the wagon's bed. "I'll be needin to make arrangements," he said.

Sheriff Carlton stepped to his side. "We'll take him on in to the funeral parlor, son. You see to your mama and your brother. You can come on in later when y'all decide what you want done." He patted the boy's shoulder but said nothing more.

John Morgan nodded to the sheriff. He reached and touched his hat brim to the other men and thanked them aloud before turning and striding toward his mother.

*

The burial was two days later, the eighteenth day of November in the year of their Lord, 1912. It being a Sunday, James Arthur Rawlerson was laid to rest beside the graves of his precious daughters, immediately following the regular church service, the last portion of which having focused on remembering his life. And when the congregation moved outdoors to the cemetery Raylene wept with shame upon seeing the wood marker that was to serve as the only record of her husband's existence. John Morgan shed no such tears. He stood ramrod-straight throughout the burial and throughout his mother's ululation, but when all had gone save they three, he turned to his mother and brother and vowed before them and God above that the wood was temporary, that he would one day see to it that his father's name and life be memorialized in stone. He swore this as a blood oath, and then he escorted home the only remaining souls with whom he shared the blood bespoke.

*

While Archie sat dozing across the table, John Morgan studied his mother as she labored at the stove. He noticed for the first time that her hair was graying, that her face was now fraught with wrinkles. The events of the past month had aged her, he concluded, rendered her old before her time. This realization troubled him, saddened him, as did the empty chairs spaced around the table between him and his brother.

"Mama," John Morgan said.

Raylene looked over her shoulder.

"Did Daddy already pay Mr. Vogler the rent money for next year?"

"No, he didn't. It's not due until January. Mr. Vogler usually sends his man around sometime early in the month."

"We got enough saved to pay it?"

Raylene shook her head. "We've only got about half, now that he upped it to seventy-five dollars."

"Reckon I'll have to sell off a few of the yearlins."

Raylene nodded. "That's just what your daddy planned on doin."

John Morgan tapped the table top with a knuckle. "Me and Arch are gonna try and bag us a turkey," he said.

Raylene spooned a pair of fried eggs from the frying pan to a plate already holding bacon and grits. She brought it to the table and set it in front of Archie, causing her youngest to jolt from his slumber and take up his flatware and begin eating. She looked at John Morgan. "You mean for Thanksgiving?"

"Yes, ma'am."

Raylene touched his shoulder. "A turkey would be just fine," she said, her unfocused gaze directed at the wall beyond the stove. "It's good that you're thinkin ahead like that. We all need to be thinkin ahead, cause ain't nothin in the past goan fill our bellies." She moved back to the stove and reached to snare two more eggs from the basket. Using a single hand she deftly cracked the pair on the edge of the pan and dropped their viscous contents in with no conscious thought needed to guide her actions.

"They're firin up that new plant that evenin," he said. "Maybe after we eat we can ride in and see if it works and all. See if them new street lamps is the wonder everybody says they'll be."

Archie stopped chewing his food long enough to listen for his mother's reply.

"I'd like to do that," she said. "I can post a letter to your Uncle Jude about what's happened. There wasn't time to let him and Aunt Betty know before the funeral, but I got no excuse not to do it now. And we can stop by the cemetery fore we come home—see how the flowers is holdin up."

"What plant you all talkin bout?" said Archie.

John Morgan rolled his eyes. "The electricity plant," he said. "The one in that brick building you'd know all about if you ever made it to school."

Archie frowned, but quickly erased the expression from his face by spooning in another mouthful of grits.

"Y'all stop your bickerin," said Raylene. "You're the men of this house now. Bout time you start actin like it."

*

Thanksgiving came and went without a turkey to grace the table, the boys finding that the birds were scarce and the time to hunt them even scarcer. They witnessed in amazement the arrival of electricity to Ft. Pierce, a simple switch closing that not only illuminated Mainstreet but forever altered a sense of permanence long held in their minds. And the day following, their amazement quickly shelved in memory, they fell to the endless menial tasks required to simply survive.

As the year sped to a close, John Morgan worked from dark to dark every day save Christmas, Archie shadowing him and sometimes lending a hand when told. They worked as a family. The first thing each morning Raylene milked the cow and fed the chickens while the boys tended to the horses and dogs, the tack or fencing that needed mending, any new problem to surface before they rode out to check on the whereabouts and well-being of the cattle, to service the hogtrap and any bounty it might hold. Each day a blurred repetition of the previous, yet each unique in its own way, days brimming with lessons and knowledge invaluable to any and all bearing for the first time the full weight of responsibility. Day by day John Morgan and his mother adjusted to the lot life had given them, but not Archie. Archie continued to seem mired in a timeless world of his own.

*

In the growing light he made his way to the dog pen, a plate of table scraps in his right hand, his brother shuffling a few steps behind with hands pocketed against the cold. A clear sky and no wind, on this the first day of the new year. A lamp shone in the pole barn where their mother milked the cow and the calf paced and bawled, where their two horses stood saddled and waiting. When he reached the pen, John Morgan unlatched the rickety gate and stepped inside the twenty-by-twenty enclosure of head-high chicken wire tacked to lighter posts, a stilted hutch at its center the dogs' only refuge against rain or sun or wind. The rank smell of feces and urine. He moved carefully so as not to step in any of the dogs' fresh deposits.

While the two younger animals bounded from the hutch to meet his approach, the older pair scarcely stirred. The older pair, a red-bone bitch and a walker male, remained tightly curled, merely eying John Morgan skeptically. On the plate he carried were pork rib bones and he tossed several to the Bluetick and black and tan before stepping forward and offering the plate to the disinterested pair.

"How come we keep feedin them dogs?" said Archie.

"Cause they'd starve if we didn't."

"All they do is eat and sleep. Old things ain't good for nothin."

"They were good dogs in their time. They deserve to get fed long as they got the strength to eat."

"We ought to put em down. Be more food for them two that earns their keep."

John Morgan cast his brother a sideways look. "You could do that? Kill old Jim and Bell like they don't count for nothin?"

"I'll cut their throats right now, if you want."

John Morgan studied his brother. "Sometimes I worry bout you, Arch. I could never kill anything that trusts me, and it pains me to hear you talk like it wouldn't mean nothin to you." He threw the last of the rib bones to the dogs then turned to Archie. "I know you don't mean half of what you say, but you go round talkin like that, somebody's goan take you serious. People will get to thinkin you ain't got good sense or somethin. You don't want that to happen, do you?"

Archie stood watching the two old hounds gingerly mouth their respective bones. "Look at that," he said. "Them things ain't hardly got a tooth left in their heads."

John Morgan sighed. "You ain't heard a word I said." He reached and thumped Archie's ear. "Come on," he said, "we got cows to ketch. I told Mr. Adams we'd have em to his place by noon."

*

The cur dog Roy found a group of twenty or so yearlings and heifers laid up in the oaks and palms bordering the west side of Five Mile Creek. The cows scattered like quail at the dog and riders' approach. John Morgan quickly identified the older heifer he reasoned to be the group's Judas, riding the cow down in the open flatwoods and turning her back northward and blocking her every attempt to deviate from that course until she slowed to a fast walk. All save a couple of heifers trailed behind the matriarch with Archie behind them and sawing his horse right and left sufficiently to discourage any attempt to stray.

John Morgan called the dog to heel by his side as he coaxed the cow forward. "Don't push em," he called to Archie. "Just keep em in line. I'd just as soon walk the rest of the way."

When they'd pushed the cows northward about two miles, Henry Adams' house and barns were there in the distance, their tin roofs reflecting the midday sun amid the palms and oaks ringing his homeplace. They rode, and when within a few hundred yards of the holding pens situated west of the buildings, they saw two men step from the shaded interior of the main barn into the bright sunlight.

Henry Adams raised a hand in greeting then walked to the trap. He slid the latch bar back and walked the gate open wide and stood holding it that it not swing and cause the oncoming cattle to shy. The other man assumed a position at the far side of the trap's open mouth, standing with arms wide that the advancing cows might see him as the deterrent he hoped to represent.

John Morgan coaxed the lead cow forward, holding his coiled catch rope and the reins in his left hand while building a loop with his right. He watched the cow closely, and when suddenly her head came up and her eyes began darting left and right in search of a way out, he urged his horse forward and dropped the loop over the cow's substantial horns and drew it tight before she could react. He threw a turn of the rope around the pommel horn and rode on into the trap, the cow stiff legged and braced to resist but having little choice in the matter and advancing on into the trap with her eyes walling and long strings of slobber trailing from her mouth.

Archie sawed his horse right and left behind the rest of the cows, waving a hand skyward and yipping them forward, the dog Roy darting from side to side, nipping at first one and then another, it playing a role in the penning drama both instinctive and practiced. When the last cow was in the trap Henry Adams swung the gate closed and stood holding it shut while John Morgan dismounted to set the cow loose. He pointed a finger as he counted to himself the number of cows penned.

"Looks like you brought nine steers and eight heifers, John Morgan," he said. "Which six was it you wanted to sell?"

John Morgan led Shorty toward the gate, coiling the rope as he came. "Any six of the steers you like," he said. "Figured it'd be easier to sort em here, if that suits you?"

Adams opened the gate sufficiently to let John Morgan lead his horse out of the trap. "That's fine by me," he said as the boy passed. "We'll sort the six, change that backwards-R of yours to my hooked-A and turn em all back out." He closed the gate and slid the bar through its slot in the post to latch it. "How you doin, Arch?" he said, shooting a glance up at the younger Rawlerson who sat his paint horse gazing at nothing in particular, his hands crossed over the pommel horn and him slouched in the saddle as if about to fall asleep.

Archie grinned and dipped his head.

Adams' hired hand stepped next to Henry. He reached and touched his cap bill, his eyes swinging from one boy to the other.

Seeing the gesture, Adams said: "You all know Duck, don't ya?"

John Morgan offered his hand to the heavyset man and the man reached and captured it with his. "I've seen you around," said John Morgan.

"Duck Gordon," the man said. "Real name's Bill but most people call me Duck, on account of how I walk, I reckon."

Adams smiled. He looked at Gordon. "You reckon?" he said, swinging his arms and scuffing the ground with a boot. He looked at John Morgan. "Well, let's get these yearlins identified. Then we can all go in the house and get you paid, get you all a cool drink fore you head out." He cast a cursory glance up at Archie.

Archie visibly jerked, as if surprised to be acknowledged. "What you got to drink?" he said.

*

In the evening after supper John Morgan sat at the table with his mother, sipping coffee and discussing their future while Archie dozed in his mother's rocker. A slim stack of bank notes and a pile of change lay on the table between them, along with the canning jar and a leather-bound ledger whose edges were worn and tattered, two yellow pencils, knife-sharpened and pitted with bite marks.

John Morgan snared one of the pencils and used it to tap the table. "That leaves us almost sixty dollars," he said, "after we pay Vogler?"

Raylene nodded. "But that don't make us rich. Time we buy our staples, seed for spring plantin, there won't be a whole lot left."

John Morgan tapped the table. "Yeah, but at least we got enough to get them things without sellin off more cows."

Raylene stirred her coffee and set the spoon on the saucer next to the cup. "And that's a blessing for sure, but we best not get too cocky. It's been my experience that trouble's not somethin easy to see comin. And trouble's always comin. That's just the way it is for folks like us tryin to get out from under."

John Morgan straightened in his chair. He reached and bumped back his hat. "Well, I don't see nothin comin we can't handle." He sipped his coffee and set the cup back on its saucer. "Did I tell you bout the calves?"

"You told me."

"They's thirty-four we've found so far. All of em doctored against the screwworms and pert as you please."

Raylene nodded. "That's good to know."

John Morgan looked at the money on the table and looked at his mother. "Did I tell you bout the new dippin vat they're puttin in up toward Ft. Drum?"

Raylene smiled and shook her head. "No, you ain't told me bout that."

"Henry says the state's goan build it, make it so anybody who can get their cows there can use it. They're even goan provide the arsenic to mix the dip with."

"Why do you need to dip the cows? Your daddy never done it. Is it to kill ticks and such?"

"Yes, ma'am. That's exactly the reason. Henry said it's the government tryin to control the fever tick problem, fore it gets any worse."

"I didn't know there was a problem."

"I ain't either, till Henry told me. He said there was an outbreak west of Okeechobee last year. Over round Fisheating Creek. Said they think it's cause of there bein so many deer in them parts."

"What's deer got to do with it?"

John Morgan shrugged. "I reckon cause deer usually got ticks. I know every one I ever dressed sure had em. Had a passel of em."

Raylene sipped her coffee. She glanced at Archie sleeping in the rocker. "How did Arch do today?"

"He did all right."

"He did."

"Yes, ma'am. He wasn't no shirker today."

Raylene eased her chair back and stood and began clearing the table. "Well, we best get to bed. Lord knows it don't take long to spend the night round this place."

"The Lord and me both," said John Morgan. "It don't never take long at all."

*

The following week he and Archie were splitting and stacking oak logs just before noon at the east end of the house when the sound of an approaching automobile gave them pause to stand wide-eyed with wonder.

The car that appeared on their lane was a cream-colored roadster the likes of which they'd never seen, a convertible with the top down, two men in the front seat, a man and a woman seated behind, the lady with a hand up and pressing a plumed hat to her blond head. The car came on and cut a wide arc through the front yard before ultimately easing to a halt when broadside to the home's front stoop, the engine not slowing to an idle until the be-goggled man driving reached and adjusted a lever protruding from the steering column. The middle-aged man occupying the front passenger seat, wearing spectacles and a dark suit with a bright orange bowtie, motioned with a hand for the boys to come forward.

John Morgan leaned and spat. He dropped the maul he'd been holding and stepped toward the vehicle. When a few feet from the seated man who'd summoned him, he stopped and reached and touched his hat brim. "Yessir," he said.

The car's engine purred softly while the lady smiled longingly up at the boy as if he were some rare thing she'd traveled far to see. The man next to her scarcely paid the boy a glance, but seemed rapt with all else surrounding him, his eyes panning the home and the outbuildings as though he might be tested later on all he saw.

The dog Roy slunk from beneath the house and began circling the auto, sniffing intently at the tires as if greatly interested in the news they carried.

"I need to see your father, son," said the suited man. "Is he available?"

John Morgan stepped and stood. He looked at the ground and looked at the man. "Nosir, he ain't." He glanced at the driver whose goggled stare seemed riveted to the front of the car, as if the automobile was his sole concern. "Who should I tell him wants to see him?"

"Jack Vogler," said the man. "I'm your landlord."

"Oh," said John Morgan. He gathered his thoughts and was about to speak but his mother stepped from the house before he could.

"Hey, Mr. Vogler," she said. She carried an envelope in her hand and she gestured with it as she spoke. "I wasn't spectin to see you. I can't remember you ever comin to pick up the rent money."

"That's not why I've come, Mrs. Rawlerson. I'm here to inform James Arthur that his lease will not be renewed."

Raylene seemed to shrink in stature. The lines in her forehead were suddenly more pronounced as her eyes swam to her oldest son. "Well, James Arthur's gone," she said.

"Gone?"

"He died back in November."

The lady seated in the car covered her mouth with a hand. "Oh, Lord," she muttered.

Vogler looked at John Morgan and looked at Raylene. "Well, someone should have told me," he said. He adjusted his position in the seat to better see Raylene. "Have you made plans? Where will you go?"

"We ain't goin anywhere," John Morgan said.

Vogler seemed not to hear the boy. He continued to address Raylene. "I'm going to put this parcel in citrus," he said, "beginning in March." He gestured with a hand to the man in the back seat. "Mr.

Barnes is going to run the operation. He'll be the new tenant on the property."

John Morgan shook a finger at the man. "So you think you can just throw us off the place, like we don't count for nothin."

"John Morgan," Raylene said, glaring at her son. She looked at Vogler, holding the envelope out to him as if thinking he may not have noticed it. "But we got the rent money all ready for you. Seventy-five dollars, just like you said."

Vogler shook his head. "I'm sorry, Mrs. Rawlerson. I'm not changing my mind. I've got my own interests to consider. You've got until the end of February to vacate the premises." He looked at John Morgan. "I don't want this to get ugly, but if you're still here come March, I'll have the authorities evict you." He reached and tapped the driver's shoulder, saying: "Let's go, Charles."

As the automobile moved away Raylene and John Morgan stood in stunned silence, watching it go. Archie shuffled around the corner of the house. He went directly to his mother and reached and tugged on the sleeve of her dress.

A few seconds on Raylene said, "What?" though her eyes were still fixed on the departing car.

"Ain't it bout time for lunch?" said Archie.

*

While Archie ate biscuits slathered with butter and guava preserves, John Morgan and his mother sat at the table weighing the few options seemingly left to them by fate. Was it fate? Raylene considered that their downward spiral may be God's own judgment, that the misery dealt them was simply punishment for them not having attended church more often, that perhaps she herself was to blame for everything, for she was the mother, the guide-on, the family's compass when it came to matters of faith.

"That's hogwash," said John Morgan. "Ain't nobody could of done better than you. Ain't none of this God's fault, either. It's just a run of bad luck, is all. Now it's up to us to change things for the better."

Raylene's eyes moistened. She reached and lightly touched John Morgan's hand.

John Morgan looked at the envelope lying between them on the table, the money that was to have purchased him another year of the only life he'd ever known. "We got so much to do, I don't know where to start," he said.

"We need a direction fore we can start. Where we goan live? How we goan make a livin?"

"What about Uncle Jude?"

"What about him?"

"He's your brother. You reckon he might know of somethin up there round him, maybe some land we could rent and still keep our stock?"

"Well, I don't know. He's only got a few acres, I think. He's workin turpentine there close to his place at Nittaw. He said in his letter that the railroad's through there now, that he could hop on a train and go clear to Jacksonville if he wanted."

"I think it's worth a shot to write him and tell him our situation, see if he's got any ideas."

"He did say to let him know if there was anything they could do."

"There you go," said John Morgan. "You write the letter and I'll take it into town. I can check that bulletin board of Mr. Cobb's. Maybe there's somethin posted there. Seems like I've seen places to rent tacked on it in the past."

*

He found nothing of interest on the bulletin board in Cobb's General Store, and it was two weeks before a response came from Raylene's brother. In the letter Jude Vickers invited them to come and stay with him and his wife, but it would have to be without the cattle. He knew of no land for lease, and he himself only held title to five acres. The cattle, he stated, were a problem for which he had no solution. He went on to say that John Morgan and Archie might find work, since there were numerous cattle ranches in his vicinity. After reading the letter and digesting its contents, John Morgan came to the conclusion that he had no choice but to start over. He would sell the cattle and move their meager belongings back to Osceola County, back to the Kissimmee Valley country from whence his father and mother originally came. The bones of his ancestors were there in that sandy soil, he reasoned, the blood of his blood. And when done reasoning, he concluded that he was simply going home, an epiphany that caused his spirits to soar and rendered him anxious to get started.

*

They were almost four weeks making ready to move. While John Morgan and Archie hunted cows, Raylene packed their belongings at the house, discarding many items that left her weeping: the twins' clothing and playthings, James Arthur's keepsakes she deemed worthless to all save him. Since there was nary a picture by which to remember the girls, she kept a doll belonging to each, along with their respective locks of hair neatly pressed in the pages of the family Bible. A few drawings and papers they'd composed at school. She kept most of James Arthur's clothing, judging that Archie's dimensions would never exceed those of his father, though John Morgan's already had. As the days slipped by she packed and discarded, doubting all the while that their lone wagon could possibly hold all that she couldn't bear to part with.

The boys were able to locate a total of one hundred and four cows and calves, along with the three mixed-breed bulls they suspected would be difficult to sell. Henry Adams paid them top dollar for twenty-nine heifers and their suckling calves. Duck Gordon, trying to build a herd of his own, bought the remaining heifers and steers for twenty-five dollars a head. The bulls they wound up selling to the butcher-sheriff, Mr. Carlton, for a paltry thirty dollars. After paying the taxes from the previous year, they had two thousand and ninety-one dollars hidden away in the wagon when they left for Nittaw.

They set forth at daybreak on the third day of February, it cold and still and the horses' breath pluming as the boys urged them forward at a fast walk. On the wagon, Raylene gave a shake of the reins and the brace of mules leaned amicably into their traces, the wagon trundling with its canvas covering hooped high over their worldly possessions and the cold eliciting creaks and pops from wood and steel and the jersey cow and James Arthur's horse tethered at the rear and slogging forward with heads up and sawing left and right with the wonder known only to the ignorant. Raylene sat tall on the wood seat, clucking to the mules, a heavy wool shawl draped about her shoulders and a yellow bonnet covering her head in expectation of the sun to come. The cur dog Roy struck out at a lope, casting right and left ahead of the procession with its black nose lifted to a wind of its own making, casting right and left yet always moving forward without so much as a glance back. They were going and, like the dog, all in the procession, both man and beast, seemed loath to look back.

That first day they traveled generally northwest across the flatwoods for about three miles, the going slow and rough and the wagon rocking and swaying over the uneven ground and them forced to change course often to negotiate ponds and shallow drains. Mid-morning they reached a dim but familiar trace running east and west that showed signs of horses and wagons having traveled it in the not too distant past. For the next several hours they followed this new trail westward, the sun passing its zenith and the air warming and the animals, though mute as stone, began to speak of their labor. When they reached another trace running north and south, they took it north and soon came to a small oak hammock where they halted in the shade to rest the animals, to rest themselves.

John Morgan stepped down from his horse and dropped the reins to trail and moved to the wagon to assist his mother as she climbed down from the high seat. "This is the old Hungry Land Trail," he said. "It'll take us to Ft. Drum."

Raylene smoothed her dress and stretched and looked at her oldest. "I remember it," she said. "It ain't changed a whole lot since your daddy and me come this way in ninety-seven." She looked out over the country, it mostly open flatwoods and the horizon so distant that she squinted to accommodate the sheer enormity of the view. "The trees seem bigger," she said. "I remember it had burned back then. There was a lot of blackened ground and your daddy and me was filthy time we come through it." She continued to gaze, executing a slow turn of her head. "But I disremember exactly where that was." She looked at John Morgan. "Reckon I never thought I'd have reason to."

Archie sidled up to them, the cur dog trailing behind him. "We goan camp here?"

"Camp," said John Morgan. "We can make another ten miles fore dark. We're just goan eat a bite and rest up the animals." He moved to the water keg strapped to the wagon side. "Fetch me that bucket. Me and you can water the stock while Mama sees to our lunch."

After nooning they moved on, the old cattle trail fairly obvious as the path of least resistance through pine and palmetto country. On several occasions they passed groups of range cattle strung out and grazing the coarse wiregrass interspersed between clumps of palmetto and gallberry, the multicolored cows all slack sided with long ears and most of the adults sporting substantial horns and bad dispositions. As they went the wagon creaked and groaned an audible record of the uneven ground over which it rolled, the horses stepping methodically with their heads sawing right and left and their ears swiveling as if seriously interested in the sights and sounds of the new world through which they traveled.

As the sun neared the western horizon they began to smell smoke, and a few minutes on they saw it: a half-dozen thin gray columns to the west, evenly spaced in a line stretching from north to south.

"What you reckon that is?" said Archie

"I reckon it's smoke."

Archie frowned. "No, shit. I mean what you reckon is goin on over there?"

John Morgan leaned and spat. "I'd say somebody's clearin land over there, burnin some piles is all."

As they continued on with the smoke still evident and the sun about to quit the day, a creek swamp loomed about a mile ahead and as they strove to reach it before nightfall a lone figure appeared in the trail ahead.

"That somebody way up there?" Raylene said.

"Yes, ma'am," said John Morgan. "Looks like somebody afoot."

"Well, I'll be."

As they closed the distance the figure took the shape of a man, a man stooped low and bracing his staggered gait with a long staff, his white hair and flowing beard in stark contrast to the dark and wretched rags he wore for clothes. A man shoeless, his toes splayed and their nails either gone missing or cracked and blackened and resembling small hooves. And when they reached the man John Morgan raised a hand to signal a halt, upon which the man did halt as well.

"Howdy," John Morgan said, his horse blowing and shaking its head while eyeing the strange little man they'd happened upon.

"Afternoon," said the man, his head cocked at an extreme angle in order to study the boy addressing him. While his right hand gripped the staff for support, his left clung to a leather strap draped over his shoulder and attached to a large canvas duffel.

"You come from Ft. Drum?"

The man nodded. "Come by there, I think." He looked at his wretched feet then craned again to look at the boy. "They was a little sign said that, anyway. Where they building the depot. Ain't never been to these parts before, so that sign's the only proof I got."

"Depot? They got tracks all the way to Ft. Drum now?"

The man wagged his head. "No. Tracks ain't laid yet. Tracks run out up at a place called Kenansville. The man told me that's the end of the line for now."

"What man was that?"

"Big feller, one that suggested I get off the train."

"Oh." John Morgan glanced westward at the columns of smoke. "Reckon that's what all the smoke is about, they must be clearin right of way on down to Okeechobee. Uncle Jude said the tracks was sposed to get all the way there, ventually."

"They layin track to somewhere all right," the man said. "I seen em. But I don't know where they headin. All I know is I got on up in Jacksonville, thinkin to ride clear to Miami. I was huntin warm weather, you see. Like to froze in Jacksonville. Don't know how they can say that town is part of Florida. Florida's sposed to be warm come winter. Least that's what I've always been told."

"You from Georgia?"

"Naw. I was born in Ohio, but I ain't been there since I was a kid. I left out of there right after the war. Been all over ever since. I've always follered the work, you see."

"You got food and water?" Raylene called from the wagon.

The man executed a little dance in the sand to get a look at Raylene. "I'm all right," he said. "Bless you for askin."

"You ever work in Missouri?" said John Morgan.

"What's that?"

"Missouri. You ever work there?"

The man shook his head. "No, not that I recall. That where you all headed?"

John Morgan dipped his head and reached and bumped back his hat. "No. I was just curious is all. We're headed to Nittaw."

The man seemed to study the ground beneath him. He flexed the fingers of the hand holding to the strap. "Guess I ain't been *all* over," he finally said.

"Nittaw's just a few miles north of Kenansville, I think. You had to come by it on the train."

The old man smiled, exposing a mouthful of neglected teeth. "Seat I had didn't allow for much sightseein."

John Morgan smiled. He gestured northward with a hand. "They any water in that creek up yonder?"

The old man made no attempt to look where the boy had pointed. "There's a bit," he said. "It's flowin, but it's got a good hard bottom. Your wagon ought to cross it all right." He gave a tug to the strap to adjust his load. "Well, I best get movin," he said. "I stand here any longer, I'm liable to take root."

"You're welcome to stay the night with us," John Morgan said, "if you don't mind backtrackin a little."

"That's very kind of ye," the old man said, him starting forward and his first steps tentative, scarcely steps at all, more like the hesitant probing of an infant when first attempting to walk. "But I'll just be on my way. I've not far to go now, so I'll be just fine."

"Miami's a long way," John Morgan said, a puzzled look on his face.

"It is?"

"Yessir. I reckon it's a hundred miles or more."

"That's good," the old man said, him gaining speed and falling into a wonky rhythm of sorts. "Yea, though I walk," he said, stepping and stabbing the ground with the stick and stepping again, moving on past the wagon and beyond without uttering another word.

They watched him go, the boys half turning their horses while Raylene leaned on the seat to see past the wagon's canvas cover.

"That man's crazy," said Archie.

"He ain't no crazier than we are," John Morgan said, turning his horse back to the north. "I reckon he's just too old to pretend anymore."

*

They passed the night camped next to the creek, dousing their cookfire and setting forth again with the sky yet adorned with stars, it near freezing and the nightwoods still and silent save for sounds perpetrated by their small procession. They traveled, and when the new sun lorded over the horizon the aforementioned depot rose out of the fog on their left. Next to the stilted structure a dozen or more men stood warming themselves by a roaring fire, dark smoke rising from the flames but briefly before reaching some invisible barrier where it diverged right and left to form what looked like a more potent shelf of the fog reef already there. A pair of wagons parked near the men, each with their six mules harnessed and standing solemnly as though the animals were yet sleeping. A freshly formed grade ran between the men and the depot. Beyond the grade in the ghostly distance stood several houses, their shake-shingled roofs above the fog and gilded by the sun. The Rawlersons did not alter their course or stop at Ft. Drum. They merely continued on, while the men around the fire, perhaps blinded by the sun, seemed oblivious of the passing wagon and riders.

All through the day they paralleled the new grade when they could, it heading slightly west of north and bound for the exact location they sought to reach. The cold of the early morning quickly abated, the day warming into the eighties, heat sufficient to resurrect the indomitable horse and deer flies in the palmetto flats, clouds of mosquitoes in and around the sloughs holding water. The going slow over the rough ground and them managing only fifteen miles before the sun was lost behind a dark bank of clouds advancing from the west. They halted for the night in a stand of old-growth pine, the most impressive trees of their kind they'd seen since beginning their journey. Later that evening, after feeding the animals and themselves, they walked out from the glow of their fire and stood gazing northward at a small cluster of yellow lights far across the flatwoods.

"That's Yeehaw," Raylene said. "They was a sawmill there when I was small. I remember going there with my daddy to fetch old scrap boards that was free for the takin."

"Yeee . . . hawww," said Archie. "That's a funny name for a place."

"It's a Indian word," Raylene said. "But I ain't never known what it means."

"How far you reckon we are from Nittaw?" said John Morgan.

"It's another fifteen miles or so past Yeehaw. Lord willin, we could make it to Jude and Betty's by tomorrow night."

"I'll be glad to get there," said Archie. "My sore behind will be real glad."

John Morgan looked at the myriad stars visible in the night sky. "All them clouds earlier, I thought sure we were in for a wet night. Now it looks clear as a bell."

The morning following before the sun rose they passed the few houses and outbuildings of Yeehaw and continued on, a fairly well-traveled road now paralleling the railroad grade and allowing them to make good time. Mid-morning they passed a single clapboard home with a good barn and cowpens. Two small boys at play in the yard stopped suddenly to stand and stare fixedly, their eyes wide with wonder as if the passing riders and wagon might be the first strangers they'd chanced to see.

When the sun was sufficiently high to pool their shadows beneath them, they did not stop to eat. One after the other the boys dropped back to the wagon to reach and take a sweet potato from Raylene. They ate as they rode and when coming to water they paused just long enough for all of the animals to drink before moving on. The cur dog ranged ahead like a forward scout, it sometimes gone from sight a good many minutes before reappearing and setting forth once again. As they moved northward there were few stretches where cattle were not in sight, some close by, but most mere brown or black or white aberrations here and there in the pale green ocean of palmettos, against the seamless gray of distant cypress. They saw few deer, but the country seemed rank with turkeys and hogs. They crossed a burn where there were so many of the big birds feeding on new growth that when they took off running it looked as though the scorched terrain itself was fleeing. As for hogs, they saw only one old boar, but their rooting presence was surely evident, the ground around every slough and drain looking as if it had been recently turned for planting. Coveys of quail were common, the scurrying birds but speckled blurs as they quit the trail ahead. Birds of every feather, hawks and crows and bluebirds, vultures riding the thermals high above, a pair of bald eagles perched at their nest in the top of a pine that was long dead and turned to lighter. They rode and they looked while their easterly slanted shadows slowly grew longer.

They reached Kenansville with there about two hours of daylight remaining, the sawmill town larger than Raylene had remembered with a general store and in the distance a two-story Piney Woods Inn. They spoke briefly with a man who sat swinging his legs atop the depot's loading dock, a man wearing bib overalls and a floppy hat and saying that he worked part time for the railroad but wore many hats and also delivered mail, when it came, to the few families scattered about from Lake Marion to Nittaw and south to Locosee. He said that he hated the name Kenansville, that he felt the turpentine folks had committed a grave sin when conspiring to name the place after the Yankee Flagler's third wife, just so the tycoon would bring the railroad closer to their operation. When asked if he knew Jude Vickers, the man said that he did and that he considered him and Betty to be good people, even though Jude himself had carved many a cat face on the pines of Osceola, collecting the sap to make turpentine. He told them that if the Vickers' place was where they were headed, they'd be well advised to cross the tracks now, for deep ditches along the grade up there would be a problem for the wagon. "They's mud up there'll bog a buzzard's shadow," he told them. When they left the man, they crossed over the tracks where he'd indicated and followed the rutted trail that was there and leading northward. For a while they talked about the man's passionate assertions as they rode, concluding ultimately that the man simply hated Yankees, them and any change they sought to bring into his world.

Just after nightfall they reached a small creek the railway spanned with a long trestle. The trail they followed made a jog to the west at that point, threading through the hardwoods to a narrow ford before arcing back east to again follow the railroad grade.

"This is Tyson Creek," Raylene said as the wagon rocked and reeled across the sandy run of the stream, it so dark within the swamp she could scarcely make out the mules, let alone her sons who rode somewhere up ahead. "Uncle Jude's is just up the hill a piece."

A few hundred yards after the trail led them back to the railroad grade, a pair of yellow lights shouted the presence of a dwelling among the trees ahead. Upon seeing the lights, Raylene looked to the heavens and breathed: "Thank you, God."

2

Nittaw

Jude Vickers welcomed his baby sister with a sincere smile and warm hug, while wife Betty—never blessed with children of her own—waddled to John Morgan and Archie, capturing a boy in each arm and drawing them into her great frame that she might pepper their cheeks with kisses of heartfelt adoration. Her nephews still firmly in her grasp, she looked at Raylene, saying, "All right with you if we bed down the animals and set down to supper? Unload the wagon in the mornin?"

Raylene, looking exhausted and wearing a serene look of thanks, released her brother and reached to remove her bonnet. She nodded her head. "We're obliged to do whatever you say, Betty—you bein gracious enough to take us in and all."

Betty released the boys. She glided to Raylene and reached and stroked her hair, a look of concern etched on her face. "My Lord, you're skinny," she remarked, rocking back and studying her sister-in-law's person. "You been feelin poorly?"

Raylene stepped and stood. "I'm all right."

The look of concern slowly bled from Betty's face. "Well, I'm tickled you're here, Sweetheart, plumb happy for the company."

Jude clapped his hands. "Well, let's get movin. There'll be plenty time for talk after we eat."

*

The modest, clapboard cypress home stood about a hundred yards west of the new railroad grade, nestled within a grove of moss-laden live oaks whose outstretched limbs cast the shake-shingle roof in perpetual shade. The structure east-facing with front and rear porches, the sawed sections of a great cypress serving as footers and fostering the appearance that the home may well have sprouted from the sandy soil. A short distance west amid the oak grove stood a sturdy pole barn, a stilted chicken coop and an outhouse seemingly tethered to the back stoop by a well-worn path.

Before sunrise the morning following their arrival John Morgan left his pallet by the hearth, captured his boots and crept quietly through the kitchen to the back porch. He sat the steps and pulled on his boots, looking and listening, smelling the musty fragrance of decaying leaves. The cur dog appeared from the darkness and settled next to him while he dressed his feet. As he rose to begin exploring his new world, the Vickers' rooster crowed, eliciting an immediate response from a turkey gobbler to the south, a mature tom, he reasoned, yet roosted in the creek swamp they'd crossed the evening before. To get clear of the house, he walked to the north a few paces where he stopped and stood looking at the eastern horizon. It was getting light, the imminent sunrise slowly easing the night westward while resurrecting the day-face of the land in front of the home. He could just make out the raised bed of the railway, it too straight and level to be harmonious with the hodgepodge of nature through which it coursed. He stood a moment looking and listening, then walked to the rear of the wagon and stopped and studied its heaped contents. Upon spying the galvanized milk pail, he wrenched it from beneath a crate of hand tools then headed for the barn. The night yet potent beneath the oaks, he stepped blindly, unsure of his course until his horse sensed his coming and nickered softly within the shelter. When he moved toward the Jersey, the cow stepped and fought her tether while bellowing her discomfort.

John Morgan stroked the cow's side. "I know," he said, setting the pail beneath the animal's swollen udder. "You promise not to kick me, I promise I'll never let you go this long agin."

*

When he returned to the kitchen the women had set the table with platters of bacon, eggs, grits, and biscuits. Uncle Jude was already positioned at the head of the table, him sitting straight as any soldier. John Morgan said "Good mornin," and, after handing the milk to his mother, crossed the great room to the hearth where Archie was yet curled beneath his quilt.

John Morgan toed the small end of the mound with his boot. "Arch," he said.

"What?"

"You need to get up."

"I don't need to do nothin," Archie said, but nevertheless flung his quilt aside and rolled to his back. He glared up at his brother, his lips pursed and his eyes narrowed initially, but his expression bleeding to one of puzzlement as his eyes began to wander. "What the hell?"

John Morgan cast a glance back at his uncle who was indeed watching, then shushed his brother before saying: "Get washed up—breakfast is ready."

Sitting up, Archie reached for his sheathed knife which lay on the hearth beside him.

John Morgan beat him to it. He snatched up the antler-handled tool and stood tall. "I'll keep this for you while we're here," he said.

A panicked look on his face, Archie reached out his hands like a pleading child. "Why?" he said.

"Just because," said John Morgan. "You'll get it back when we leave."

*

When all were seated, Jude said grace and they fell to eating without further formality and only scant few words spoken until all

81

had had their fill and sat back in their chairs to enjoy the main course of conversation.

Jude rolled a cigarette using tobacco and paper fished from the bib of his overalls. After lighting up, he blew smoke toward the lamp that hung suspended from a hook in the low ceiling. He cut his eyes to Raylene, gesturing in the air with the hand holding the cigarette and his eyes not holding his sister's gaze but darting about the room. "Now that y'all are here," he said, "what you wantin to do? I mean, how long do you reckon you'll be wantin to stay?"

Raylene looked at the porcelain cup on the table before her and looked at her brother. "I reckon we want to get busy findin a place of our own. We don't want to put y'all out no longer'n we have to."

Jude cut a glance at Betty, his wife, whose unblinking stare made him squirm in his chair. He looked at Raylene. "You're family," he said. "You're welcome to stay as long as you want."

Betty suddenly unseated herself from the table and stepped to the stove. She got the soot-blackened coffeepot and brought it to the table and began topping off the cup of each and every person without question. "Lord, Raylene," she said. "Like I told you last night, I'm tickled to death for the company. It gets mighty lonesome out in these here woods. You and the boys are a godsend for me. You surely are."

Raylene smiled up at her sister-in-law. "I'm glad you feel that way, but we just got here. I reckon before long you'll be just as tickled to see us gone."

Jude smoked. He watched Archie at the far end of the table, the boy slouched with head dipped and arms crossed about his chest and him listing to one side as if on a slow journey to the floor. Jude looked at his sister. "You lookin to buy a place?"

Raylene nodded. "You know of any for sale? Or even for rent? We'll rent if we have to."

Jude reached and tapped his cigarette ash into his coffee mug. He shook his head. "I don't know of anything, but I can ask around. It may be we'll have to take a ride to Kissimmee one day—ask the people in the courthouse. They belong to keep track of what's for sale and all. Least, that's what I been told."

John Morgan straightened in his chair. He reached and captured his cup but immediately set it back on the table. He looked at his uncle. "You reckon me and Arch can find work hereabouts?"

Jude shrugged. "Maybe, long as you ain't too particular."

"Well, ranchin's what we know, but we'll take anything that pays wages."

"Well, they's plenty of ranchin goes on round here. Cows is one thing this hard land seems suited for, them and snakes and skee-ters." Jude paused and winked at John Morgan. "We got plenty of snakes and skeeters, but far as I know, ain't no wages bein paid to work em."

John Morgan returned his uncle's smile but then shifted his gaze to his mother, to the food on her plate she'd scarcely touched. "Me and Arch will unload the wagon," he said. "You just sit and visit with Aunt Betty."

*

Outside the morning cool was now consigned to the deep shade beneath the oaks, the sun's slant rays instantly warming all they touched. While the boys began unloading the wagon, Jude offered assistance when he thought it needed, along with advice as to where each item should be stowed within and without his home. When they were almost done he drew John Morgan aside, sug-gested to the boy that there was something he needed to show him on the far side of the house.

At the east-facing front porch he asked his nephew to sit with him on the steps. They sat in silence for a moment, arms resting loosely on their knees, their dark shadows cast slant across the porch by the late winter sun. Finally, Jude, him staring straight ahead as if rapt with something beyond the bounds of his vision, said: "You all been through a mighty rough stretch."

John Morgan glanced sideways at his uncle then looked at his own boots. "Yessir," he said.

Jude removed his cap and looked in its bowl and placed it back on his head. "How you reckon your mama's doin? I mean, she seems awful puny to me. Heck, she ain't hardly eaten a bite since she got here, and from the looks of her, I'd say it's a habit she's had for a while."

John Morgan wiped at something on the toe of his boot. "She's all right," he said.

Jude looked at him. He shook his head. "She ain't all right. Might be you been too close to see it. But I see it. It's plain as the nose on my face that somethin's wrong with her." He studied his nephew. "My guess is she's been too busy mournin to take care of her own self. Lord knows she's got good reason." Pausing again, he sat looking around, his eyes panning the distant horizon. "She ain't complained about nothin, ain't mentioned feelin poorly or somethin?"

"No, sir. Mama ain't never been one to complain."

Jude nodded. He unseated himself from the step and stood dusting the seat of his breeches. "Well," he said. "I hope I ain't upset you with all my questions. I'm just worried bout my little sister is all."

John Morgan shook his head. "You ain't upset me. I been totin around the same questions for a while now. I just ain't had the guts to ask Mama."

*

In the days following he and Archie began to look for both work and a place they might possibly buy or rent. They had no immediate success and Archie, content to stay behind and be coddled by his Aunt Betty, left his brother to continue searching alone. And John Morgan did doggedly continue to search, an exercise in futility until late in March when his uncle suggested he might find work with a fellow who owned practically all the land from Nittaw to Lake Kissimmee.

As directed by his uncle, he rode west from the house until striking a cattle trail snaking northward through the sandy scrub country. The spring morning cool and all through which he rode glistening with dew, a smattering of pines but mostly scrub oak and palmetto, the occasional cypress head girdled with gallberry, broom sage, and wax myrtle. Quail and turkeys calling. A great migration of incessantly cawing crows leapfrogging from treetop to treetop while moving ever northward, their dark exodus not ordered by thought but by an ancient directive long hardwired in their tiny avian brains. He rode, and when he'd followed his shadow for almost an hour, the trail intersected a rutted wagon road, an east-west trace his uncle had said would lead him to the Williams' place.

After he'd followed the road westward for about a mile the scrub on its south side abruptly ended at a manmade clearing, a ten-acre rectangle of carpet grass that was treeless save for a pair of live oaks rising like great umbrellas at its south end. Beyond the oaks stood a tin-roofed house and, to its right, several outbuildings and a large holding pen. Upon seeing the house his horse quickened its step, began lifting its forelegs in high elegance as it followed the ruts in a gradual arc toward the dwelling.

The sandy yard surrounding the home had been recently swept clean of debris left by winter's hand, yet the cycle of life already conspiring to erase the efforts of man, as evidenced by a brownish-yellow haze that now covered the ground. John Morgan guided his horse into the yard and on toward the home's front steps. There was no wind and his horse's hooves raising brief clouds of the fine pollen until he halted it a few yards from the porch and called to the house. "Hello in the house," he said. With his words still in his ears a brindle dog he'd not noticed launched from a rocker on the porch, a heavily muscled cur similar to his own, growling a menacing warning yet not leaving the porch but instead pacing at the top of the steps with hackles raised and glancing repeatedly at the closed door behind it. When the door eventually opened inward, the dog immediately settled on its haunches and turned to stare intently at the mounted stranger.

A middle-aged woman appeared in the doorway but did not cross the threshold. She stood in her bare feet with her left hand gripping the door edge and her right obscured by the ankle-length housedress she wore. She squinted against the outside light to better see who was calling but said nothing.

John Morgan reached and touched his hat brim. "Mornin, ma'am," he said, "I come to see Mr. Williams."

The woman studied him. She looked at the dog and looked at the boy. "Don't get down," she said. "You step down and Butch is apt to take offense."

"No, ma'am. I seen right away he had his knife out. I'll set right here."

"Who should I say is callin?"

"John Morgan Rawlerson, ma'am. I come to ask Mr. Williams about a job."

"You're lookin for work."

"Yes, ma'am."

The woman dipped her head slightly and briefly surveyed the land beyond the boy before returning her gaze to him. "Where'd you come from? We don't get many visitors out here."

"Nittaw, ma'am. I'm stayin over there with my Uncle Jude and Aunt Betty."

"The Vickers."

"Yes, ma'am."

The woman nodded. She released the door and stepped through the threshold and onto the porch, revealing a big Colt revolver in her right hand. She motioned with the gun toward the several rockers on the porch to her right. "You're welcome to sit and wait if you want. It's almost noon so Bill should be here directly." She gestured to the barn and pens west of the house. "Tie your horse out there, so he don't sully my nice clean yard."

John Morgan looked where she indicated and reined his horse around to go there but then halted and looked at the dog, it still planted at the head of the steps and watching him fixedly.

Smiling, the woman said: "He won't molest you now. I done told him you're all right."

John Morgan touched his hat. "That's good to know," he said. "Thank you, ma'am."

The woman nodded and turned and stepped into the house, swinging the door shut behind her.

He rode to the trap by the barn and stepped down and cinched a rein to the top board. When turning to walk back to the house, he realized the cur dog had followed him, it now close to his person and sniffing at his breeches and boots in a relaxed manner. He reached down and patted the dog's shoulder. "Good boy," he said, and then he straightened and headed for the house.

He'd been sitting and rocking a few minutes—the dog next to him, lying sphinx-like and still as stone—when the woman came from within the house carrying a big mug of steaming coffee.

John Morgan rocked forward to stand but she motioned for him to remain seated. "It's got cream and sugar," she said, handing him the mug. "You look to be about the same age as my Will, so I fixed it like I do for him."

John Morgan smiled and nodded. "Just the way I take it," he said, "but you shouldn't of gone to the trouble."

"Wasn't no trouble," said the lady. She stood and watched him take his first sip then turned to go back inside but paused at the door. "I'm Diane," she said, "but most people just call me Mrs. Williams."

When he smiled and nodded she stepped from view and he set about sipping his coffee and waiting. A few minutes on a pair of hen turkeys appeared at the field's north end. He sat watching the birds' slow search for insects, marveling at their wariness, the two naked blue heads never down simultaneously but one always up and watching. He watched and when the birds were midway of the opening the pair suddenly halted and stood with heads stretched tall. He thought for a moment that the distant birds had somehow caught a movement of his. But when suddenly they broke and sprinted back to the scrub from whence they'd emerged, he noticed the source of their panic: a pair of riders entering the northwest corner of the clearing.

He watched the riders come, the leader carrying the weight that comes with age but sitting his big buckskin well while the one trailing, though slimmer and taller, seemed all wonky atop the sorrel he rode. The pair, both wearing white blousy shirts and dark felt hats, skirted the west edge of the clearing, heading not for the house but for the trap where his own horse stood with its head high and watching them come. They came on, and when the older man reached the trap he stepped down from his horse and tied a rein to a fence board. He reached and bumped back his hat and briefly stood looking at the bay gelding before turning to head for the house.

John Morgan set the coffee mug on the floor. When he unseated himself from the rocker, the dog beside him rose and stretched and together they descended the porch steps and walked to greet the approaching man.

When the man was within a few paces, John Morgan reached and touched his hat brim. He introduced himself and stated the reason for his visit. To this Bill Williams nodded and offered his hand and they shook and then proceeded up the steps and onto the porch. The boy Will soon joined them and they each claimed a rocker and sat down while the cur dog circled and dropped to the floor next to Mr. Williams' boots.

"So," Bill Williams said. "You're lookin for work."

"Yessir."

The boy Will rocked forward to see past his father. "How old are you?"

"I'm fifteen."

Will smiled and slapped his leg. "Shoot," he said, "I'm sixteen."

Bill Williams looked at his son and looked at John Morgan. He gestured toward the trap where the horses stood swishing tails and bobbing heads. "Your rig says you work cows."

"Yessir. I did for bout ten years, I reckon. We had us a place down near Ft. Pierce, was buildin up a pretty good herd till the feller that owned the land up and wouldn't rent to us no more."

Williams cocked his head quizzically.

"He figured there was more money to be made in citrus. That's what he told us, anyways."

Williams nodded. "I've thought about puttin some in my own self," he said. "But you ain't rode all the way up here from Ft. Pierce, have you?"

John Morgan shook his head. "No sir. I'm stayin with my Uncle Jude, over at Nittaw—just till we can find us a place of our own."

"You got cows over there?"

"No, sir," John Morgan said. "We sold em off, fore we left out down there." He paused and looked at Williams. "You know of any land for sale around here?"

Bill Williams rocked. He reached and removed his hat and laid it in his lap, his thinning brown hair all wild and damp with sweat, and he briefly tried to tamp it down with a hand then quit to look at John Morgan. "Only place I know of is the piece that lays between me and Lake Kissimmee. Feller that owned it lost it for not payin his taxes, so I reckon the state'll sell it to anybody who will."

"Anybody that'll pay the taxes?"

Williams nodded. "That's what they told me at the courthouse, back when I had the notion to maybe buy it myself."

John Morgan scooted forward in his chair and shifted his position to better see Bill Williams. "How many acres is it?"

"It's right at twelve sections, plus or minus, dependin on how high the lake is and all."

John Morgan pensively cupped his chin with the fingers of his right hand. He looked at Williams. "You know how much tax is owed?"

"It was about eight thousand when I asked, but that was a couple years ago. I don't know if it keeps growin with nobody ownin it. If it does, it's got to be more than that now."

John Morgan sat back in his chair. He looked at the dog lying at Williams' feet. "How come you didn't buy it? I mean, if you don't mind my askin."

Williams set his hat on his head and bumped it back. "Naw, I don't mind," he said. "I'm land-poor as it is. I got more'n thirty sections I'm payin taxes on. Besides, my cows already use that property, been doin it for years, so me buyin it just didn't make no sense to me. No sense at all."

"They's some good fishin on that property," Will injected. "You like to fish?"

John Morgan looked at the boy and nodded. "I like it, but I ain't done it in a while." He looked at Bill Williams. "You reckon they'd be willin to sell me part of that property, say a couple sections maybe?"

Williams shook his head slowly. "I doubt it. If I ain't mistaken, the whole tax bill has got to be paid fore they'll sign the property over to somebody new. And, it's got to be cash money. They won't carry a note on a tax sale." Williams watched his words bring a dejected look to the boy's face. "Course I could be wrong," he continued. "If y'all are really interested in the place, you ought to have your daddy go to the courthouse, get it straight from the horse's mouth, so to speak."

"Yessir," John Morgan said. He looked at the sleeping dog on the floor to the right of his boots, its ribcage rising and falling and rising and falling. He felt a slight breeze suddenly cool his left cheek. He looked at Bill Williams. "I'll work hard for you," he said.

The man shifted in his chair, his eyes swimming from the boy to his own son and back again, as if having been profoundly moved by the simple statement but not knowing exactly how to respond. "Well, I reckon you will," he finally said. "Can you be here at daylight tomorrow morning?"

"Yes, sir," John Morgan blurted. He stood and extended his hand, causing the dog to leap to its feet. And when father and son stood he shook their hands in turn while expressing his thanks and goodbye. He then turned and bounded down the steps and virtually floated across the yard toward his horse, his obvious elation eliciting smiles from the Williams and a curious cock of the head from their dog.

*

His mood quickly changed when he got back to his Uncle Jude's. Archie was sitting on the back porch floor, him slump-shouldered and seeming to study something on the ground below until the sound of John Morgan's approach caused him to look up. And when he saw his brother Archie dropped from the porch and trotted to him, his face the blank page of the hopelessly addled.

As John Morgan stepped down from his horse, Archie stood watching like a curious dog until his brother turned to acknowledge him. "Uncle Jude ain't here," Archie said.

"I know. He's at work."

Archie kicked at the sand and leaves with a bare foot. "No, he ain't. He didn't go to work."

John Morgan began leading his horse to the barn with Archie shadowing him. "Well, where'd he go then?"

"He went huntin a doctor."

John Morgan stopped walking, reaching back a hand to stop his horse as well. He looked at his brother. "A doctor?" he said. "Damn it, Archie. Quit beatin around the bush and just tell me what's goin on. Why'd he go for a doctor? Who's sick?"

Archie stuffed his hands in his pants pockets and shrugged his shoulders. "Ain't nobody sick. I reckon he went cause Mama didn't get up."

"What?"

"Mama didn't get up. She's still in bed, far as I know."

"Shit," said John Morgan.

He quickly tied his horse in the barn then ran to the house. The kitchen and living room were eerily quiet as he passed through them and on to the spare bedroom. The door to the room was open and when he stepped through the threshold his Aunt Betty rose from a bedside chair to greet him, a handkerchief clutched in her right hand and her eyes bloodshot portraits of sorrow.

Betty stepped toward her nephew who stood staring at the still form in the bed with a look of disbelief. She reached and drew him in to her, holding him tightly while telling him repeatedly how sorry she was. She held him and she told him what a good woman his mother was, what a blessing it was for God to take her as she slept.

When his aunt released him John Morgan continued to stare at the old woman his mother's lifeless body had become. A moment on he reached and patted his aunt's shoulder. His lower lip palsied and his eyes swimming. Then he turned suddenly and left the room. He walked from the house and down the steps like a figure in a dream, continuing on past the barn and into the scrub beyond. He walked blind to all around him until in a sandy clearing he sagged to his knees and began to weep. He wept a shower of tears, and the sandy soil below instantly absorbing the salty drops, devouring them as if proof of human suffering was surely the nourishment for which the ancient land had always hungered, would always hunger.

*

It was getting dark when Jude arrived with the doctor, a portly native of Kissimmee named Lowery, noted for his quiet demeanor and the flask of whiskey always hidden within his dark linen coat. After examining Raylene's body, he could only confirm the obvious, stating that, after hearing the woman's history, she'd likely died of misery, that she was simply "give out" after all that had happened. When he'd gleaned information needed to record the death, he declined Jude's request that he spend the night. Saying that he liked to ride of a night, he simply climbed into his buggy and left them to mourn without the distraction a houseguest inevitably presents. And when the departing horse and buggy had been swallowed by the darkness, they four shuffled one by one into the house where they settled in the chairs surrounding the kitchen table.

Jude asked that they bow their heads so that he might petition God's mercy and guidance for Raylene, his beloved sister whose suffering He'd saw fit to end so suddenly. And when he'd done that, he asked the same for those of them left to suffer her passing.

He said amen and then he sat tall in his chair to look at the two boys orphaned on this sad day.

"I don't much feel like talkin," he began. "But I know it's something needs doin." He looked at the two boys and looked at his wife. "Best to air things out. It surely is."

Archie, sitting at the far end of the table, slowly raised a hand.

"Yes, Archie," said Jude. "You got a question?"

"We goan eat supper? I'm awful hungry."

Betty issued a little moan. She rose from her chair and stepped to the larder next to the stove. "I'm sorry," she said. "Y'all go ahead and talk. I can fix us something and listen too."

Jude looked at John Morgan. "We need to make arrangements for the burial."

"Yessir. I been thinkin on it."

"Well, I figured next to Mama and Daddy, in the Vickers' plot. What you been thinkin?"

John Morgan shook his head. "She'd want to be with Daddy and the twins."

"At Ft. Pierce?"

"Yessir."

Jude stared blankly at the table, his forehead furrowed and his jaws ruminating slowly. "Well, I reckon that presents a problem, son. I got to work. We bury her down there, you're talkin bout four or five days at the least. Naval Stores will let you go, if you miss three days runnin. Besides, a body won't keep that long, without it bein embalmed and all."

"I can get there in two," said John Morgan, "and I don't need no help." He paused to read his uncle's reaction, and recognized immediately that it was not good. "I don't mean no disrespect. I just know it's what Mama would want. And the plot is paid for. Daddy took care of that when the twins died."

Jude placed his hands on the table, his fingers drumming the hard wood while his eyes focused on nothing save the morbid thoughts spinning in his mind. He looked at John Morgan. "The body won't keep."

"No, it won't. Embalmed or not, it won't, but Mama will." He pressed his right palm against his chest. "She'll keep right in here, long as I live."

Jude was silent, and his silence prompted Betty to come to him and place her hands on his shoulders. When he looked up at her and she simply nodded, he turned his gaze back to John Morgan. "All right," he said. "But I'll prepare her for travel. That's no job for a young feller like you. Besides, it'll give me time to say my good-byes."

John Morgan nodded his agreement. "Thank you," he said. "I appreciate you understandin." He then paused and sat thinking for a moment. He looked at his uncle. "How long you reckon it'll take you?"

A puzzled look on Jude's face, and then him saying: "To prepare the body?"

"Yessir."

"I don't know—two, maybe three hours to build the coffin. I got some cypress lumber already sawed in the barn. I should be done well before noon, I reckon."

John Morgan nodded. "If you don't mind, I'll use that time to ride and explain to Mr. Williams. He's expectin me to show up for work in the mornin."

"He hired you?"

"Yessir, he did. Course I don't know how he'll take me needin time off, before I even started."

"He'll understand. Bill Williams is a good Christian. He knows what's important."

"Yessir. I kindly got that feelin from him right off."

Just then Betty came to the table and set flatware and a thick ceramic plate before Archie. On the plate was a steaming mass of meat, potatoes, and carrots swimming in brown gravy, a large mis-shapen biscuit slathered with butter. As Archie bent to the plate, she turned to her husband and John Morgan. "Y'all best eat some, too," she said. "It ain't much, but it's hot and y'all are going to need your strength."

*

In the morning he did his daily chores in the predawn darkness before saddling his horse and leaving for the Williams' place. He made the round trip in just under two hours, his sense of urgency a companion that would not let him dawdle. By the time he'd cared for his horse and hitched the two mules to the wagon, Jude had completed the coffin and stood waiting for John Morgan's assistance in placing the body within the crude but sturdy casket.

Together they carried the box to the bedroom. Betty was waiting in the room, having already wrapped Raylene's body with cheese-cloth kept on hand to shroud meat before hanging it to cure, the gauze-like material being their only defense against the insidious blow flies sure to come. When they'd set the box on the floor by the bed, Jude and the boy stood looking at the mummy-like form, the anonymous look of it startling yet somehow easing the dread they harbored for the tasks they were about to undertake.

After a moment of silence, Jude looked at John Morgan and said: "You all right?"

John Morgan nodded that he was and stepped to the head of the form and slipped a hand beneath each of the bound shoulders. Jude followed his lead, initially gripping the paired feet but moving to the knees for better leverage when realizing that rigor mortis was waning, that the body was no longer completely rigid. Together they lifted and they gently lowered the body into the box and then stood back to gather themselves before continuing on, before facing the next dreaded step of a journey only just begun.

*

It was almost eleven by the time he had the wagon loaded with everything he thought he'd need: a shovel, his rifle and jacket, and a gunny sack of jerked meat and sweet potatoes, another filled with cracked corn and oats for the mules. He stuffed fifty dollars of their savings in a pants pocket, the same pocket home to the wooden disk the girl had given him in his other life. And when thinking

95

himself ready to go, he noticed Archie sitting atop the wagon seat and quickly realized he'd forgotten something of great importance.

Looking up at his brother, he said: "You better stay here, Arch."

Archie stubbornly shook his head. He wouldn't look at his brother.

"I ain't gonna stop."

"I don't care, if you're goin, I'm goin."

"Shit," John Morgan said, forgetting his aunt and uncle were on the porch behind him. He turned to look at them. "Sorry bout that. I reckon Arch is goin with me. I ain't got time to fight him."

Betty's arms shot out, her palms raised and signaling "Wait." She turned and went into the house, saying as she went, "That child's gonna need some things."

Jude watched her go then looked at John Morgan. He swung his arms and gave a single clap of his hands. "Well," he said, "least you'll have some company, some help unloadin and all."

John Morgan nodded. "I didn't figure on him goin, but I reckon it is only right."

Jude cracked a broad smile. "I believe you just made your mama awful proud of you." He swung his arms. "Yessir, that's what I believe."

*

After last-minute advices from his aunt and uncle, John Morgan gave a wave and a shake of the long reins and the mules obligingly stepped forward, their long ears bobbing and swiveling to the sounds of their world and them blessedly ignorant of all purpose and destination. They went, and the boys not uttering a word until they'd crossed Tyson Creek and resumed following the railroad bed, at which point, Archie raised a question. "Where we goin?" he said.

John Morgan, stunned by his brother's plea, was slow to reply. "We're goin to Ft. Pierce," he eventually said, "to bury Mama next to Daddy and the twins."

"All right," said Archie. He then reached and slipped his knife from its sheath and, with it, began cleaning his nails.

They traveled, crossing the tracks and passing Kenansville a little after noon according to the sun. The day warm with only a few billowy clouds to occasionally dull the sun's intense presence, until that nearest of stars finally sank below the horizon as they trundled past little Locosee. They moved on, and the sun's distant cousins in their billions took command of the sky and their reign of the night autonomous until a grand misshapen moon rose to power in the east. And in the moonlight their way was clearly revealed and they made good time, passing the lights of Yeehaw and coming to the small drain where they'd stayed the night a month before, where their mother had offered a rare glimpse of her youth. Before crossing the shallow run, John Morgan halted the mules and stepped down from the wagon to stretch while the animals drank their fill. He stood looking at the lights far across the flatwoods, remembering his mother's words of that night. And though saddened by the memory, he recognized it as a keepsake to be treasured forever. He looked and he remembered, standing there in the blueish glow cast over all, his thoughts the only sound save for the drip, drip of water from the mules' muzzles. When he quit looking and climbed up to the wagon's seat, Archie was not there. He found him in the wagon's bed, wrapped in his quilt and sleeping, curled in a fetal manner with his back pressed to the coffin and his head resting on the sack of feed.

He clucked the mules on, making a good many miles before the sun rose and Archie parted the canvas flap to view the passing world, his face wearing its customary look of befuddlement. "Where we at?" he said.

"On the Hungry Land Trail—a couple miles north of Ft. Drum, I reckon."

For several minutes Archie continued to kneel in the wagon's bed, his hands gripping the front edge of the wooden seat and him half in and half out as if loath to trade his canvas womb for the light of a new day. He rode, rocking and swaying to the whims of the uneven ground, and then he said: "I'm hungry."

John Morgan paid his brother a glance. "Well, reach back there and fetch that sack Aunt Betty give us. Bring it out here. I could eat a bite myself."

They went on, sating their hunger as they traveled and not stopping until well past Ft. Drum. At a flag pond holding water, John Morgan fed and watered the mules. He and Archie satisfied their own thirst with water dipped from the side-mounted keg. They each in turn left the wagon to relieve themselves in the privacy afforded by tall palmettos girding the shallow pond. Then they climbed aboard the wagon and went on.

It was getting dark when they turned east on the old Cracker Trail and the night full grown by the time they quit it to head southeast across the trackless property they had once called their own. The going suspect and the mules balking often until the moon rose and its dead light resurrected familiar landmarks to guide them on. They traveled and when the moon was near its zenith they laid tracks through a yard where they'd in the past laid thousands, the house dark but an automobile parked before it and telling of the lives now housed within. In the yard the mules tried to halt, their senses filling them with false hope that surely their work was done. John Morgan coaxed them on, yet their heads sawing and them trying to look back until reaching the Okeechobee Road where they once again fell into the mindless gait suiting them so well. They crossed the bridge spanning Five Mile Creek and soon the faint glow of Ft. Pierce was evident ahead. At the outskirts of town they turned north and went directly to the church grounds, halting at the graveyard within a few feet of their family's plot.

John Morgan looped the reins around the brake lever and sighed deeply. He turned and parted the canvas flaps to check on Archie. A faint odor hit him when he looked in, the smell instantly causing a pang of sadness to rise in his chest. Though it was too dark to see, he heard his brother's slow, deep breathing and, deeming it best to let him sleep, he closed the flap and climbed down to the ground. He walked to the side of his father's wooden marker where he paused and stood looking at it as well as the two small granite slabs memorializing his sisters. There were no lights at the church or at the parsonage. As he stood looking and listening, one of the mules shook its harness. An owl called far to the west. He judged by the moon that it was around three o'clock. He walked the perimeter of his family's graves, seeing that the next closest ones were at least twenty feet away. Then he went to the rear of the wagon to fetch the shovel.

On the opposite side of the twins from his father's grave, he began outlining the extent of his task ahead with the shovel, working carefully as not to violate the grave of his sister, Marcy. He dug methodically, heaping the sandy loam neatly along the south edge of his creation. His mind numbed by fatigue, his thoughts rarely wandered beyond the next placement of the shovel, the next dump of its purchase. He worked and he soon was drenched with sweat. He paused frequently to catch his breath, to stand with his hands paired atop the shovel's knob and his eyes unconsciously measuring his progress until his breathing slowed, until bending once again to his labor. And when there was light enough to make out the bottom of the hole he judged it sufficient and set about trying to extricate himself from within it. By summoning what seemed the last of his strength, he used the shovel to chisel toe-holds into one earthen wall and used them to climb up and out where he planted the shovel in the mound before grabbing his knees and gasping for breath.

Exhausted and filthy with dirt and sweat, he eventually stood tall. He looked around, the eastern horizon set aglow by the sun to come. A light now shone from one of the parsonage's windows and, seeing it, he began trying to beat the dirt from his person, flailing with his hat and stomping the ground like a man afflicted. He went to the wagon and dipped water from the keg. He washed his hands and face as best he could then donned his hat and began walking toward the light.

Reaching the red brick home, he momentarily stood before the door like some beggar hesitant to plead his case. Then he rapped on the wood with a knuckle and stood back. And when the door opened he was struck dumb by the face staring out at him, a face familiar but one belonging to a man whose name he'd suddenly lost.

The man, sensing the boy's distress, smiled and asked: "Can I help you?"

John Morgan stepped and stood, his hands groping about as if needing a hat to hold. He nodded. "Yessir," he said, gesturing back with a hand at the vicinity of the wagon. "I was hoping to get you to say a few words over my mama."

The preacher looked at the distant wagon and looked at the boy. He slipped his hands into the pockets of the dark robe he was wearing, as if suddenly aware of the morning's chill. "You're the Rawlerson boy, aren't you?"

"Yessir. I'm John Morgan."

"Has your mother passed?"

"Yessir. I brought her down here to bury her next to Daddy and the twins." He looked at his boots and looked at the man. "My brother and me. We brought her together."

The preacher reached a hand up and ran its fingers through his gray hair. "Well, this is a bit unusual. I usually have some notice. Have the authorities been notified?"

"Yessir. The doctor did that. He recorded it up at the courthouse, in Kissimmee."

"Kissimmee?"

John Morgan nodded. "We live up in Osceola County now."

The preacher nodded. "I remember you moving." He looked around. "Well, how soon do you want me to perform the service? You'll want time to spread the word, I suppose."

John Morgan shook his head. "Ain't no time for that. I was hoping you would do it now. I got the grave dug, and all."

"You dug the grave?"

"Yessir."

The preacher shook his head. "I gather from your sense of urgency that the body's not been seen by a mortician."

"No, sir. There wasn't none to be had."

The preacher nodded. He looked around. "Well, let me get some clothes on," he said. He started to turn but stopped and again looked at the boy. "You want to come in? I'm certain June would be happy to fix you some breakfast."

"I appreciate it, but I'm not hungry. Reckon I better go wake my brother, anyway. I know he'll want to help, and all."

When the preacher nodded and turned to go, John Morgan did likewise, striding toward the wagon at a rate belying the fatigue he felt.

*

As he maneuvered the coffin to the rear of the wagon a male cardinal called incessantly in the nearest oak, the crested bird with its spring song pleading to the world its desire to mate. Though Archie stood listening to the bird's music, John Morgan, so focused, was incapable of hearing such frivolity. "Give me a hand," he said.

The words startled Archie. He quick-stepped to his brother with a hand outreached and him wearing a mischievous smile.

John Morgan released his grip on the coffin's rope handle and circled his brother. "Quit cuttin the fool," he said. "You grab a hold of this end, and don't pull till I tell you." He leaned into the wagon sufficiently to reach the coffin's far end. "All right, slide it on out."

They carried the box between the dug grave and that of Marcy, John Morgan backing to the foot of the hole before stopping and indicating with his eyes that they set it down. He walked back to the wagon and got a coil of manila rope. Returning to his brother, he unfurled the rope and with his pocketknife halved it into two lengths that appeared about equal.

Archie watched as his bother then knelt at the head of the coffin and secured one of the lengths to the rope handle already there. "What's that for?" he said.

John Morgan got to his feet. "So we can lower it down," he said. "You can't just drop it in."

"I knew that," said Archie. He suddenly frowned, scrunching up his nose and exhaling: "Somethin stinks."

John Morgan looked at his brother. He shook his head and then moved to the foot of the coffin where he attached the second length of rope in the same manner. He stood tall and turned to look at the parsonage. "Yonder comes the preacher," he said. "When he gets here, you pay attention to what he's got to say." He turned back to look at his brother. "You hear me?"

Archie now stood gazing up into the oak where the bird was still singing. When finally he lost interest and looked at his brother, he raised a hand and pointed beyond him. "Here comes somebody," he said.

*

The preacher brought his wife as a witness, them both dressed in dark finery well suited to the occasion. After greeting the boys, he called for a bowing of heads and when all complied voiced to God and all present the name and good character of the daughter whom He'd called home. He said amen and he opened his worn Bible and read several passages aloud, them all so familiar he scarcely glanced at the page as he spoke. He read and then he closed the Bible and asked the boys if them capable of lowering their mother into the grave. And when they replied that they were, he instructed them to do so and they did so, taking wide stances and leaning back against the weight until their mother's body completed its final journey, whereupon they severed their last earthly connection by tossing in the ropes and stepping back to stand gazing into the hole, frozen in time, as if turned to stone by the finality of what they'd just done.

"You may fill in the grave now," said the preacher. And when John Morgan grasped the shovel and began to do so, he added, "She came from the earth, and to the earth she now returns."

The preacher's wife then stepped to the boys each in turn, patting their shoulders and stating that she was heading to the house and that they were to come there when finished, that they were not to leave before sitting down to a proper meal. And when she'd gone the boys took turns with the shovel while the preacher stood watching, clutching his Bible and trying to impart some wisdom as to why they'd been subjected to so much suffering over the course of their young lives.

"I once heard it said that life is like a sad song," he began, "the lyrics one sad verse after another yet the melody so beautiful in its entirety that we cling to it—we never want it to end." He paused and studied the boys as if to allow them a comment, or perhaps only wanting an amen. When they offered neither, he continued. "Only the dead ever see the end of suffering. Suffering is every man's burden, a part of every man's life." He paused and watched John Morgan work. He watched Archie wander some distance away, shuffling his feet and seeming to search for something on the ground as he moved aimlessly among monuments to the dead. He looked at John Morgan. "You understand that you are his keeper now," he said, lowering his voice that only the older boy might hear.

John Morgan looked. "Yessir," he said. "I pretty much always been."

"What will you do?"

"We'll go back to our uncle's place, I reckon. I got me a job waitin up there."

The preacher nodded. "It's good that you'll have a place to stay."

John Morgan worked. "It's only temporary, though. I aim to get us a place of our own, a place where me and Arch can raise cows and horses and all."

"With God's help, I'm sure you'll get it."

John Morgan stopped shoveling and stood tall to look at the preacher. "Mama always said that God helps those that help themselves. And I believe her to be right about that, so I ain't lookin for no help—from Him or nobody else. It's up to me, I figure."

The preacher shook his head. "No man is an island, my son. There's no shame in asking for help. No shame at all. I believe God wants us to ask. I believe it lets Him know we've not forgotten Him."

John Morgan was silent, as if digesting what the man had said. He turned and resumed shoveling. A moment on he stopped and again looked to the preacher. "Reckon I can't agree with you on all of that, cause I'm feelin some shame right now."

"Why is that?"

"Cause I need to ask you a favor."

"Ask it."

"You reckon if I give you the money to cover the cost, you could see about gettin stone markers made for Mama and Daddy? I'd do it myself, but I need to get back and go to work."

The preacher smiled. "I'd be honored."

John Morgan nodded. "She was born in eighteen-eighty," he said.

"You can give me the specifics at the house. I don't want to trust my memory on something so important."

"Yessir. I reckon not." John Morgan looked over his shoulder to locate his brother then looked at the preacher. "What day is it?"

"It's Thursday."

"I mean what date?"

"April second. You buried your mother on the second day of April, nineteen-thirteen."

John Morgan slowly shook his head. "That's what I thought," he said. "We buried her on my birthday."

"Today's your birthday?"

"Yessir. I'm fifteen today."

The preacher's eyes grew moist. He stepped and stood, glancing at the Bible in his hand before refocusing on the boy. "And life goes on," he said. "And life goes on."

*

In the days following his return to Nittaw, he settled into working for the Williams while Archie, convinced that his brother would never be too far away, assumed the role of his Aunt Betty's little helper.

On an evening early in May, John Morgan made cow camp on the east shore of Lake Kissimmee. He settled there for the night beneath a lone oak with two men long in the Williams' employ, men whom he instantly liked though he'd only just made their acquaintance that very day. Their three hobbled horses cropping grass while the men sat Indian-fashion about a small fire whose flames danced and writhed to a wind coming off the lake. They sipped a clear liquid that was not water from tin cups and gazed into the flames. The muffled sound of waves lapping and lapping and there nary a light save for their fire and its lesser likenesses replicated in their six eyes. It overcast with a low ceiling of clouds and on the wind the sweet threat of rain distinguishable from the dank, piscatorial breath of the lake.

"I once knew a feller named Rawlerson," said Irish Frank Finney, his faded blue eyes leaving the fire to focus on the boy. "He served with me during the war. I disremember his Christian name, but I remember he rode a mule he'd named Ethel. After his wife, he'd named it. Said that mule was the second most stubborn female he'd ever known." Finney leaned forward and spat in the fire. He chuckled. "Funny the shit you remember." He removed his floppy hat and used it to fan smoke from his face, revealing a distinct border above his brow where darkly tanned skin of his face met that of his near-white forehead, his yellowish-white hair. He again looked at the boy. "Your folks come out of Kansas?"

John Morgan shook his head. "No, sir. Not any that I know of. I was told my great granddaddy come here from South Carolina, way back, when Florida still belonged to the Spaniards."

The third man, Barely Thompson, tall, lanky, and sporting a wry grin, looked at the boy but gestured with his cup toward the old man. "What was his name? Old Frank here might of knowed him."

"Ha, ha," said Frank. "As usual, you're barely funny." He gestured to the boy with his hat. "You want to hear somethin funny, ask him how he come by that name of his."

Thompson laughed. "I knew I should of never told you that story."

"Yeah, well, you done let the cat out of the bag, so go ahead and tell it."

"Or you will."

"That's right. And I don't tell it near as good as you."

Thompson smiled and took a sip from his cup, grimacing when he swallowed. "Whooooeee," he said. He looked at the boy. "You'll probably think small of me after I tell this."

Frank slapped his leg. "I guarantee it," he said.

John Morgan's eyes sparkled, swimming from one man to the other. He sipped his drink and then shook all over against its bite. He focused on Barely Thompson. "Go ahead and tell it," he said, "while I can still hear."

A round of chuckles and then Thompson improving his position, pulling a small branch from beneath him and pitching it into the fire. "Well," he said, "I was told it was given to me right when I come out of my mama, right when the old colored midwife that delivered me held me to the light, to see iffen I had all my fingers and toes, to confirm my sex and all." Thompson paused to sip from his cup. "Old woman's name was Morris or somethin. Anyways, she holds me up and is checkin me out when Mama asks her iffen I'm a boy." He looked at John Morgan. "My folks already had two girl young'uns, you see. They'd been prayin long and hard for a boy, I was told."

John Morgan nodded while Frank Finney shook his hat at Thompson, urging him to continue.

"Oh, hold your water, old man," he said to Finney. "I'm gettin to it." He looked at the boy. "Anyhow, when Mama asked if I was a boy, the old woman up and shouts 'Barely.' Well, my mama hears this and she goes and repeats the blame word. She hollers, 'Barely! What does barely mean?' And the old woman fires back, 'Means just what you think it means. Means this young'un's thing so small I barely see'd it."

John Morgan laughed aloud while Frank Finney beat the ground with his hat and erupted in a fit of coughing.

Barely Thompson watched with a sheepish grin. When the commotion died down, he looked at the boy and added: "You see my daddy was in the next room and overheard all this, and him bein the jokester that he was, he just couldn't resist. I been Barely ever since."

When the boy and old man were able to calm down, they sipped their shine and shook their heads. "That story gets better every time you tell it," said Frank. "It surely does, and you a good sport about it, too."

"It don't bother me none to tell it now. Now days, the girls don't have no problem sexing me. Now days the girls get happy when I drop my breeches."

The men laughed again. When they settled, Frank cast Barely a sideways glance. "Yeah," he said, "but that's just the Lee sisters."

Thompson cocked his head. "Lee sisters? What Lee sisters? I don't go with no Lee sisters."

Frank winked at John Morgan. "Sure you do," he said. "Only old gals I ever see you with is a Lee, either Ug or Home, one. So don't tell me you ain't knowin the Lee sisters."

Barely momentarily looked puzzled, then burst into laughter. "Ah, shit," he said. "Reckon I do know them gals."

They laughed and they sipped more shine and the pendulum of conversation swung back toward the more serious. Thompson gave it a shove that direction by mentioning Frank Finney's colorful past. "Old Frank here used to be a sure enough outlaw. He rode with Quantrill during the war, the James boys and all."

John Morgan's eyes widened. "Jesse James?"

Frank Finney shrugged. "Yeah," he said, "but I ain't drank enough to dredge up them memories. That was a long time ago. I wasn't no older'n you when I done them things. And I ain't proud of none of it. I'd just as soon forget I ever done any of it."

A gator bellowed up the shore to the north, and they all three turned as one to listen for a repeat performance but when none came turned back to once again gaze into the fire. John Morgan looked at Frank. "So you spent some time in Missouri, I reckon."

"Hell, I was born there."

"You ever hear of Joplin?"

The old man flashed a quizzical look at the boy. "You ever hear of Tampa? I'm from Missouri. Course I heard of Joplin. I spent almost three years in that hellhole, workin the zinc mines back in the eighties."

John Morgan lay back in the grass and kicked his right leg out straight in order that he might slip a hand into his pants pocket. He withdrew the wooden disk and righted himself. He leaned and reached out the wafer to the old man and Frank took it and began turning it this way and that, trying to capture the fire's light to better see the object.

"Where on God's green earth did you get this?" he said, his eyes fixated on the disk as though it were an old friend, one he'd never expected to see again.

"A girl give it to me. Do you know what it is?"

"Hell, it's a poker chip," said Barely. "Ain't you ever played poker?"

Frank Finney shook the chip at Barely. "This ain't just any old chip. This is a high-dollar one from the House of Kings, the place where I lost my shirt, my virginity, and my good reputation, all in one night." He looked at the boy. "This thing's worth a fortune, if they ain't gone under. That girl must of thought the world of you. You must of showed her a real good time."

John Morgan smiled sheepishly and shook his head. "I don't even know her. I just met her outside the store in Ft. Pierce one day. Her and some other tourists had got off the train there, just to stretch their legs, I reckon. She handed me that, said it was where she lived, that if I was to take it there, they'd give me money for it."

Finney reached and handed the chip back to the boy. "She said she lived there?"

"Yessir. That's what she said."

The old man shook his head. "Well, that's just mighty peculiar."

John Morgan studied the old man's expression, his raised eyebrows and pursed lips. "Why's that?" he said.

"Well, I got to know several of them gals that lived there—back then in the eighties. I was real fond of em all, and them me. At least they acted like they was. But I never knew one to give money to nobody. Hell, they always had their hand out for yours. The only thing they ever give me was a good time; that, and a dose of the clap every now and then."

"Whoooeee," said Barely. "Sounds like my kind of place." He looked at the boy. "You ever had the clap?"

John Morgan looked at the fire and looked at Thompson. He shook his head. "Not that I know of."

Barely slapped his leg and looked at Finney. "The boy don't even know what it is."

The old man flashed Barely a coarse look. "Course he don't, numbskull." He looked at the boy. "This girl what give you the chip, was she pretty?"

John Morgan nodded. "Prettiest I ever seen."

Finney nodded. "And you got it in your head to go and find her one day."

"I didn't say that."

"You didn't have to."

John Morgan looked at the chip in his hand. "Yeah, well, I might of thought it a time or two."

"Well, you listen to me. You ever decide to act on that notion, you best be real careful. Many a man has walked into the House of Kings only to never be seen again. It's a rough place, rough as they come."

"Yessir," John Morgan said, him turning the chip in his hand. "I'll keep that in mind." He looked at Frank Finney. "How much you reckon this is worth?"

"I don't know for sure. I only seen a gold one like that a few times. Only the big shots ever played with gold ones, and even they wouldn't show but one or two." The old man paused and scratched his head. "I don't know, but I expect it's worth more'n you could make in ten years, workin here. Hell, ten, maybe even twenty."

"Damn," said the boy.

Barely Thompson reached and nudged the old man's shoulder. "You keep talkin like that, you'll have the kid gone tomorrow. He'll be lit out for Missouri, huntin money and pretty little whores."

John Morgan's eyes narrowed. "Sarah ain't no whore."

"Sarah?" said Barely. He leaned and spat in the fire. "Hell, kid, you wouldn't know one if ye saw one."

"Maybe so, but I know she ain't one."

Barely uncrossed his legs and sat with his arms draped about his knees. He looked at the old man and looked at the boy. "All right," he said, "if you say so. I ain't never met the woman. Hell, she could be pure as spring water, for all I know."

"And that ain't much," said Frank.

Barely looked sideways at the old man. "Ain't much what?"

"What you know."

"Shit," said Barely, "I might just know more'n you think."

"I doubt that. Long as I known you, you ain't surprised me yet."

"Y'all hold on now," said John Morgan. "I didn't mean to start no argument." He lay back and stuffed the chip into his pants pocket then righted himself. He motioned with his hand in the air. "Let's talk about this here land we're on."

Both men looked at him. Frank Finney plucked his hat from the grass beside him and set it on his head. He uncrossed his legs, his old bones issuing several pops loud enough to be heard over his drawn-out groan, a rusty hinge sound voicing perfectly the pain he found in such a movement. He sat briefly with his upper torso leaning forward over his outstretched legs, reaching and grasping his knees before rolling to his left and pressing to all fours. He then teetered there, on hands and knees, as if perhaps it was the position he'd sought all along.

"You goan make it?" said Barely, jumping to his feet to assist his friend.

"I'm all right," said Frank, but him nevertheless accepting the hand offered by the younger man. When upright, he dusted his breeches and backed close to the fire where he stood warming his backside. "Reckon I'm gonna have to start totin a chair every-

where. Damn ground got to where it just don't want to let me go."
He turned his head to look at the boy. "What you want to know
about this land?"

"Everything," said the boy. "Mr. Williams said it's for sale."

"I didn't know that," said Barely Thompson, settling again by the
fire. "Course I ain't never asked about it. I give up on owning land a
long time ago, so why bother askin what's for sale and all."

"Well, I ain't give up. I never will. I will get a place for my brother
and me, one way or another."

Thompson looked at Frank Finney. "Listen to that," he said. "You
recollect ever thinkin thataway?" He turned his gaze back to the
boy. "You got a lot to learn, boy. After you been throwed a few
times, you may think twice about gettin back on that horse."

John Morgan was silent. He reached and laid a piece of fatwood
on the fire and sat watching the flames eagerly accept his offering
of new life.

Frank Finney watched the boy. "Don't pay him no mind," he
said. "The way I see it, a feller can get anything he truly wants. It's
just that most of us, like old Barely and me, is born bein a little too
easy to please. We never wanted much in the first place." The old
man paused and rubbed the seat of his pants. He gave a little start
when realizing the cloth too hot and quickly turned to face the
growing fire. He looked at the boy. "You want a place of your own,
don't let nobody dissuade you from tryin to get it. Foller your
heart, is what I'm sayin. Your heart is the only compass you should
ever trust, if you want to find happiness in this here world." He
paused and looked at the boy, awkwardly, as though perhaps
embarrassed by his own words. "That's just my opinion, anyway.
For what that's worth."

The boy nodded to the old man. "I aim to do just that," he said.

*

In the months to come, through his work for the Williams, John
Morgan came to know well the lay of the land surrounding Nittaw.
He ranged as far east as Bull Creek and north to the tiny hamlet of
Holopaw. He once was gone ten days, skirting the shores of Lakes

Marion, Jackson, and Kissimmee in search of cattle gone wild as deer yet wearing the Williams brand and him alone responsible for their return to the land from whence they'd wandered. Save for his horse and his dog Roy he was always alone but never lonely, surely born again hard from the womb of the hungry land through which he rode. And as time passed his skill as a cow hunter did not go unnoticed and his pay soon increased from four to six dollars a week, pay he willingly surrendered to his aunt and uncle for the room and board provided him and his brother. Thus he worked but could not save and so, in August of his seventeenth year, he finally summoned the courage to reveal to his aunt and uncle the plan lodged so long in his mind.

He broached the subject after supper, as his uncle reached for his tobacco and before Betty could rise to clear the dishes from the table. He told them he had something to discuss with them and he rose from his chair and fetched a cigar box to the table, a relic from his past holding the remaining money they'd brought from Ft. Pierce. He then took his seat and said: "Reckon y'all can put up with me bein gone a while?" He studied his aunt and uncle's faces, his brother's, whom he knew was not going to like what he had to say.

Jude looked at his wife and looked at John Morgan. "What's old Bill got you doin now? He sendin you on a trip somewhere?"

"No, sir. I done give Bill my notice. This is something I got to do for myself, for Archie and me."

Jude dragged on his cigarette. "You quit Bill?" he said, exhaling a cloud of smoke along with his question.

"Yessir. A week from today will be my last to work."

Jude looked at the plate before him and looked at his nephew. "Six dollars a week is good pay these days." He paused and shook his head. "Where you think you gonna find better pay than that?"

"I'm goin to Missouri."

Jude's eyes narrowed. "Missouri? What in hell makes you think you'll find good work in Missouri?"

John Morgan shifted his position in his chair. "I got my reasons," he said.

Jude watched his nephew, obviously waiting for further explanation, but when none came he simply shook his head and frowned. "That ain't no answer."

"I know it sounds crazy, but my mind's made up. Workin for Mr. Williams ain't never going to get me and Arch a place of our own. So I'm goin to try somethin else." John Morgan looked at his Aunt Betty and looked at Jude. "I can't thank you enough for lettin us stay on like you have. You been nothin but good to us, and we won't forget it. But it's time we started lookin out for our own selves, give y'all some peace and quiet for a change."

Betty pushed her plate forward a few inches and raised her hands in a pleading manner. "Peace and quiet," she said. "I'll take company over peace and quiet, any day. Havin y'all's been a blessing. You're like my own boys now." She reached and repositioned the fork on her plate, her eyes beginning to swim and focused not on the boys but on the meaningless task at hand. She looked at John Morgan. "What if y'all don't come back?"

John Morgan shook his head. "Arch ain't goin with me. This is something I got to do alone."

Archie, seemingly awakened by the mention of his name, looked at his brother. "Ain't goin where?" he said.

John Morgan turned to his brother. "I got a job to do. When I get back, you and me will get us a place of our own."

Archie stared blankly for a moment. "I can wear my knife, then," he said.

John Morgan shook his head. "If that's all it takes to make you happy, sure, you can wear it."

Archie merely grinned.

John Morgan turned back to address his aunt and uncle. He gestured with a hand to the cigar box on the table before him. "I'm takin fifty dollars with me. Feller at the depot said it ought to be plenty enough to pay my fare all the way through. The rest in here—reckon it's about two thousand—if you'd hold it for us, I'd be grateful." He looked at his uncle. "You're welcome to use what you need, iffen you have to. Lord knows, it's the least I can offer for you taking us in and all."

Jude gave a wave with his hand, as if shooing a pesky fly. "Your money will be here when you get back." He paused and gave a deep sigh. "If you get back, is more like it. You ain't never been north of Holopaw. Thinkin a kid like you can get all the way to Missouri is foolish, plumb foolish."

"I'll do it."

"But why, John Morgan?" said Betty "Why Missouri? Can't you at least tell us that?"

"It wouldn't make no difference. Y'all would still think me foolish."

They sat without speaking a moment longer, until Jude snuffed his cigarette in a bight of gravy left on his plate and looked at his nephew and said: "We'll pray for you. Reckon that's about all we can do, if your mind's made up."

3

An Odyssey of the Blind

September, 1914

It cost him nothing to get as far as Jacksonville. The brakeman on the first northbound train of September—Tim Edwards, a man he'd helped load cargo on several occasions—situated him beneath a tarp covering naval stores bound for the port city. The sun was about an hour high when the train begin to move. The car on which he rode was an open flatbed and its tarp covering rowed barrels of turpentine his only protection against the elements. It was seasonably hot. He sat with his sweat-soaked back pressed against an oak barrel, his arms hugging his drawn-up legs while his right hand gripped the wooden handle of a motley carpet bag. His only view was of the blurred and ambiguous ground passing on his left. This, together with the swaying of the car and the rhythmic clack announcing every division of rail, soon lulled him to sleep. He slept with hat pulled low and head dipped between his arms, dreaming dreams in which his family was once again whole, tranquil scenes in which he'd have willingly stayed forever had the train not slowed to a crawl. When it reached full stop, a surge of adrenalin realigned his thoughts to the harsh reality of the moment.

The sun was setting when he climbed to the ground and stood looking around. He heard the huff of an engine far ahead, the faint din of some sort of machinery. The smell of woodsmoke riding another biting odor he could not place, an odor he found offensive and one he'd come to classify as the unmistakable scent of human misery. A long blast from a steam whistle far to the west. Buildings of varying heights formed the east and west horizons with the railroad right-of-way a seemingly endless void stretching north and south. There were many tracks other than the ones he'd arrived on and he walked westward picking his way across two sets to reach a service road running parallel to the rails. He followed the gravel road north toward a building with loading docks and a great sign on its south-facing side proclaiming: Jacksonville. People coming and going on the trackside of the building. Reaching the dock, he climbed its four steps and walked to an open window.

"Excuse me, sir," he said to the man seated within. "When's the next train to Joplin, Missouri?"

The man swiveled his stool to look at John Morgan. Studying the boy, the man's thin line of a mouth evolved into a smirk. "It's not that simple, kid."

John Morgan stepped and stood. He shifted his bag to his left hand. A pair of men wearing pin-striped overalls and short-billed caps passed behind him on the loading dock. The men were talking and paid him no mind.

The ticket agent turned to his left and reached and captured a map affixed to a plank of wood. When he turned back to the window he oriented the map for the boy to see. "You need to take the eight o'clock to Atlanta," he said, tracing with a finger the route he proposed. "From there you'll want to take the next available to Birmingham. They can tell ye there what you need to do to get to Memphis." He looked at the boy, studying him up and down, then turned back to the map. "Memphis's where ye need to be to cross the river into Missouri."

John Morgan looked at the man and looked at the map. "How much you reckon all that will cost me?"

The man cupped his chin pensively. "Can't say," he said. "It's twenty dollars to Atlanta, but I don't know about the rest, them being different lines and all."

"It's twenty dollars to Atlanta?"

"That's right." The man watched him. "Course, if ye got no objection to riding in one of the freight cars, I'll put ye on for a sawbuck."

"A sawbuck?"

"Five dollars." The man adjusted his visor and leaned back on his stool. "Anybody ketches ye in there, ye ain't never talked to me. Understand?"

The boy nodded. Half turning from the man, he slipped a hand into his right pants pocket and fished out a small roll of bills. He pulled a single note from the rest then slipped the roll back into his pocket, his eyes not on his actions but shifting right and left, watching his surroundings.

When he'd paid the man, the man pointed to a line of boxcars sitting idle on the spur furthest from the depot. "Pick any one you like," he said. "They all going to Atlanta. If ye wait till it gets good and dark, ye can go ahead and climb aboard. Won't have to worry bout oversleepin."

*

Once the sun had set, a potent darkness settled over the railyard, it so dark he was unsure that the cars he reached were the ones indicated by the man. There was not yet a moon and the only light was one directly above the depot's ticket window. He stood briefly studying the light and gauging where he was, then began feeling for the cold steel of the latch lever to open the sliding door of his chosen car. Once inside, he slid the door closed and latched it. A smell that reminded him of an outhouse hit him. He felt his way to a corner and, after feeling for any obstacles, settled to the wooden floor, sitting with his back pressing against the two perpendicular sides of the car. He sat for a moment, marveling at the degree of darkness within the car. Then he felt to open his bag and locate the biscuits and jerky he knew were somewhere inside.

Sometime in the night a rumbling sound awakened him. A surge of adrenalin doubled his heart rate when he realized the car's door had been opened. So dark he couldn't be sure he'd opened his eyes.

He listened as someone climbed into the car and slid the door closed. A rattling cough, then shuffling steps fading to the far end of the car.

John Morgan lay listening to his own heart. He thought that maybe he should cough himself, but decided against it. He merely lay still, his mind racing and him knowing full well that sleep was now out of the question.

After what seemed an eternity, a dim light slowly began framing the boxcar's sliding door. He heard sounds of activity outside in the yard: the steam whistle he'd heard the evening before, faint voices and some sort of machinery. He strained to make out the far end of the car but could see nothing. Then out of the darkness came a plea both sudden and startling, spoken words causing every muscle in his body to contract.

"You got any smokes over there?" the voice raspy, scarcely more than a whisper.

"No, sir," John Morgan replied. "I ain't took the habit up, yet."

"Didn't figure you had."

"Why's that?"

"Didn't smell it on you."

"That how you knew I was in here? You smelled me?"

"That's right, soon as I slid the door open."

"Damn."

"Now don't go huntin a washtub or nothin. You smell sweet, compared to most."

John Morgan dipped his face to a shirt sleeve and inhaled deeply. He sniffed again then dropped his arm to his lap. "You headin to Atlanta?"

"Not especially. I'm just ridin."

"You ever been to Missouri?" John Morgan said, subconsciously slipping his hand into his boot to feel the wooden disk stowed in his sock.

"I been all over. Tracks go there, I been there." The man fell silent for a moment, then continued: "This is your first time ridin the rails, ain't it?"

"Yessir. I ain't never been on a train till yesterday."

"Well, let me give you a piece of advice. You ain't likely to meet Jesus in one of these cars, but you sure as hell will meet the devil, you do it long enough. Ain't none of my business, of course. It's just that I judge you to be a good kid, and I'd hate to hear you've come to harm cause I ain't bothered to warn you and all."

"Yessir. I thank you for tellin me."

"You keep to yourself. Don't go tellin nobody your business. And don't never let a brakeman get near you. Them sons of bitches are a sadistic lot. Ever last one of em is lookin to crack your skull."

John Morgan felt the car lurch. "We're movin," he said.

"Yeah. Won't be long we'll be in Waycross."

"Does this train stop there?"

"Briefly, takin on a few more cars, cypress lumber mostly, headed north."

"How long till we get to Atlanta?"

"Should make it by sundown, I reckon."

"You reckon there'll be a train headed to Birmingham?"

"Sure they is. The night run leaves at seven-ten."

"How will I know it? I got to ask the ticket agent?"

"Naw, don't do that. I'll see that you get on the right one. I might just take it myself." The man coughed several times, each exhalation more violent than the previous. He cleared his throat and spat. "You a Florida boy?" he said.

"Yessir, born and raised."

"I got some oranges, do you want one. They wasn't quite ripe when I picked em, but they comin on pretty sweet now."

"Well, I thank you for offering. Reckon I can eat an orange, all right."

*

The sun had set by the time he helped the man down from the car, the man whose features remained a mystery in the dim light of the enormous railyard in which they now stood. He thought the man light as a child and much older than he, short in stature, stooped with age and moving with a strangely cautious gate, clinging to his offered arm as though in great need of his company. They walked slowly, the man whispering directions while John Morgan looked with awe at the great terminal building dominating the west side of the yard. "That's the biggest damn building I ever seen," he remarked to the man. To which the man merely shushed him and said, "Quiet, boy. I'm countin rails."

They walked, crossing tracks and the old man muttering to himself various destinations, the names of states and distant towns and cities as if the ground over which he shuffled were surely a map long etched in his mind. Stationary cars on several tracks ambiguous in the dark, solemn barriers they negotiated by crawling over cold steel couplings and continuing on. Then the man halted the boy at a string of cars, saying: "Here we go. This'un will take us all the way to Tupelo. Now find us one ain't locked."

"Tupelo?" said the boy. "Man said I need to go to Birmingham."

"You got to go through Birmingham to get to Tupelo, boy."

"Oh," said John Morgan.

"Whereabouts is it in Missouri you wantin to get to?"

"Joplin."

"Well, there you go. We get to Tupelo, you can ketch the next train to Memphis. You got to go to Memphis to cross the river, you know."

"Yessir. I been told that."

"The other side of the river is Arkansas. There, you'll go through Jonesboro and on to Springfield. Now you're in Missouri. It ain't but a short piece from Springfield to Joplin, not more'n a couple hundred miles." The old man paused to cough. "Why the hell you want to go to Joplin? Been my experience there ain't nothing there but zinc mines and trouble."

"Yessir, I been told that, too. It's just somethin I got to do."

"All right, ain't none of my business, nohow. Find us a car ain't locked while I ease over here and take a shit." The old man reached and found the boy's arm. "Somethin you might ought to think about doin yourself. It'll be a while fore we get another chance."

*

It was mid-morning when they arrived in Tupelo, the sun so bright when the boy opened the door of the boxcar that he had to stand for a moment to let his eyes adjust. Then he hopped down and set his bag on the ground and turned to assist the old man. It was the first time since meeting the man that he'd seen him clearly, and what he saw took a few seconds for his mind to process. The man stood in his rags in the open doorway, a fruit picker's bag slung over his shoulder and him gazing down in the boy's direction but yet his eyes glazed over like those of a long dead fish, and surely just as useless. "You're blind," the boy blurted.

"No shit," said the old man, stooping and groping the air for the hand he knew was being offered. "You just now figuring that out?"

"I had no idea," said the boy. He reached and took the man's weight and set him to the ground.

"I'll take that as a compliment," said the man. "Now let's get out of here. Won't be no train to Memphis till tomorrow morning." He began moving with his cautious shuffle, stepping across the nearest rail as though seeing it clearly.

"Where we going?"

"They's a patch of woods down here a piece. Apt to be some friends of mine there will feed and water us."

They walked along the tracks following their elongated shadows and the morning sun warm on their backs and causing the polished rails to shimmer ahead like parallel lines of poured mercury. A smattering of houses here and there after they passed the depot, dogs barking and the faint sound of organ music, voices lifted in song.

"Reckon today must be Sunday," said the old man.

"Yessir," said the boy. "By my count it is."

A motorcar chugged across the tracks some distance ahead, traveling on a marl crossroad beyond which a mixture of pine and hardwoods rose like a great wall to seemingly define the town limits.

"Model T," commented the old man.

The boy looked at him and looked at the now empty crossroad ahead. "You could tell that by the sound?"

"Yep. The blame things is gettin to be everywhere. I got to ride in one a while back. Feller just stopped and asked me did I want to experience the future."

"Did you like it?"

The old man shrugged. "It was all right. Kind of startled me a bit, the way it took off so quick. Not like ridin a train, I'll tell you that. More like ridin an ornery horse."

When they crossed the marl road the old man guided the boy to a path leading into the woods as though having perfectly good vision. A short distance on they came to a clearing where several crude shelters ringed a firepit in whose midst lay the charred remains of a dead fire. Tin cans and bottles of all description scattered about. An assortment of clothing hung from a line strung between trees at the clearing's edge. A still form wrapped in a blanket lay fetal-like beneath a lean-to fashioned from an old wagon sheet and black gum saplings.

John Morgan stood eyeing the sleeping man. He turned to his blind companion, gesturing toward the lean-to. "There's a feller sleepin in this one," he said.

"Tip," the old man said, saying it louder than needed to address the boy.

The man wrapped in the blanket visibly jerked, then slowly freed himself and sat up, wearing tattered long johns sporting a pinkish hue, a full beard streaked with gray as was his long unkempt hair. The man squinted against the brightness of the morning. A hand shot to his face and began probing amongst its whiskers, as if attempting the capture of some sensed intruder. Done scratching, the man shook his head as if to realign its contents. "Long time no see, Pick."

"Long time," said the old man. "Where's everybody?"

Tip shook his head. He looked around as if wondering the same thing. He looked at the boy. "Who's your friend? Don't believe we've met."

Pick waved a hand toward the boy. "This is Florida Boy. He ain't a regular. He's just going somewhere."

Tip raised a hand to the boy and dipped his head hello. "Nice to make your acquaintance, boy going somewhere."

"Yessir. Nice to meet you, too."

Struggling to a standing position, Tip emerged from beneath the tarp and stepped a few feet to his right, his bare feet starkly white against the trodden ground. He turned to face the woods, dropped the flap of his drawers and began to urinate. "Boy's got manners," he said. "Don't find that much these days."

Pick cocked an ear to the man. "Ain't that the truth," he said.

When done relieving himself, Tip reached within his bedroom and dragged out a pair of bib overalls. Dressing himself, he looked at the boy. "You headed to Florida?"

"No, sir. I'm headin west."

"What with winter comin, thought you might be headed home." Tip studied the boy momentarily, as though wanting a reply. When none came he stooped to retrieve a pair of brogans from his hovel, then sat in the dirt to don them. "I winter in Florida most every year, down around Palatka. You know Palatka?"

"No, sir. I ain't never been there. I ain't been a whole lot of places."

Tip flashed the boy a toothy grin. He looked at the old man. "What about you, Pick? You going with me, ain't you?"

Pick stepped and stood. "If you're still here when I get back," he said. "I'd kind of like to go on with the boy a ways, make sure he don't get lost."

Tip got to his feet. He dusted the seat of his breeches. "Blind leadin the blind," he said. He smiled and shook his head. "Well, I'll wait for you. Good company's hard to find nowadays."

*

They piddled most of the day, the two men talking of old times while the boy gathered enough firewood for the coming night. Late afternoon Tip left without saying where he was going. He returned an hour later carrying a flour sack laden with cans of pork and beans, their supper, sans any explanation as to how he'd come by it. By the time the sun had set the boy had a good fire going, the beans simmering in a blackened kettle set on coals he'd raked to one side of the flames.

They three sat on the upwind side of the fire, Tip and the boy watching the flames while Pick merely listened, the fire's hiss and crackle forming in his mind a view all his own.

"I hear there's a war done broke out in Europe," said Tip. "Heard Germany first declared it against France, and then the Brits went and fell in with the French." He paused and reached to stir the beans with the large spoon he had in hand. "Now they sayin a bunch of other countries are loadin their guns, fixin to jump in too."

"They'll always be a war going on somewheres," said Pick. "It's just man's nature. Long as it don't come over here, it don't mean nothin to me."

Tip gestured to the boy. "It'll mean something to the boy here, do we wind up gettin in it. He might have to go fight for you and me."

"Well, I pray we don't get in it," said Pick. "Anyway, that's enough talk about war. Ain't them beans hot yet?"

They ate and were still eating when three men suddenly walked from the woods and into the ring of light cast by the fire, men with scraggly beards and who all wore dark floppy hats and predacious looks. "What's for dinner?" said the oldest of the three, a little pump action rifle resting in the crook of his arm. As the one man spoke his companions sidled right and left respectively, as if intent on encircling those sitting at the fire.

"Beans," said Tip. "We only got pork and beans, but you're welcome to have some."

The boy laid his spoon in his tin plate and then set the plate on the ground beside him. He watched the men, his heart racing, the hair on the nape of his neck standing instinctively.

The man swung the little rifle from the crook of his arm and leveled it toward the fire. "Don't want no beans," he said.

Tip's eyes widened. "You ain't got to point that rifle, mister. You all can take whatever you want."

John Morgan felt Pick's hand grasp his right arm. "Run," the old man whispered. "They's killers, but they won't hurt me."

"Yes, we can," the man said, simultaneously shouldering the rifle and firing a single shot.

Tip went limp, his chin dropping to his chest as the plate in his lap began to fill with blood draining from the hole in his forehead.

"Run!" said Pick, yet he needn't have said anything.

The boy had already bolted from beneath his own hat. He charged headlong at the leftmost man, the man squatting back on his heels and reaching for a big knife sheathed at his side but the move too late and the boy on him and knocking him senseless with a right to the chin. The crack of the rifle and the blow to the man's chin sounding as one and the boy continuing on past the falling man, sprinting for the cover of the woods while the older man jacked in another cartridge. The rifle barked again as he sailed into the wall of night, his pumping arms staving off bushes and limbs and his eyes blind to any path. He ran thusly for what seemed a long time, until his legs would no longer carry him, upon which time he pitched headfirst into some sort of scrubby bushes that scratched and clawed at his passage. He lay still, his lungs burning as he gasped for air. He felt nauseous but managed to keep his supper. For a good while he simply breathed and listened for any sign that he was being pursued. He was thankful for the darkness. The darkness was his friend. Finally, satisfied the men weren't coming, he thought to get up and it was then he realized that something was wrong, that the left side of his shirt was soaked with something other than sweat.

The bastard got me, he thought. He rolled to his side, moving slowly as to evaluate his condition. A numbness at the back of his left shoulder quickly transitioned to a sharp pain as he used his arms to sit up. He sat for a moment, his legs outstretched. He could feel his heart beating where the bullet had found him. Drawing his right leg up, he reached and confirmed the chip was still in his sock. He rolled to his knees and struggled to stand, the bushes into which he'd fallen stubbornly clinging to his person as if loath to let him go. Shaky. He looked around but could see no faults in the darkness. Overhead through the canopy he saw stars but couldn't name them. He gave a deep sigh and said: "Shit." Then he began to walk.

Having no bearing, he decided to move at a right angle to the line he'd been on when he fell, hoping he'd come to the railroad grade. If he could find the tracks, perhaps he could find his way back to Pick. He hadn't heard any more shots, so he thought maybe the men had not harmed the old blind man. That's what he prayed for, anyway.

He walked with his right hand raised and groping the night, keeping his left arm pressed to his side, his left thumb hooked in his waistband to keep the arm as still as possible. He'd not gone far before realizing his legs were curiously heavy. He quickened his steps, pleading with his useless eyes to locate some semblance of hope in the seamless dark ahead. And suddenly it was there, but just a glimpse then gone: a light, he was sure of it. He halted and took two steps back and the light was there again, a steady yellowish-white light. He moved on toward the light, altering his course when needed to keep his goal in sight. Stepping forward until suddenly he staggered from the woods into the well-kept yard of a home.

He momentarily stood catching his breath and eyeing the house. A light shone through a window, the light that had led him from the woods. He thought to continue on to the light, but the thought was cut short when the light suddenly went out, when suddenly he was floating above a familiar room, watching his sleeping sisters and marveling at their beauty.

*

He had been listening to the hounds for a long time, imagining them surely hot on the trail of fox or deer, until it suddenly occurred to him the monotonous baying was that of penned dogs. He opened his eyes. A strange room with not one accoutrement familiar to him. He cocked his head to look around and came face to face with a woman whose kind eyes immediately set him at ease.

"Well," the lady said, "I'm happy to finally see them handsome eyes. Praise the Lord. Believe you goan be all right."

The boy stared at the woman, obviously befuddled that a woman of color could be so much like his own mother. He thought to speak but found his mouth so parched it was difficult to form the words.

Recognizing his distress, the woman fetched a tumbler from a table by the bed. The glass in one hand, she slipped the other beneath his pillow and raised him up sufficiently that he might drink. When he'd had his fill she stepped back and stood holding the glass as though anticipating he would soon want more.

"Thank you," the boy said. He saw his clothes on a trunk to the side of his bed, neatly folded and obviously having been washed and pressed. His boots standing at the foot of the trunk. He looked at the woman. "Where am I?" he said.

"Well, you in my house," said the woman. "My young'uns found you layin out in the yard, yesterday mornin. They thought you was dead. Give em an awful fright, you did." The woman chuckled. "Ain't every day we find a man layin out in the yard. Specially one's all bloody and tore up the way you was."

John Morgan lay thinking. He eyed the white material wrapped tightly around his upper torso. "Who doctored me?"

"Me and my man, with the Lord's help of course. Won't no doctor come out here. Sides, you bein shot and all, we din't know what all you been up to. Thought maybe it best we not let on to nobody, bout you bein here and all." The woman paused momentarily. "We got the little 'ol bullet out. It near about come all the way through."

She gestured toward him with the glass. "Found it just under the skin, high on your chest there. Didn't hit no bone, so you should heal up all right."

"Well, I sure thank you for your trouble." He reached out his arms and tried to rock forward but pain, weakness, and a brown hand quickly erased that notion from his head. He lay back with a deep sigh.

"You don't need to be movin around. You'll be bleedin agin, do you not lie still." The woman smoothed the sheet covering him. "You welcome to stay here long as it takes. You need to get word to your people, you just tell me how."

The boy wagged his head from side to side. "I ain't from around here," he said. "There's just a feller I met on the train. He was with me when I got shot, and I'd like to know he's all right."

The woman said, "Oh, Lord," and turned and set the glass on the table. She looked at the boy. "Word is they found a man up the tracks there in them woods yesterday. Shot dead by somebody."

"One man?"

"That's what I heard."

The boy nodded. "That's good, I reckon."

The woman watched him. When he said nothing more, she turned to leave the room but stopped in the doorway and said: "You can call me Loretta. Loretta Smith is who I am."

A moment after Loretta had shut the door he threw back the sheet and sat up in bed. He swung his legs over the side and sat long enough to catch his breath and steady himself. A bit mortified that he was completely naked, he slipped from the bed and stepped tentatively across the wooden floor to his clothes. He searched the pockets of his jeans and found that his money was all there, his knife and the wooden chip as well. Then, after putting everything back as it was, he returned to the bed, exhausted yet filled with a feeling of complacency.

*

He is almost a month with the Smiths, the family of five treating him as one of their own, treating him so well he is reluctant to leave them. Yet on a cool night in early October he does leave them. He leaves a note expressing his thanks along with twenty dollars and slips from the house sometime after midnight. Following directions he'd gleaned from the eldest Smith boy, he walks through the night along the main road leading to Memphis. Not long after daybreak, where cotton fields stretched to the horizon on each side of the road, an automobile overtakes him and slides to a halt when the goggled driver applies the mechanical brakes.

"Where you headed, boy?" the portly man shouted over the revved engine. He tugged at a lever on the steering column and the motor slowed to an idle. "Confounded contraption," he muttered.

"Memphis," said John Morgan.

"Well, climb in. I'm headed there myself."

The boy eyed the car's door hesitantly. He gathered himself to climb up and over but the man stopped him.

"The latch there," the man said, gesturing with a gloved hand. "Pull the damn latch. She'll open pretty as you please."

"Yessir," he said. He did as told and climbed in and shut the door. "I ain't never done this before."

The man reached and adjusted the throttle lever to rev the engine then slipped the car in gear and let out the clutch. The car lurched forward and the man guffawed. "Hold on, boy. We going to Memphis."

John Morgan held on. He sat watching the rows of cotton sliding by, faster and faster until the bolls became a blurred mass of flickering white atop a sea of green. The wind whipping his hair and causing his eyes to tear.

"Where you from?" said the man, his large belly almost reaching the steering wheel and him in his goggles and gray suit resembling some sort of talented toad out for a drive.

"Florida."

"Florida! Well, you done walked a long damn way, ain't you."

"No, sir. I rode the train, mostly."

The man nodded. "You got business in Memphis?"

"No, sir."

The man looked at the boy and looked at the road. "You're not in the habit of talking much, are you?"

"No, sir. I reckon not."

"Well, all right. You may as well catch you a nap then. We'll be a while gettin to Memphis."

John Morgan looked at the man. "I appreciate you givin me a ride."

"Shoot," said the man. "I know you do, boy. Now set back and get some rest. A man on the move needs all he can get."

It was just after noon when they got to Memphis, it pleasantly cool and the city bustling with activity. The man drove Main Street and let him off in front of the newly built Terminal Station, John Morgan having told him of his intention to catch the next train to Arkansas.

"You stay out of trouble, boy," the man told him.

"Yessir, I'll do my best. Thanks again for the ride."

"You best get you a coat. I don't like to see a man half naked with winter comin on."

"I aim to do that."

The man reached and pulled off his goggles and shook them at the boy. "Well, goodbye to you, and good luck."

"Yessir," said the boy.

He shut the door and the man nodded and raised a hand and turned the car around in the street and went back the way he'd come. John Morgan watched him go, then turned and walked to the great double doors of the station house.

*

He purchases a ticket that will get him as far as Jonesboro and then wanders the streets of Memphis just to kill time. In a department store he uses the last of his money to buy a cheap cotton coat, a loaf of white bread, and a wedge of cheese. He sleeps on a bench inside the Terminal Station until told to move by a uniformed man with a gruff demeanor. He sits outside on the curb the remainder of the night and at dawn he boards the westbound train's only

130

coach. There are few passengers and he chooses a window seat on the starboard side of the car, a window through which he watches with wonder as the train traverses the great Mississippi via the Frisco Bridge. He sees the New Bridge under construction and wonders what may be wrong with the old. He is very tired but does not sleep for fear of missing some new wonder. As the world passes beyond the glass, he suddenly feels very small, a sense of regret. He slips a hand in his pants pocket to hold the wooden disk, and holds it still when the conductor enters the car and announces they've come to Jonesboro.

He thinks to hop the next train to Springfield but is caught when trying to board and beaten senseless by an unsympathetic brakeman. He finds work at a livery on the outskirts of town. He eats and sleeps with the horses. The owner is a middle-aged widow who is greatly impressed by his way with the animals. In only a few days the woman invites him into her home. She gives him clothes and a Stetson hat that had belonged to her late husband. He succumbs to her advances. He sleeps in her bed and she teaches him pleasures beyond his wildest dreams, yet after only a month he tells her he must go. Their parting is amicable and the heartbroken woman pays him with a good buckskin mare and tack. On the first snowy day in December she stands by the road and watches him ride out of her life forever. Her name is Marion, and he will not forget her.

Two weeks later he is in Springfield. He works at odd jobs for day wages and found, and then moves on. In January he feeds penned cattle for a man named Crawford on a ranch a few miles east of Joplin. He feels a kinship with the stern yet fair man and stays with him through the summer. Having saved every dime he's been paid, he quits the man on the first cold day in November and rides on to Joplin. In the heart of the business district on Main Street he halts the horse he's given the name Girl and steps down and stands looking up at a sign that reads: House of Kings. Both motorcars and horses travel the wide street, and at its center on one of two sets of tracks a horse-drawn trolley with clanging bell trundles southward. He looks at the sign on the three-story building and breathes: "Finally."

131

4

Sarah Over the Street

November, 1915

It was almost noon when he crossed the street and tried the Saloon's double doors. He found them locked so he strode back to his horse and stood looking up and down the broad street. A cold breeze channeled by the shoulder-to-shoulder buildings chilled his left cheek while shouting the impotence of his cheap coat. He stood, and a half-wild-looking dog trotted past, it eyeing him suspiciously with its pointed muzzle lifted and testing the air as it veered to avoid him and his horse. A pair of ladies came out of the Woolworths down the street, the pair in their ankle-length dresses swinging handled bags and lost in conversation. When the women had gone he turned and mounted his horse. He clucked Girl to a walk and rode with the breeze back the way he'd previously come.

At the edge of town he boarded his horse with a wheelwright whose shop doubled as a stable. It was almost two by the time he'd walked back to the House of Kings and now one of the doors stood open. He entered the building, pausing just beyond the entryway to allow his eyes to adjust. A grand staircase on his right as he moved on into a great room with many square tables atop which stood upturned chairs. A small, raised dance floor lay beyond the tables, along with a circular platform holding a piano and several chairs. A long mahogany bar with its brass footrail and spittoons spanned the width of the room's south wall. An ornately framed mirror on the wall and girded by paintings of nude women, all of the ladies a bit plump and reclining in alluring attitudes of repose. He walked to the bar and stood eyeing the row upon row of bottled spirits lining the back bar when a tall lanky man emerged from a doorway to his right.

The man carried a wooden crate of tinkling glasses. He hesitated briefly upon seeing the boy but continued on and deposited the crate out of sight on the floor behind the bar. He stood tall, looking at John Morgan, his eyes seeming to fixate on the boy's hat.

"What'll ye have, Tex?"

"Howdy," said the boy. "I'm lookin for a girl named Sarah."

The man smiled. "You and a lot of other fellows," he said. "She's upstairs but she's not open for business. You need to come back after seven."

"After seven."

"That's right. Now, what are you drinking?"

The boy stepped and stood. "Nothin right now," he said. "I was just hoping to talk to her. Reckon she'd see me?"

The man shook his head. "Not before seven. No customers allowed up those stairs till then." The man watched a puzzled look come to the boy's face. "Look, kid," he added, "come back tonight and give your two dollars to Miss Betsy. Then you can talk to Sarah till your heart's content."

"Miss Betsy?"

The man nodded. He gestured toward the staircase. "She'll be seated at that little table there."

John Morgan turned to look and turned back to the man. "All right," he said, reaching and touching the brim of his hat. "I'll come back tonight."

*

He killed time by simply walking around, from one end of the town to the other. At sunset he entered a café and ordered the day's special, roast beef, green beans, and mashed potatoes, the first professionally prepared meal he'd ever eaten. He thought the food good, and he left a quarter on the table as he stood to leave, mimicking what he'd witnessed other patrons do as he ate. Outside the night was full grown yet the street well lighted as he strolled to the House of Kings. A number of automobiles were now parked one behind the other along the sidewalk. Several buggies with their harnessed horses standing three-legged, heads hung low as though sleeping. He walked and the sound of fiddle and piano grew louder with each step he took.

The double doors were propped open and he walked through them into a haze of smoke and din of noise. The great room was alive with activity. Several couples on the dance floor sashayed and stomped to a lively tune played by two musicians seated on the platform. The boy stopped in front of the stairs and stood marveling at all the commotion. He noticed a woman seated at the table next to the stairs and he stepped before her and reached and touched his hat brim hello.

"Howdy," he said. "I'd like to see Sarah."

The woman, her face painted so gaudily with makeup as to resemble a circus clown, smiled up at him. "Well, Sarah it is," she said. That'll be two dollars, hon."

He paid her the money then stood like a man suddenly realizing himself lost when the woman said nothing more. "Where's she at?" he said.

The woman issued a little chuckle. She gestured toward the ceiling. "Same place she's always been: third floor, second door on the left."

He nodded to the woman and turned and started up the stairs. At the second floor landing he heard garbled voices and laughter emanating from beyond a closed door. Next to the door sat a man in a dark linen suit, a swarthy, muscular man perched on a stool with arms crossed about his chest and eyeing John Morgan with a look of contempt. The boy lifted a hand in greeting, yet continued on without pause when the man did nothing to reciprocate. He climbed the next flight of stairs to the third floor landing, to a long hallway cloaked in darkness save for a dim red light at the far end.

135

Before proceeding down the hall, he noticed a door on his right that was barred and sporting a heavy padlock. He walked, feeling his way down the hallway, until locating the second door on his left. He stood before the door, studying the thin wedge of light bleeding beneath it and then looking right and left before raising a hand to knock. He removed his hat and stood turning it in his hands. A few seconds on the door opened and a young woman with blond hair and striking blue eyes stood gazing up at him.

"Hey," she said.

John Morgan's gaze dropped from the woman's eyes to the long nightgown she wore, the garment's fabric so sheer that little was left to his imagination. "I'm lookin for Sarah," he said.

The woman smiled. "Well, you've found her," she said, opening the door wide. "Come on in, and I'll introduce you."

He stepped past the woman, his eyes quitting her to pan the small room's interior. A single bed girded by twin nightstands, a lamp dimly glowing on one stand and a basin with matching pitcher on the other. A highback chair holding a stack of folded towels. He turned back to the woman, a puzzled expression obvious on his face.

"Is something wrong?" said the woman.

"Where is she?"

"Where's who?"

"Sarah."

The woman cocked her head curiously. "I'm Sarah," she said. "What kind of game are you playing?"

John Morgan shifted his hat from one hand to the other. "I ain't playin no game," he said. "Is there another Sarah lives here? The one I'm lookin for has got dark hair and eyes. She's younger than you."

The woman glided to the bed and sat on it. She studied the boy's face. "What makes you think her name is Sarah?"

"She told me."

"So you've talked to her?"

"I did."

The woman's eyes narrowed. "That's impossible," she said. "I know for a fact that window don't open."

"What's a window got to do with it? I talked to her when she come to Florida."

"Well, that must have been a long time ago. The year I've been here, she's never set foot out of that room."

"What room?"

The woman stood. She shook her head to free her long hair from her shoulders then grasped the sides of her gown and began to slowly pull it up. A coy smile on her face, she watched the boy watching her legs as the gown's hem rose higher and higher. "You didn't come here just to ask a bunch of questions, did you?"

"No, ma'am," said John Morgan. "I'm here cause I thought you were the Sarah that invited me here. At least, I think that's what she meant." He slipped a hand in his pants pocket and withdrew the wooden chip. He showed it to the woman. "She give me this, said I could get money for it, if I was to come here. Was she telling me the truth?"

The woman stared wide-eyed at the chip. She released her gown and again sat on the bed. She nodded yes. "That's a ten thousand dollar chip."

John Morgan slid the chip back in his pocket. "So who do I see to cash it in? Sarah ain't told me that."

She shook her head. "Unless you can come up with a better story, I'd advise you to keep that chip to yourself."

"Story? I ain't told you no story. I told you the truth."

"Maybe. Maybe not. All I'm saying is nobody is allowed to win that kind of money in this place. Nobody."

John Morgan stepped and stood. He looked at the floor and looked at the woman. "Well, how do I get to see Sarah?"

The woman's eyes narrowed. "Forget about her. Seeing her in that window is the closest you'll ever get to that Sarah. If Sarah's even her name. We call her Sarah Over the Street, on account of how nobody's ever seen her out of that room, the one overlooking the street." The woman paused. She stared blankly at her hands that were in her lap and kneading the material of her gown in a worrisome manner. "I don't dare tell you any more about that girl." She looked at the boy. "I've said too much already. I've probably said enough to get me killed, if you repeat it."

"I won't do that. You and me just had a good time, is all. We ain't talked a bit."

The whore stood and stepped to the boy. She embraced him and nuzzled his neck. The heat from her body. The sweet musky smell of her hair. "That's my sweet boy," she said. "Now why don't we have that good time, so at least part of your story will be true."

*

After sleeping in the stall with his horse, he rose before sunrise and returned to the Crawford place. Bob Crawford and his wife Sue were surprised to see him but didn't trouble him with too many questions. They fed him breakfast and discussed the day's work schedule as though he'd never left.

The Saturday following he saddled his horse in the frigid pre-dawn darkness and rode to Joplin, both his and the horse's breath pluming proof of life in the seemingly dead world through which they moved. No sound save the clop of the horse's hooves and the creak and jingle of tack and over the town ahead a full moon in its slow descent toward the horizon. He rode, and by the time he was on Main Street the moon was already gone, the sun to come already subduing stars in the eastern sky.

Across the street from the House of Kings he dismounted and tied his horse to one of the sidewalk's roof support posts. His horse shook and blew, its pluming breath jetting from its flared nostrils as though some inner fire had been stoked against the morning's cold. John Morgan, his hands stuffed in his coat pockets, stood looking at the uppermost part of the building across the street. He waited, and the world began to take shape around him, as did the lone window of the House of Kings' third floor. As he watched the window, a horse-drawn milk wagon passed on the street, the driver huddled in his heavy coat and lifting a gloved hand in passing. A tabby cat emerged from beneath the sidewalk and slinked to mid-street where it paused briefly to arch its back and cast a threatening stare at the horse before moving on. When he refocused on the window, the sun's first rays were slowly painting a portrait within its frame. He was stunned by what he saw, and though the street was suddenly alive with activity, he did not notice. The naked figure at the window was all that existed, was undoubtedly the girl of his memory though now obviously a woman. Moving like a man in a dream, he removed his hat and raised it as though saluting the woman. When she lifted a pale hand in return, he began to tremble.

*

Sarah watched as Miss Etta stepped from the trolley and crossed the street. The Florida boy was still sitting on the walk, but nothing in Etta's demeanor said that she'd noticed him. When the trolley had moved on she waved to the boy, and he immediately reciprocated. *He sees me. He definitely sees me.*

She turned and started for the door but stopped midway across the room and came back to the window. Upon seeing the boy had not moved she skipped to the door and stood waiting, stepping and standing and waiting until sounds beyond the door seemed to release her. She skipped back to the window and again waved to the boy.

Miss Etta, a stack of folded white towels under one arm and a look of concern on her face, glided through the door and swung it shut behind her. She moved directly to the bed with scarcely a glance at Sarah. She set the towels on the bed and stood staring at them as if suddenly paralyzed by some sight or sound or, perhaps, mere thought.

"Come see," said Sarah. "Did you see him?"

Etta turned to face the girl, her fists pressed to her substantial hips, elbows flared wide. "I seen him," she said, her brown eyes wide and swimming.

"It's the Florida boy."

"I know who he is," said Etta. "And I know who he ain't."

Sarah looked. She left the window and came to stand before Miss Etta. "What do you mean?"

Etta reached out her hands and cupped the girl's bare shoulders. "My sweet child," she said. "My poor sweet child."

Sarah studied the brown face, the kind eyes in whose dark pupils she could see her twinned self. "What did you mean?"

"I mean he ain't never goan be what you want him to be."

Sarah's eyes began to swim. "He's come here to see me."

Etta looked the girl up and down, her eyes widening as they returned to focus on the porcelain face. "Shoot," she said. "That all he wanted, he might as well go on home. He done seen all your treasure. Course that ain't how the world works, is it? You done ruined that boy. You done struck that boy stupid. Ain't nobody goan be able to talk sense to him now."

Sarah's eyes narrowed. "Good," she said.

*

It was midafternoon when the colored woman exited the House of Kings. He watched her board the northbound trolley then mounted his horse to follow at a distance. It was cold and the gusting wind into which he rode brought tears to his eyes. The lady departed the trolley at its turnaround, at the town limit where she continued on by walking the road edge. He never saw her glance back, but felt sure she knew he was following. After walking the road for several hundred yards, she quit it to follow a dirt path into a stand of pines. The path led him to an unpainted clapboard house where the woman sat waiting for him on the home's front porch. She sat rocking in her chair, watching with one raised eyebrow as he stepped down from his horse.

"Howdy, ma'am," he said. "Reckon you know why I'm here."

The woman nodded. "Pretty sure I do, Florida Boy" she said. "You goan try and use me to get to Sarah."

John Morgan stepped and stood. He removed his hat and set it back on his head. "Yes, ma'am. You got me figured out."

"What's your name? She goan ax me, so you might as well go on and tell me."

"John Morgan," he said. "John Morgan Rawlerson."

The woman nodded. "I'm Etta. Etta Nix is who I be."

He also nodded. "I aim to court Sarah," he said. "If she'll let me."

"Shoot, you all that child's talked about, ever since we seen you in Florida."

The boy squirmed a bit in his chair. "I was hoping you could tell me about her. I don't even know her last name, you see. Who do I need to see to get permission to court her?"

"She ain't got one," said Etta.

"Ma'am?"

"She ain't got no last name." Etta gestured with a hand to the rocker beside her. "Come on up here and set down, and I'll tell you a story bout Sarah. Liable to get me kilt, but I just don't care no more. Believe God done told me it's time to do the right thing by that child, so I'm goan do what I can."

John Morgan ascended the steps and sat in the rocker. He removed his hat and looked at Etta, it not so cold on the porch, what with the afternoon sun full on them and the surrounding pines blocking most of the wind. The buckskin horse obligingly waiting before the steps, head up with ears pricked toward its master as if awaiting instructions.

"Sarah's folks used to own all the land up there where the main mine is now. They was farmers, raised a few cows and pigs, grew corn and cotton. They was young, I was told. Sarah was their first child, and her just about a month old when Mista King brung her to that room. He come and got me cause I'd done raised a passel of young'uns. I did all the cleanin for him back then, so he knew I was scared of him, and wouldn't say nothin to nobody."

"Why were you scared of him?"

Etta cut her eyes to the boy. "Shoot," she said. "Everybody scared of that man, everybody still livin, anyways."

John Morgan looked at the hat in his lap. "So what happened to Sarah's folks? How come King to have her?"

141

"He said they was burned up in the fire that took their house. Said they wasn't nothin left of them. Said Sarah din't have nobody else so he was goan do the Christian thing and see she got raised proper." Etta paused to look at the boy. "He ain't no Christian, but I've often thought he sure as hell might be the devil himself. I've suspected it for a long time."

John Morgan rocked. "So you think he killed Sarah's folks."

"Sure he did. He wanted their land. Wasn't a month after the fire fore he owned that ground and was settin up to mine the zinc under it. Made him one of the richest men in Missouri, it did, killin them people and takin their land." Etta reached and touched the boy's arm. "Now I know what you're thinkin. You're thinkin, if I know all this how come him to get away with it. He got away with it the same way he still gets away with things today. He owns the law in these parts. They all in his pocket. Ain't a week goes by you won't see ever last one of em in his place. He owns em, so don't never go lookin for help from the law round here. Shoot, Mista King is the law round here."

John Morgan was silent. He seemed to be watching his horse. "So what is Sarah to him? I've heard she never leaves that room. Why would he treat her that way?"

"Cause he owns her. He's clipped her wings just like he's done to all them birds he keeps up there. Just like he done to me. She ain't nothin to him but a play-pretty and, just like his birds, he'd rather kill her than see her free to fly away."

The muscles in John Morgan's jaws flexed as though he were chewing but he was not chewing. He looked at Etta. "So how are we gonna get her out of there? Have you got a key to that lock?"

Etta shook her head yes. "He'll find you, though" she said. "If you don't kill him, we all dead—you, me, and Sarah. They ain't no place you can hide from that man."

"I ain't come here to kill somebody. There's got to be another way."

"If you kill Mista King, I don't believe Andre and the others will bother to hunt you. I spect they'll be too busy fightin over Mista

King's things to worry bout you and Sarah. You kill Mista King and all his birds goan think they can fly."

"Who's Andre?"

"He the big galoot that does Mista King's dirty work. He usually on the gambling floor, makin sure don't nobody win too much. He likes to cut people, so don't never let him get too close."

John Morgan nodded. "I think I seen him." He brought a hand to his chin and rubbed it pensively. "I need to come up with a plan," he said. "We got to get this right the first time, if this King feller is all you say he is."

Miss Etta nodded. "It ain't easy to fool the devil."

"Does he live there, in the House of Kings?"

"Mista King? Naw, he stay out at his place west of town. He got a big mansion out there, near bout to the mine."

"Does he see Sarah every day?"

Etta shook her head. "He always come on Sunday evening, less he be sick or somethin. Place is closed on Sunday, so he can slip in and out without nobody seein what he's up to. Rest of the time you just don't never know. He might be in town on business and just pop in. But that don't happen too often, thank God."

"So there's nobody there on Sunday?"

"Nobody ceptin Andre. He always there. He sleep in that room off the gambling hall, so ain't nobody can take Mista King's money."

"They keep money in the building?"

Etta nodded. "In that room." She looked at the boy sideways. "You thinkin to rob Mista King?"

"I ain't plannin on it, but I will if I have to." He looked into Etta's eyes. "Tomorrow's Sunday," he said.

Etta cocked her head. "I know that."

"Is there anything keepin you here, besides Sarah?"

"Why you want to know that?"

"I'm takin Sarah tomorrow, and I'd like you to come with us."

"To Florida?"

John Morgan nodded.

Etta looked at her hands in her lap and looked at the boy. "I got nobody here. All my young'uns still livin moved off long ago. I don't even own this house; it belong to Mista King."

"So come with us."

"But how? How we goan go?"

"I'll take care of the how. You just bring a few things with you tomorrow. Be ready to go once I've done what I have to do."

"Oh, Lord," said Etta. "Don't know if my ol heart can take all this citement."

"Do you have a key to the front door?"

Etta nodded that she did.

"What time does King get there?"

"After dinner. Round six-thirty."

"I'll be at the front door at three o'clock."

Etta nodded. "I'll let you in."

"What about Andre?"

"He usually lay out on Sunday, sleepin off all the liquor he drink the night befo."

John Morgan slapped his leg. "All right, then. Tomorrow at three." He paused and looked at his horse and looked at the hat in his lap. "Do you think Sarah will go with me?"

"She'll go. I think that sweet child been knowin you was comin for her since that day in Florida."

He looked at her, a smile growing on his face. "From here on out, I'm from Texas."

A smile then formed at the corners of Etta's mouth. Her eyes sparkled. "So we goin to Texas then."

John Morgan nodded. "If anybody wants to know," he said. He unseated himself from the rocker and set his hat on his head. He looked down at Etta. "Thank you," he said. "See you tomorrow at three."

"Pray," she said.

"Ma'am?"

144

"Pray bout all this. We goan need the good Lord's help with all this."

The boy stepped and stood. He looked at his horse and looked at Etta. "I ain't sure He knows who I am."

"Shoot, boy. He standin right there next to you. Plain as day. I spect He been whisperin in your ear since that day in Florida. Now get on and take care of our business. Sarah and me dependin on you."

*

It was almost nine when he strolled through the double doors and into a din of smoke and revelry. The place was packed with people, virtually every table taken by diners, the bar lined with men and women from every rung of the social ladder. Though the musicians were absent from the bandstand, the great room hummed with conversation and laughter, the clink and tinkle of flatware on china. He wove his way through milling people to stand at the bar. A boot propped on the brass footrail, he waited to catch the eye of the lanky bartender he'd seen before. He watched the man, marveling at his tireless efficiency, at his uncanny ability to detect a simple lifting of a hand amid the turmoil around him. And when he raised one of his, the man did not disappoint.

"Evening, Tex. What can I get ya?"

"A beer, I reckon."

He sipped that beer, and then ordered another, leaning into the bar just looking and listening. He read the plethora of humorous plaques affixed here and there on the wall. He studied the nude women of the paintings, the enormous deer antlers lining the wall near the high ceiling. Eventually the sound of instruments being tuned drew his eyes to the large mirror. In the glass he saw five musicians in all, the same pianist and fiddle player as before, but now joined by banjo, guitar, and a plump female accordionist. When the quintet struck up a lively tune, couples began making their way to the dance floor. He briefly watched the dancers reel and stomp and sway, then quit the bar and worked his way to the stairs. He tipped his hat to Betsy and climbed to the second floor.

He reached the landing just as two men with gaited sleeves dragged a lifeless man from the room beyond the door. The swarthy man he'd seen before emerged behind the laboring pair, a bloody stiletto clearly visible in his right hand. "Hold on," the man barked.

When the pair halted and stood tall to look at the man, John Morgan eased back against the wall. He watched as the muscular man knelt and wiped the knife clean on the suited corpse's pants leg — as he stood and folded the knife shut before secreting it within his pin-striped coat. "Go ahead," the man said to the waiting pair. "Get rid of it."

As the men bent to their ordered task, the swarthy man turned to focus on the boy. He didn't have to say anything.

John Morgan gestured to the doorway. "I was just headin in," he said.

The man frowned and swung an arm toward the room then turned and climbed aboard the stool that sat in the corner. "Shut the damn door behind you, kid," he said, his eyes riveted on the boy as if something about him had piqued his interest.

Inside the enormous room John Morgan stood briefly to orient himself, the sights and sounds completely foreign to him. Tables of different shapes and sizes where men leaned in as if shooting marbles, or perhaps playing jacks. The only thing familiar was the few round tables where men sat playing cards. He'd seen men playing cards, but had never played himself. Everywhere on all of the tables were chips like the one in his pocket, yet not one he saw was gold in color. He stood taking it all in, cigar smoke so thick in the room he could scarcely breathe. Bright red drops of blood on the floor next to one of the card tables. In a far corner a man with gaited sleeves and wearing a visor stood behind a counter within what looked like some sort of cage. The boy watched as this man exchanged chips of various colors for cash money. He watched several patrons at the window before walking there himself.

"I want to cash in a chip," he told the man behind the bars.

The man studied the boy. He bumped back his visor and spread his hands in the air. "Well," he said. "Let's have it."

John Morgan fished the chip from his pocket and held it up for the man to see. "It's a ten-thousand-dollar one," he said.

The visor gave a little jerk as the man's eyebrows raised. "So I see," he said. "You mind telling me where you got it. I haven't issued one of those in weeks, and I'm certain it wasn't to you, kid."

"Feller give it to me in trade for cattle back in Texas. He's the one told me what it's worth."

The man leaned closer to the boy. "Look, kid. I won't cash that chip for you. You just need to slide it over here and walk away." He paused and looked about the room. He looked at the boy. "I'm trying to do you a favor," he whispered. "Now that I've seen it, I can't let you leave here with that chip."

John Morgan looked at the disk and looked at the man. "Can't you at least give me somethin for it?"

"I'm offering you your life. Isn't that something?"

The boy briefly studied the man's eyes, then slapped the wooden disk on the counter and slid it beneath the iron crossbar to where the man could reach it. "Yessir," he said. "If I'm going to get killed, it won't be over that piece of wood."

The man snatched up the chip and deposited it somewhere below the counter. He looked at the boy. "I didn't take you for a fool. Glad to see you prove me right."

He felt every bit the fool as he strode through the double doors and into the street. When he got to his horse he declared it aloud to the animal, reaffirming it several times on the way back to the Crawfords'.

*

As John Morgan sat eating his breakfast, Bob Crawford sipped coffee and watched his every move as if keenly interested in the boy's culinary habits. When the boy noticed, he stopped chewing and sat with a forked wedge of fried egg suspended in the air over his plate. "Somethin wrong?" he said.

Crawford set his cup on the table. He looked at the boy. "How old are you, John?"

"I'll be eighteen in April."

Bob glanced at his wife who stood washing dishes at the sink. He looked at the boy. "We'd like you to stay on permanent, if you've a mind to. You been a big help to us. And Lord knows we ain't gettin any younger. If you'll stay on, we'll make it worth your while. We got no one else, you know."

John Morgan laid his fork on the plate. He sipped his coffee. "I appreciate that you think that highly of me. You've made me feel like family. I don't know what I would've done if you hadn't took me in and give me work, but I can't stay here. I got a brother back home that depends on me. I don't think he'll make it without me."

Sue stopped what she was doing to look at the boy. "Bring him here," she said. "We got plenty of room."

The boy shook his head. "It ain't only him. I come here for a reason. Once I do what I come to do, I'll have to disappear. I won't have no other choice."

Bob's eyes widened. He leaned in close to the table. "Disappear? You fixin to do somethin stupid?"

"I reckon most will think so, but I ain't going to let that stop me. My mind's made up. I'm fixin to help somebody that needs helpin, and that's all I'll say about it."

A look of puzzlement on his face, Bob scooted his chair back and folded his arms about his chest. He looked toward the boy yet his eyes not focused on anything.

Sue dried her hands with a dishrag and tossed it on the counter. She stepped to the boy's side and placed a hand on his shoulder. "It's obvious you been raised up right," she said. "If you feel you're doing the right thing, you probably are."

John Morgan nodded and smiled up at Sue. "I hope you're right."

"How soon is this going to happen?" said Bob. "Your disappearing and all?"

"If everything goes as planned, tonight."

"Tonight," said Bob, shaking his head. "You're going to disappear tonight."

"Yessir, and I could use your help. I'm sorry to have to ask, but there's no one else I can trust."

"What kind of help?" asked Bob, his eyebrows arched like angry cats.

"I need to borrow your buggy."

"Our buggy. Well, that ain't no big deal. You're welcome to use it, long as you bring it back."

John Morgan nodded that he intended to bring the buggy back. "Well, there's more to the favor I'm askin. When we get back here, I was hoping you'd drive us on to Springfield, drop us off there."

"Us, you say. Who's going to be with you?"

"A girl," John Morgan answered.

Sue Crawford grabbed the boy's shoulders. "Well, you scoundrel, you. So that's what this is about. You're eloping with your sweetheart."

"It's a little more complicated than that. But, yeah, that's basically it."

"What time do you expect to get back here?" Bob said.

The boy shrugged. "Don't know for sure. I hope it's not too late."

"Me, too. Springfield's almost fifty miles. I got cows to milk in the morning."

"I'd drive it myself, but there wouldn't be no way to get your buggy and my horse back to you."

"You're leaving your horse?"

John Morgan nodded. "She's yours if you want her."

Bob reached and scratched the back of his head. "Sure, I'll take her, but not without payin you for her."

"You already are. What you're about to do is more than enough payment."

Bob stood. He swung his arms as if limbering up for some sort of competition. "Well," he said, "if you say so. There anything else we can do to help you?"

John Morgan thought for a moment. "Yessir," he said. "If any-body comes around askin bout me, I'd appreciate you tellin em I went home to Texas."

"So you're from Texas now?"

"Yessir."

Bob nodded. He looked at his wife. "You hear that, Mama, the boy's going home to Texas."

*

Main Street was virtually deserted when he drove the two-seated buggy past the entrance of the House of Kings. A short distance later he turned the buckskin across the two sets of trolley tracks and urged it back south until directly across the wide thoroughfare from the double doors. He lifted a boot to apply the brake then stepped down to the ground and strolled across the street, to any-one watching his demeanor relaxed yet his eyes sawing right and left like those belonging to a hunter. He halted just short of the sidewalk and stood facing the doors, his dark replica stretching leftward from his boots, a taller and thinner self grotesquely dis-torted by the raised walk and building wall beyond. He stood wait-ing, looking and listening, his eyes occasionally casting right and left but mostly fixated on the two brass doorknobs ten feet away. Though the afternoon was cool, he soon felt beads of sweat sprout-ing on his forehead. He stepped and stood, his mind beginning to race when a sudden click at the door caused him to execute a com-ical little two-step, as though the notion to dance had come and gone in the same instant.

When Miss Etta swung the door inward, he darted past her and turned to watch as she eased the door closed. She raised a finger to her lips and then gestured to the stairs. She led the way and was breathing audibly by the time they'd reached the second floor land-ing where she halted and turned to face him. He could see her breath, it was so cold in the building.

She pointed to the gambling room's closed door. "He in there," she whispered. "It ain't locked."

John Morgan nodded. "You go on up. I'll be there directly."

Etta briefly studied his face then lifted her skirts and turned to do as told.

Easing to the door, he quietly opened it and moved on into the great room. A naked bulb over a door to his right offered the only light, so he stood until most of the room's features were discernable then slowly advanced toward the light. At the door he halted and pressed an ear to the smooth wood. Breathing, faint but deep and steady. He tried the door's knob, turning it slowly and then easing the door inward an inch at a time. He stood for a moment reading the lay of the small room with the aid of the dim light he himself had let in. He sidestepped left and could see better. The man was a still mound of covers on a cot positioned against the room's back wall. A pair of brogans and a pile of clothing on the floor next to the cot. A reek of stale beer and cigar smoke together with the stench of a man obviously averse to bathing. A steamer chest was to the boy's left, and above it on the wall were three long guns resting on a rack fashioned from deer hooves. He watched the man, easing to the gun rack where he selected from it a lever-actioned rifle. He felt the weight of the weapon. He slowly worked the lever to open the bolt sufficiently to see it was loaded with at least one cartridge. He closed the bolt and stepped close to the sleeping man. With a measured movement he swung the rifle like an axe, a chopping motion with the man's head as his target. At the barrel's impact, the man exhaled a single guttural grunt then lay still.

Setting the rifle on the pile of clothes, John Morgan pulled a coil of pigging string from his jacket pocket. He stripped the covers off the man and reached and rolled him onto his stomach. Red flannel long johns that looked to be new. Using the string, he hog-tied the man, hands to feet, then gagged him with a strip torn from the cotton bedsheet. Standing tall, he proceeded to search the room.

The money he had feared would be locked away in some sort of safe or vault, turned out to be in the unlocked trunk. There were stacks of wrapped bills along with several cloth sacks containing both gold and silver coins. When he'd counted out ten thousand dollars from the paper bills, he placed it in one of the sacks containing twenty-dollar gold pieces. He cinched the sack closed and stood, amazed that the trunk still looked full, that he could scarcely tell any money had been removed. Before leaving the room, he fetched the rifle from the floor and bent to verify the man was still breathing. Satisfied the man was not dead, he left the room, closing its door as well as the outer one once he'd gotten to the landing.

He heard voices and laughter when he reached the third floor, the sounds coming from one of the rooms on the left side of the hallway. He listened briefly, then knocked softly on the door to his right. As he waited, movement down the hall caught his eye. The whore, Sarah, stood highlighted by the light escaping her open door. She was there then gone, as both she and the light ducked back into her room. "Shit," John Morgan hissed, the word scarcely past his lips when the door before him opened.

Etta stood with one hand on the door's edge and the other motioning him in. Warmth escaping from the room and feeling to him like the greeting of an old friend. He stepped inside and Etta swung the door shut. Every muscle in his body tensed as she grasped his elbow and ushered him forward. When he saw the girl, all fear and dread and regret was gone in an instant. He felt as if he might be floating. Sarah stood haloed beneath the suspended oil lamps, her hands clasped before her waist, dressed in a sky blue dress that fell to just below the knee, a matching blue ribbon in her raven hair and all the light that ever existed held captive in her dark eyes. "Hey," she said to him.

"Hey," he said, the sound of his voice apparently foreign to the caged birds and them all suddenly vocal and sounding like an orchestra in dire need of direction.

Etta shook his arm to gain his attention. She pointed to the rifle and sack in his left hand. "You did it?"

"He's tied up," said John Morgan, his eyes still fixed on Sarah. "He won't bother anybody for a while."

"Tied up?" said Etta. She released his arm and began to sway from side to side. "Oh Lord," she said. "Sure do hope Mista King don't decide to look in on him."

The boy looked at her. "Does he do that?"

"I don't know. I don't think so. He always act like he don't want nobody knowing he come here, but he don't tell me his business."

"There ain't no reason to worry. If we hurry, we'll be long gone before King gets here."

Etta shook her head. "I done told you. If we don't kill that man, he'll find us. He the devil. We got to wait for him and do it soon as he steps through that door, fore he can work that black magic of his."

"I don't know if I can do that. I've never even met the man."

"You just wait. You'll do it when you see how he treat this child. You'll be proud to do it when you see what I been seein all these years."

Sarah came to them just then. She stood close to the boy but did not touch him. "You are very beautiful," she said.

"Handsome," Etta injected. "He handsome, not beautiful. You beautiful, he handsome."

"She is that," said the boy, his cheeks flushed by Sarah's words and uninhibited demeanor. When he managed to shift his gaze from her to Etta, he simply said: "I'll do it."

*

Etta prepared dinner in the restaurant's kitchen and brought it up to them, saying they best not deviate from their normal routine for fear King, with his "supernatural powers," would somehow alert to their treacherous intentions even before arriving at the room.

It was almost six when they finished eating so Etta quickly shooed John Morgan to the water closet, fearing that King might be early and open the door at any time. "He don't knock," she told him with a chuckle. "He just waltz right in like he own the place."

While he waited, the boy marveled at the indoor facilities, having never before seen such luxury. He also studied the rifle, realizing it was no ordinary 1873 Winchester but a one-of-one-thousand that had been hand tooled and was likely quite valuable. He waited, listening to the muffled voices of the two women, until suddenly all went quiet. He didn't hear the door open, but he definitely heard it shut. Then he heard a raspy male voice, heard it clearly ask: "Why do you disobey me? You are never to be clothed unless I request it. And what's this? Have you had a guest?"

Easing the closet's door open, he moved out into the room, the Winchester leveled at the elderly man who stood examining the dinner dishes and had not yet seen him. Though he was careful not to make a sound, the man nevertheless turned to look at him, casually, as if not the least bit surprised by what met his eyes.

"Good evening," he said. "I've been expecting you."

The boy stepped closer to King, angling toward the room's door to discourage any notion the man might have to flee. "I doubt that," he said. "Otherwise you wouldn't be here."

King studied the boy over his wire-rimmed glasses. "Well, maybe not you, per se, but surely some unfortunate soul like you. You're not the first to ogle my sweet Sarah's charms through that cursed window. But then I'm sure dear Etta has told you about the others. No?" He glanced at said window then looked at the boy. "I'm not prone to make mistakes, yet not eliminating that window is one I must admit to. If not for that window, I doubt that time and chance would ever have brought us to this juncture in our lives."

Etta had moved to Sarah and now stood embracing the girl. She looked at the boy. "Don't listen to him," she said. "He tryin to charm you."

King turned to look at Etta. "You go too far this time, my dear."

"Look at me," John Morgan said.

King looked. "Certainly," he said. "You're holding the rifle. Andre's rifle, I see. Did you kill him? I presume so. That weapon is his pride and joy. He would never part with it willingly."

"Shut up and listen to me," the boy said "We're fixin to leave here, and there ain't nothin you can do about it."

"Of course," King said. "I'm just a helpless old man. What could I do?" He reached into his coat pocket and withdrew a pair of surgical shears and held them up to the boy. "I'll just see to my birds. You all may leave at your leisure. I'll not try to stop you."

John Morgan motioned with the rifle toward the table. "Put them scissors down, there on the table. I don't trust you holdin em."

King did as told and looked at the boy. He gestured to Etta. "She's said that you must kill me, has she not?"

John Morgan did not answer.

"Yes, I thought so. But I trust you can't do it. You don't have a killer's eyes. Etta has always been a poor judge of character; it's a failing of hers I've come to rely on in situations like this."

As King spoke, Etta released Sarah and moved to the table. She picked up the shiny shears and with them punctuated King's final statement by deftly snipping his right carotid artery, the movement so swift and the scissors so sharp that for an instant King's reaction was to have no reaction at all. He simply stood still focused on the boy, oblivious to the dark arterial blood that spurted from his neck and was rapidly painting a portrait of his death on the floor below. And then his legs buckled. The man dropped like a deflated balloon, his legs folded beneath him at impossible angles while his upper torso remained an upright heap of mere clothing if not for its human hands and head.

For a moment the three witnesses looked like subjects in a photograph, mouths agape and eyes riveted on the horror between them, then they began to move. Etta dropped the shears and turned to console Sarah who looked as if she had no clue that she had just witnessed a murder. John Morgan lowered the rifle to trail by his leg. He stood thusly for an instant, trying to stop shaking, to think. Then he took a deep breath and hurried to Sarah. The sack of money in one hand and the rifle in the other, he opened his arms and gathered her in. He held her, whispering that everything was going to be all right, that he knew she was too good for him but that he'd do his best to be the man she surely deserved. And when he tried to release her, Sarah would not let him go.

"Do not leave me," she said.

John Morgan smiled. "Never," he said. "I'm yours for as long as you'll have me. Now gather your things. We've got a long way to go."

*

They were a little over an hour reaching the Crawford ranch, it dark and snow beginning to fall. Bob Crawford surely has questions yet does not voice them. He merely takes control of the reins and with Etta beside him coaxes the horse forward on the road to Springfield. The boy is seated next to Sarah who is huddled in a full length, fox-fur coat, the pale oval of her face turned to him but him staring straight ahead as if perhaps he is frightened by her close proximity. They ride thusly but a short distance before Sarah's mittened hand captures one of his and gives it a squeeze. He looks at her and she scoots close, the warmth of her glorious even through their heavy clothing, and he frees his hand and drapes his arm about her shoulders. Her head pressed to his neck and the smell of her hair surely the scent of happiness and the snow falling and the world passing yet he is aware only of her.

It is sometime after midnight when they arrive at Springfield's Frisco Station. It is no longer snowing and a profound silence there to greet them amid the buildings of man, a silence that is broken by the creak of wheel and harness, the clop of hoof and the buckskin's blowing, sounds of their own making. They quickly gather their things and exit the buggy. They thank Bob Crawford and bid him farewell then enter the station terminal, the women carrying their carpetbags and the boy the blanket-wrapped rifle and the cloth sack holding their future.

5

A Sun for Sarah

December sixth, 1915

The sun was just above the southwest horizon when they stepped from the boxcar onto the Nittaw Depot's small loading dock. They looked haggard and tired. There had been no coaches on the last leg of their journey, the southbound run from Titusville via the Okeechobee Extension of the Florida East Coast Railway. Tim Edwards, the brakeman who'd seen him off more than a year earlier, was there to greet them. While John Morgan and he briefly talked, Sarah and Etta stood gazing at the lone dwelling nestled beneath live oaks a few hundred yards to the west, it warm for December with only a few wispy clouds to sully an otherwise bright blue sky.

"Well," said Etta, "he say Nittaw be small. Ceptin for that house over there, I don't see nothin at all."

Sarah, in her one blue dress, her bag in one hand and the fur coat in the other, tilted her head back. She closed her eyes and felt the sun's warmth on her face. "I think I love it," she said.

Etta watched her. "Old sun do feel good," she said. "But we got to be careful. White as you be, you'll cook fore you know it."

Just then a double blast from the train's whistle and it beginning to move, the brakeman poised on the dock until the caboose rolled past and then him reaching and grabbing the handrail and swinging onboard. He stood one-legged on the bottom step, his other leg sawing in the air and him raising his free hand in an unspoken goodbye.

John Morgan, the wrapped rifle resting in the crook of his arm, turned to the ladies. "That's my Uncle Jude's place," he said, gesturing to the house.

As they walked the worn path leading to the house, Sarah's head swiveled right and left as she took in what was, to her, exciting and new: a pair of vultures riding the thermals high above, a jersey cow to their left with head high and contentedly chewing its cud while watching them pass. They walked and suddenly Etta stopped and bent to inspect her skirts.

"What kind of misery this be?" she said, reaching a hand to try and rid her dress of some thorny hitchhikers. "Ouch," she said. "They's sharp as a needle."

John Morgan chuckled. "Sandspurs," he said. "You ain't got them in Missouri?"

"Lord, no. Not that I ever seen."

Nearing the house they were met by the cur dog Roy, the animal growling and slinking toward them with raised hackles. "Put your knife away, Roy" John Morgan called to the animal. "It's only me." At the sound of his voice, the dog immediately stopped and stood tall. A look of recognition coming to its eyes, it came to him with not only its tail but its entire body whipping from side to side.

After briefly petting the dog and introducing it to the women, he moved on to the back porch where he paused before the steps when his horse, Shorty, whinnied to him from the pole barn beneath the oaks. He smiled and turned and called out to announce their presence. "Hello in the house," he said.

Footsteps within the house, then the screen door opening as Aunt Betty emerged onto the porch. Upon seeing the boy she squealed and pointed to him with the dishtowel in her hand, her bare feet tattooing the wood floor briefly before she barreled down the steps to her nephew. She hugged him and kissed his cheek, then stepped back to look at him. "Would you look at you," she said. "You're a grown man. My Lord, you'll have to duck to get through the door. And look at those shoulders . . ." Her eyes shifting to Sarah, she suddenly seemed aware her nephew was not alone. A look of puzzlement coming to her face, she looked again to John Morgan.

John Morgan gestured to the girl. "This is Sarah, Aunt Betty. She's with me now."

Betty, her eyes taking stock of the woman before her, extended her hand. She smiled. "I'm pleased to meet you, Sarah."

Sarah looked at the hand and looked at John Morgan.

John Morgan nodded. "It's okay," he said.

Sarah lowered her bag to the ground and offered her hand and Betty took it and pulled her in, hugged her and then stepped back to admire her some more. She looked at John Morgan. "She's an angel," she said, "a sure-enough angel."

John Morgan smiled and turned and gestured with a hand to Etta who had halted a step behind him and Sarah. "This is Etta," he said, "Miss Etta Nix from Missouri. She's with me, too."

Betty nodded to Etta then looked at her nephew, the look of puzzlement returning to her face.

"It's a long story," he said, his eyes shifting to the house. "Uncle Jude and Archie ain't here?"

"Jude's not home from work yet," said Betty. "He'll be here directly." Her hands worried the dishtowel. She looked at the women and looked at her nephew. "I don't know what's become of Archie. He run off back in June—slipped out one morning fore daylight. We ain't seen him since."

John Morgan shifted the rifle to his other hand. His eyes panned the land beyond the clearing then returned to his aunt. "Y'all looked for him, I reckon. Ain't nobody seen him?"

Betty shook her head. "One of the railroad men said he probably hopped a train, said they find where people been in them cars all the time. None of the horses was missing, so we figured that's what he done: hopped a train to somewhere."

John Morgan scuffed the ground with his boot. "Damn," he said.

"He got real sullen a month or so after you left, started pacing round here talkin to himself. Jude caught him skinning one of them stray cats used to hang around the barn. Said Archie just done it out of pure meanness, wasn't no other explanation for it."

John Morgan sighed and shook his head. He looked at Sarah and Etta and looked at his aunt. "Well, reckon there ain't nothing I can do about it right this minute."

Betty shook her head. "Y'all come on inside and let me fix you something to eat. Troubles don't seem half as bad when your belly's full."

*

Jude is home by sunset. He is elated to see John Morgan and enthralled by Sarah. He seems unable to take his eyes off her, and comments repeatedly on her beauty. He is obviously happy for the most part, yet when forced to acknowledge the presence of Etta his mood suddenly darkens. He invites John Morgan outside on the pretext of checking the stock. A full moon is lodged in the trees beyond the railroad bed and they circle the house casting potent shadows in its hoary light. They sit the front steps and Jude is quick to expose an ugliness bequeathed him by circumstance, an indelible belief so engrained at this point in his life as to leave him helpless before its demands.

"That Sarah is a peach," Jude began. "It's easy to see why you latched on to that darlin, but what the hell were you thinkin bringin that colored woman here?"

John Morgan straightened. He looked his uncle in the eyes. "If it wasn't for that colored woman, I wouldn't be here. If it wasn't for her, Sarah and me both would likely be dead."

"Yeah, well, ain't no colored woman stayin under my roof."

"Then I won't be stayin either."

Jude looked at his nephew and looked at the moon. "Shit," he said. "Where you goan go? You and Sarah can stay. And us happy to have you. But ain't no wife of mine cleanin up after no colored."

John Morgan deep sighed and shook his head. "I ain't seen this comin," he said. "You're my mama's brother. How can you be so different? Mama would've welcomed Etta with open arms, especially when she saw how important the woman is to me." He paused and reached and removed his hat and looked in its bowl. He looked at Jude. "You claim to be a God-fearin man, don't you?"

Jude looked at him but said nothing.

"Well, how you reckon He feels about how you're actin right now?"

Jude pulled a splinter from the step and tossed it into the yard. "Well, you and that girl ain't sleepin in the same room. Till you're married, you'll abide by my rules."

"Never intended to. I'll sleep in the barn. Sarah and Etta can have the bed in there."

Jude looked at him. He shook his head. "If you wasn't so big, I'd whip your tail right now."

John Morgan smiled. "Does that mean we got things sorted out?"

Jude leaned forward and spat. "I don't know what it means."

*

It didn't take Etta long to earn the respect of her hosts by pitching in and helping with not only the household chores, but ones involving the livestock and garden as well. Christmas week, Jude took all of the women into St. Cloud to Holland's Mercantile where he treated them to material for new dresses. Upon returning home, both he and Betty were pleasantly surprised to learn Etta was a master seamstress, adept with all the latest patterns available.

On that same day John Morgan rode to see Bill Williams for advice on purchasing land. The day pleasantly cool, and his bay gelding stepping smartly on the ride over as though thankful to once again be at the work it was born to do. At the house the boy sat the porch with Bill, sipping sweet tea and exchanging tidbits of one another's experiences over the past year. When Bill mentioned that the property west of him was still available to anyone capable of paying the back taxes, John Morgan's interest piqued.

"If I'm able to get it," John Morgan said, "reckon you could sell me a few head to seed it with?"

Bill rocked. He sipped his tea then set his jar on the floor by his chair. He looked at the boy. "You come back wealthy, did ya?"

"Not exactly, but better off than when I left."

Bill smiled and set to rocking again. He watched the boy's horse which obligingly stood untethered below the porch. "Well, you tie up that land over on the lake, and I'll sell you some pregnant heifers to get you started. I only got one bull that's worth a damn, so I can't help you there. Course you'll probably get his services for free, them heifers come into season again. Old Mixey gets around. I spect he's sired plenty of calves I don't know about."

"Yessir. I know that. I done seen plenty of em."

"Well, just let me know how you come out. We can cut out a few heifers and use the trap right here to hold em, so you can mark and brand em."

John Morgan nodded. "Yessir," he said. "That would be a big help. Lord knows how long it'll take me to build my own pens."

"You goan need help, ain't ya?"

"Yessir, eventually."

"Well, I know two good fellers what's likely lookin for work."

John Morgan looked.

"I had to let Barely and Frank go. I hated it, but my sister's boys needed work."

John Morgan smiled. "I can't think of any two I'd rather have," he said. "But I reckon you best not mention it to em yet. A lot has to happen fore I can think about hirin anybody. A whole lot." He unseated himself from the rocker and adjusted his jeans. "I'll let you know soon as I can."

Bill stood and they shook hands and the boy descended the steps and mounted his horse. "Good luck at the courthouse," Bill called as the boy turned his horse, and the boy raising a hand and touching the horse's flanks with his heels and the horse stepping forward at a brisk walk. "Thank the missus for the tea," he called back.

*

Sarah's knowledge of Christmas consisted only of what Etta had been able to tell her on the sly. The cutting of a tree and the decorations to follow were all new to her, as well as the exchanging of gifts and the turkey dinner with said prayers of thanks for the birth of Jesus and the good He'd brought to the world. She seemed lost during all the festivities so John Morgan asked her to come with him outside. He saddled his horse, instructing her in all the details necessary to accomplish the task then hoisted her into the saddle, to sit sideways to accommodate her dress. Since she had never been on a horse, he reassured her that he'd let no harm come to her then climbed up to sit behind her. With the reins in his right hand, he slipped his left arm around her waist and clucked the horse forward, feeling her body tense to the sudden movement.

"You all right?"

"Yes," Sarah said. "You are with me."

They rode south from the house to Tyson Creek, it cool but not cold and the warmth of their closeness a thing to be relished, a gift to rival any exchanged in the world on that day. At a wide spot in the small creek, John Morgan halted the horse among great cypress trees whose knees were here and there like wooden stalagmites rising from the sandy soil. He stepped down from the horse and reached and grasped Sarah's small waist and set her to the ground as if she were no heavier than the frilly white dress she wore. He stood holding her, looking at his twinned self in her incredibly dark pupils, at the perfect white teeth revealed by her smile.

"There's no hurry," he said.

Sarah cocked her head quizzically.

"It ain't your fault that so much has been kept from you. We've got the rest of our lives to learn all we don't know."

"The rest of our lives together?"

"Yes. I want to marry you."

"Marry you. You mean like Uncle Jude and Aunt Betty."

"Yes. I'll be your husband, and you'll be my wife."

"Will I still be Sarah?"

John Morgan chuckled. "You'll always be Sarah."

"Will you want to touch me?"

He flinched at the question yet did not look away. "Only if you want me to."

"I want you to. Etta has told me it is okay with you. She said that God will smile when He sees us touch."

"I reckon God can't help but smile when he sees you, no matter what you're doin."

"You reckon. What does this mean, this reckon word you speak so often?"

John Morgan cocked his head in puzzlement. "Reckon? Well, I ain't never thought about it. I reckon . . ." He shook his head. "It's a word same as think or guess or maybe suppose."

Sarah smiled. "Ah," she said. "That's what I reckoned."

John Morgan looked at the ground and looked at Sarah. "You're messin with me now," he said. "Will you marry me, or not?"

Sarah smiled coyly. "Yes, I will marry you. I will be yours to have and to hold for ever and ever."

John Morgan released her and stepped back, his mouth agape and eyes wide. "I don't know whether to kiss you or spank you. Where did you hear that?"

She stepped to him and embraced him, her cheek pressed to his chest. "Don't be angry with me," she said. "Miss Etta told me about marriage in the long ago, right after I saw you that day in Ft. Pierce."

"And here I been going on like a fool tryin to teach you somethin you already know."

Sarah nuzzled his chest. "You are no fool. There is much I don't know, and I'm happy it is you that will be teaching me."

*

He revealed his plans to Jude on the first Tuesday of the new year, the day dawning cold with a heavy frost blanketing everything not sheltered by trees. They were splitting oak logs atop the great lightered stump just north of the pole barn, the boy swinging the ax while his uncle gathered and stacked the fruits of his labor. Their every exhalation the pluming proof of an inner fire stoked by exertion. They worked, and as the sun's first rays found them, the boy began to alternate statements between swings of the ax.

"Bill says that property along the lake is still for sale."

"Oh yeah? How much they askin?"

"Don't know for sure. Whatever the back taxes come to, I reckon."

Jude positioned a new sawn section of oak on the stump. He stood tall and looked at the boy. "There something you ain't told me?"

John Morgan stood ready with ax. "There's a heap of somethins I ain't told you." He released the head of the ax, let it drop to the ground next to his boot while still holding the handle. "I appreciate you not pressing me for answers, bout what all went on out there."

Jude chuckled and scuffed the ground with his boot. "Well, I have to tell you it ain't been easy. I seen that fancy rifle, I knew darn well you got to be holdin secrets."

"Yessir, I am, some that I won't never tell. But I'm bound to tell you enough to keep you and Aunt Betty safe if somebody shows up here lookin for me."

Jude's eyebrows arched. "You got people lookin for you?"

"I hope not, but it's a possibility. Sarah was bein held prisoner by some bad people out there in Joplin. They didn't let her go willingly. I took her, with Etta's help."

"Damn," said Jude.

"And she ain't all I took." He released the ax and gestured to the pole barn. "Let's walk over to my bedroom. I want to show you somethin."

They walked beneath the barn's roof and on to the stall where John Morgan's blankets and pillow lay atop the hay stored there. The boy dropped to his knees and began digging in the hay with his hands. He fished out the cloth sack and turned and emptied its contents onto his blanket, the stacks of paper bills along with several dozen gold coins.

"Shit," said Jude. He stared in disbelief at the money. "You ain't robbed a bank, have ya?"

"No, I ain't done that. This was owed to me and Sarah; course the people who had it didn't see it that way."

"So you took it."

"Yessir, it and her."

Jude shook his head and stepped and stood. "Damn," he said. "Almost wish you didn't tell me. Now I'll be lookin over my shoulder for sure."

John Morgan began returning the money to the sack. "I had to tell you somethin, cause I'm goin to the courthouse tomorrow. I was hopin you'd come with me. Didn't want to have to explain this money in front of strangers."

"Well, I thank you for that. I'd of probably fell out when I seen it."

John Morgan stood, still holding the sack. He looked down at it and looked at Jude. "I'm hopin that this, together with what's left in the cigar box, will be enough. We get that land, you won't have to put up with us much longer."

"Shoot," said Jude. "Your Aunt Betty's dreadin the day y'all leave. She done got attached. She won't know what to do with herself."

"Will you come with me tomorrow?"

"Sure I will. It's too cold for sap to flow, and I got nothing else won't wait."

John Morgan smiled. "Good, I can use your advice on something like this, you already done it and all."

"Well, that was a long time ago. I don't know how much I remember, but maybe it'll come back to me once inside the courthouse." Jude paused and looked at the sack and looked sideways at the boy. "When you planning to marry that girl, if you don't mind my askin?"

"Is Reverend Holland still preachin in Kenansville?"

"Far as I know. He's there two Sundays a month. He should be there this Sunday coming."

"Well, there you go. We'll catch him right after the morning service."

Jude kicked at the hay around his boot. "Shoot," he said. "That Sarah must be an agreeable woman. Sounds like you just thought this up. Have you even asked her?"

John Morgan nodded. "She said yes."

"What about her folks? Hell, I don't even know her last name."

"She's an orphan. She goes by Overstreet, I reckon. Overstreet is her last name, at least it is until Sunday."

"An orphan."

"Yessir."

"Reckon I'll have to give her away, then."

John Morgan smiled. "I think she'll be proud to hear that."

Jude smiled and swung his arms. "Well, all right," he said, "all kind of big doins this week." He rubbed his hands together and stomped his feet. "Well, I'm bout to freeze. Let's get that wood hauled inside, grab us some breakfast and hot coffee."

*

They left before daylight with it not as cold as the previous day yet they could still see their breath. They took Jude's buggy drawn by a long-legged mule he called Old Trotter after its stubborn refusal to accept any other gait. "Once he's in harness, he's either standin or trottin," said Jude. "My hand to God, I've never known the blame thing to run or walk."

Kissimmee seemed still to be sleeping when they parked in front of the red brick courthouse, the sun's rays backlighting the handsome two-story building with its surrounding oaks and well-swept grounds. They went directly to the clerk's office where a pair of middle-aged women sat sipping coffee and talking in the open area behind a long counter. Upon seeing the two men, the women hushed and looked at them expectantly.

"We'd like to ask about a piece of property," said John Morgan, at which one of the women stood and stepped to the counter.

"And what property is that?" said the woman, her graying hair worn in a severe bun and her wire-rimmed glasses seeming about to slide from her nose.

John Morgan set the cloth sack on the counter. "It's out on the east shore of the lake. I ain't got a name for it, but if you've got a map I reckon I can show you."

The woman thumbed her glasses back in place. She eyed the sack then looked at the boy. "What lake?" the woman asked. "Tohope-kaliga?"

"No, ma'am. Kissimmee—it's about ten sections, I reckon, layin just east of Bird Island. I understand it can be bought for back taxes."

The woman nodded. "I think I may know the parcel you mean." She turned and walked to a bank of wooden cabinets lining the rear wall of the room. She slid open a great drawer and began rummaging among its contents. Withdrawing a pair of leather-bound ledgers, one of which was quite large, she brought them to the counter. She opened the larger of the two and began thumbing through its pages. "Here we go," she said. She rotated the open book that the men could see the plat maps therein, saying: "This where you mean?"

The boy looked where she indicated with her finger. He studied the map, recognizing the lakeshore, the small island, and an outlined portion of the shore he believed to be the property. "Yes, ma'am. I believe that's it. How many acres you reckon it is?"

The woman looked at him over her glasses. She smiled and reached for the other book. She opened it then looked back to the map, tracing with her finger. "Samuel Smith," she said aloud, then began flipping through the pages of the smaller ledger. Halting at a page, she again traced with her finger. "Nine thousand, one hundred and one point one," she said. "Give or take a few depending on how high the lake happens to be."

"Nine thousand," John Morgan said. "So a feller named Smith used to own it?"

"Yes, he did," said the woman. "He forfeited it three years ago for failure to pay the taxes."

"Reckon he couldn't make a go of it."

The lady shrugged. "I don't know why. I see he lives out of state, so he may not have ever seen the land. Your guess is as good as mine why he let it go."

John Morgan nodded. He looked at Jude and looked at the lady. "What will it take to buy it?"

The woman walked to the desk where the other lady still sat. She returned with a pad of paper and a pencil and once again looked to the smaller ledger. She was several minutes jotting figures on the pad. Her calculations completed, she looked at John Morgan, holding the pad up so he could see. "Eight thousand, two hundred eighty-one dollars and ninety-one cents," she said. "That's ninety-one cents per acre to cover the six years of back taxes."

John Morgan smiled and looked at Jude who wore an expectant look, then looked at the woman. "I'll take it," he said.

The woman looked over her glasses. "You'll take it?" she said. "You mean right now?"

"Yes, ma'am. Right now."

The lady turned and looked to her cohort. "Can you get George in here? Tell him he's got some work to do."

*

The morning was almost warm. He and Sarah were in the pole barn before sunrise, saddling Shorty and Archie's paint horse, Lester. Sarah in a pair of Archie's old jeans with the cuffs rolled up and a length of rope for a belt—Aunt Betty's broad-brimmed straw hat and a too-large, long-sleeved shirt for protection against the sun. John Morgan took his time readying the horses, patiently explaining the purpose for all he did. When done, he helped Sarah into the saddle and walked her through the rudiments of riding before mounting his own horse and leading her forth to see their new land. They brought with them food and water and the Winchester rifle, having the notion it would likely be tomorrow before they returned.

They rode northwest through the scrub country dotted with cypress heads, John Morgan incessantly looking back at his beloved and her always rewarding him with a smile. Birds of the morning singing in the day, calling to their like kind as birds will do and have done for as long as there have been ears to hear them. They followed the ancient cattle trail until reaching the Williams road whereupon they turned west. Having scarcely spoken thus far, the path of less resistance provided by the road seemed to awaken a need to talk. John Morgan slowed his horse until Lester brought Sarah alongside him. "You doin all right?"

Sarah nodded. "There is so much to see," she said, "so many things I have only seen in the picture books." She threw up a hand and pointed ahead. "Look," she said.

John Morgan looked in time to see the latter half of a black racer flow into the palmettos bordering the sandy ruts. "Black racer," he said. "It's a good snake."

"There are bad ones?"

"There's some around here you don't want to mess with, rattlers and cottonmouths mostly. You see any snake, you stay away from it. Best not to take any chances until you know what you're lookin at."

"Serpents," Sarah said.

John Morgan looked at her. "Serpents?"

"The only picture of a bad snake I have seen is the one in Etta's Bible, the serpent that spoke evil to Adam and Eve in the garden."

John Morgan chuckled. "Well, the snakes round here don't say much. All they ever say to me is stay back."

"Stay back," Sarah repeated. She reached and stroked Lester's neck. "Tell me about Archie. Why do you think he has gone away?"

John Morgan shrugged. "Beats me. That's just Archie. He ain't the easiest feller to figure. I spect he probably left looking for me. We ain't been apart for more than a few hours before now."

"Is he good, like you?"

"Shoot, you just ain't been around many people. Far as Arch goes, he's all right. I mean, he's got his warts and all, but he's my brother. I got to where I hardly notice em anymore."

"Warts? I do not know this word, warts."

"It's a ugly growth on your skin. You get em from frogs, people say. But Archie ain't really got warts. I just meant he ain't perfect. Reckon I should of said he's got his faults."

Sarah nodded that she understood.

They rode and they passed the Williams place and he told her about the family that lived there and how Bill was going to sell them cattle to stock their future, how that one day they too would have a home place such as the Williams'.

An hour on they halted the horses in a grove of squatty live oaks and stood down to stretch their legs and rest. By the sun he judged it to be around ten o'clock. The horses stood in the shade, swishing tails, their heads hung and their eyelids sagging while John Morgan and Sarah seated themselves at the base of an old oak. They each ate a square of cornbread and drank water from a stoppered bottle that had once held vinegar. They talked and then they caught up their horses and continued on.

With the sun almost due south they watered the horses in a strand of cypress holding water and then moved on, now heading generally southwest. They crossed several small drains, mere snaking ditches carved through the sandy soil by countless downpours over the years, excavations accomplished by water and gravity, not the hand of man. "This leads to Lake Jackson," John Morgan would say at each crossing. To which Sarah would simply smile and nod, though having no clue where such lake resided. They rode and at a time he judged to be near three o'clock, John Morgan signaled a halt and they sat the horses gazing westward. The boy was silent for several minutes, just staring at the distant trees portending a hardwood hammock, him silent so long it prompted Sarah to speak.

"Is something wrong?" When he turned to look, she saw that his eyes were swimming.

He shook his head. "I just wish my daddy was here to see this. This land would of made him very happy."

"Are we there? Is this our land?"

John Morgan turned and looked over his shoulder and turned back to look at Sarah. He nodded. "I think we're on it. It's hard to tell for sure, but I'm pretty sure we are."

Sarah pointed a finger toward the distant hammock. "It looks different over there. Is that ours too?"

"Yep, that's Orange Hammock. There's good orange trees in there, and a sure-enough Indian grave. Least, it looks like a grave to me. The mound is too straight and perfect to be accidental."

"A grave?"

John Morgan looked. "It's where people are buried in the ground. When people die, that's what you do. You bury them, and then you call it a grave."

"When I die, will you bury me there, in Orange Hammock?"

John Morgan frowned. "That's a question I ain't ready to consider. We need to talk about livin, not dyin."

Sarah cocked her head to cast him a serious look. "Etta says that we all have to die, that it is simply the end of our story here on earth so that we may begin our new one in heaven."

John Morgan looked at her and turned away to look at nothing. "We need to get movin," he said. "We still have a ways to go, to reach the spot I have in mind to spend the night."

They crossed the great expanse of flatwoods, heading to the right of the sun until reaching the hardwood hammock's edge, whereupon they turned south and followed its edge until the oaks and palms and sweet gums transitioned into a strand of old cypress. John Morgan turned them into the cypress and again headed west. The great trees bone colored and standing in water the color of coffee, water so dark and deep in spots as to reach the horses' bellies and cause them to thrash and lunge with uncertainty until reaching dry ground on the strand's far side. The water cold and the horses dripping and steaming in the late afternoon sun when they emerged from the wax myrtles bordering the strand. John Morgan signaled a halt and stood in his stirrups to look at the vast openness ahead. "Lake Kissimmee," he said, then settled in his saddle and clucked the horses forward.

A quarter-mile of switch grass belly-high to the horses dipped and rose to the breeze coming off the lake. They rode westward through the grass toward a lone live oak perched on a small rise and more and more of the shimmering lake there as they went. Reaching the oak, they halted and sat the horses just taking in the view, the horses also looking with their nostrils flaring and contracting, reading from the breeze what no eye shall ever see.

"Oh, my," gasped Sarah. "It is a gift to see such as this."

"It's pretty, all right, specially with the sun bout to set."

"I can see so far," she said. She gazed into the distance, a tear streaking her left cheek. "Now I am truly incorrigible."

John Morgan looked, noticing the tear and feeling a bolt of sadness shoot through him. "I don't know what that means," he said. "Are you all right?"

Sarah looked at him, smiling through her tears. "A bird that has flown is incorrigible. It will never again submit to the cage. To cage a bird it must have no memory of flight."

John Morgan slid from his horse and walked to her side. He reached and lifted her to the ground. He removed her straw hat and let it fall and held her to him, stroking her hair and whispering softly: "You don't have to worry about that no more. Now you're free as a bird ought to be. But you need to open all them cages in your mind, let all them memories fly away."

Sarah lifted her head from his shoulder to look up and capture his eyes. She tiptoed to reach his lips then kissed him passionately. The horses blew and stomped and shook their bridles yet they humans were oblivious to all save each other. And when they came up for air, though the horses, the lake, and all about them seemed as before, they both knew in that brief moment the world had changed forever.

*

He is tending to their small fire when Sarah without a word sheds her borrowed boots and rises. He watches as she strips off her clothes and walks naked into the night. Stunned, he hesitates but briefly before rising to follow. She is standing with the lake lapping at her knees, the replicated moon on the water's surface before her and her pale form in its cold blue light ethereal as though not flesh and bone but perfection shaped from moonlight itself. He leaves his own clothes there on the shore and goes to her, the water cold and him tensing against it but continuing on until he stands beside her.

"Can you swim?" he asks.

"I don't know."

He takes her hand and leads her into the lake, it so dark with nary a false light save their fire beneath the oak. When he is chest deep he is holding her afloat and she wraps her legs about him to ease his labor and they kiss and remain so positioned until both are shivering from the cold. All the while there are countless eyes watching them, eyes for which the darkness is surely no impediment and whose owners' primitive minds are surely incapable of finding fault with their actions. Yet John Morgan's sense of being watched comes not from these eyes but from a feeling about Sarah so engrained as to cause him to lead the woman he loves out of the lake and back to a lesser fire.

Later he is awake in their blankets, holding Sarah as she sleeps. He is certain that he is a fool, yet contemplating the days ahead he is a happy fool, and one who will later sleep like a baby.

*

The morning following they leave the lake and cross back through the cypress strand. They ride south to a hammock he remembered from his days hunting cows for Bill Williams. The north edge of the hammock is high ground sporting handsome oaks and a few sable palms. A large flock of turkeys scattered before them as they entered the trees, some flying but most running to effect their escape. The big birds gone, they sat the horses in the deep shade offered by the trees.

"What do you think?" said John Morgan.

"I think it is beautiful here."

"Do you reckon you can live here, if I build you a nice house here under these oaks?"

Sarah nodded. "I reckon I can," she said with a smile.

John Morgan smiled and shook his head. He continued to study his surroundings. "Drivin a well pipe should be easy, close as we are to the lake. And they's plenty of cypress not too far away. Cypress is the best wood to build with, you know."

"I did not know that," Sarah said, standing in her stirrups and repositioning herself in the saddle, a look resembling anguish on her face.

"Are you hurting?"

"Yes, the insides of my legs and my buttocks."

John Morgan laughed. "Your buttocks? That's a fancy word for a butt. I ain't heard that one before." He looked at her, the smile bleeding from his face. "Reckon I shouldn't of took you on such a long ride. Sittin a horse all day takes some gettin used to. I'm a little sore myself."

"It is a good soreness," she said.

"Oh yeah? Well, we ain't home yet."

Sarah's eyes were wandering, studying her surroundings with what looked like a keen interest. "But I think we are," she said. "It certainly feels like it to me."

*

While they'd been gone Aunt Betty and Etta had been busy. They'd fashioned a long white gown for Sarah, one they felt suitable for the wedding. Now that they had access to Sarah, they spent Friday putting the finishing touches to their work. Since John Morgan owned no Sunday clothes that still fit him, he and Jude rode into St. Cloud, leaving the women to fawn over Sarah.

They were married on the eighth day of January, 1916, the day dawning warm with a dense fog shrouding the land. The five of them attended the regular ten o'clock service in Kenansville, Miss Etta's presence with the family drawing nasty looks from a few in the small gathering, looks that were quickly squelched when met by even more ominous ones from not only John Morgan but Jude as well. Bill Williams and his wife were part of the congregation but no one else the boy recognized. When the service ended the fog had lifted and the day outside pleasant with only a slight south-easterly breeze. Reverend Holland, a handsome man with thinning hair and kind eyes, stood at the small building's door, bidding his flock goodbye and reiterating that they were invited to attend the wedding ceremony about to be held beneath the lone oak on the grounds. A few proceeded directly to their transportation, but most milled about waiting for the preacher to escort them back to the oak.

When they did circle the building and go to the oak, John Morgan was surprised to see Barely Thompson and Frank Finney standing beneath the tree, both men stepping and standing in their ill-fitting suits, grinning prodigiously at his approach. After much hand shaking and back slapping, the preacher pulled John Morgan aside for a brief conference then assumed his position and said a prayer for the couple about to be joined.

During the short ceremony, John Morgan and Sarah stood gazing at one another as if oblivious to all else until he slipped his mother's ring on her finger and kissed her to the sound of applause and cheers. Both Miss Etta and Aunt Betty cried while Barely and Frank hooted and howled, the pair stomping out a little dance that looked like they might have discovered a snake and were trying to kill it, without getting bit.

"Congratulations, son," said Uncle Jude, pumping the boy's arm and slapping his shoulder.

Barely, finished with his dance, came to the pair and stood grinning and eyeing Sarah. "Whooee," he said. "You wasn't lying, was you."

Frank quickly stepped to his friend's side. "Behave yourself," he said. "Quit actin like a heathen." He reached and touched his hat brim. "Pleased to meet you, ma'am. You got yourself a fine man, here. You surely do."

Sarah nodded and smiled. "Thank you, Mister Frank."

Barely moved to John Morgan's side, leaning in close as if about to disclose secrets. "Here," he said, easing a pint bottle of some sort of unlabeled spirits from his coat. "I brung you a little courage for tonight."

John Morgan took the offering and briefly studied it. He smiled and shook his head. "This some of that Bull Creek poison?"

Barely grinned and nodded his head with authority.

"Well, I thank you, but I damn sure don't need it."

Barely's eyes drifted from John Morgan to Sarah and back again to the boy. He shook his head and grinned. "I hear that," he said.

John Morgan looked at both of his old friends. "Y'all found work yet?"

The men shook their heads. "It usually has to come find us," said Barely with a smile.

"Well, it just did," John Morgan said. "I'll be needin you in a few weeks. I'll let you know."

Both men smiled and nodded their acceptance.

Jude suddenly appeared and grabbed John Morgan's shoulder. "The preacher's taken care of," he said.

John Morgan nodded. "Thank you, I appreciate it."

"Now you and Sarah need to take a little walk." He gestured west toward the two-story Piney Woods Inn. "Just tell the man who you are. He's expectin you all."

John Morgan looked at the building and looked at Jude.

"You got two nights on Betty and me. I'll come get you Tuesday noon."

He and Sarah thanked Jude and said goodbye to Barely and Frank. They walked to Etta who stood waiting next to the wagon with Aunt Betty. They each hugged the women in turn, an act which produced more tears and smiles of satisfaction. Then they said their goodbyes to the Williams and all who remained and, lifting their bag from the wagon, strolled toward the inn with their shadows fittingly conjoined and them arm in arm and their shod feet scarcely touching the ground like lovers in a dream. Their loved ones watching them go and they to a person silently praying it would always be so.

*

When they'd returned to the Vickers home Etta insisted he take his rightful place in the spare bedroom with Sarah but John Morgan waved her off, saying he thought it better that nothing change. He stated that no woman should have to sleep in a barn, that since he would soon be away building their future it made no sense to alter their sleeping arrangements. Yet in the coming days, while he laid his plans for their new home and the purchase of cattle from Bill Williams, Sarah rarely slept in the house. For almost two months she slipped from the house in the dead of night to join her husband in his bed of hay where they'd make love with only God and the occasional horse or mule or cow as witness. Sometimes, if the mosquitos were especially bad, he'd send her back to the house, yet those times were few and she usually slept in his arms until the rooster's first crow, at which point she'd kiss him good morning and slip silent as a cat back into the house. All in the home were aware of the newlyweds' charade, yet their knowing went unspoken, a telling smile every now and then but nothing more.

One evening in late March John Morgan took stock of the money they had left. The Missouri money left over from the purchase of the land, together with the eighteen hundred from the sale of the Ft. Pierce cattle, totaled four thousand, two hundred and nineteen dollars. The man in the courthouse had told him the taxes for the first year would be approximately eleven hundred, so he immediately subtracted that amount from the total he had to work with.

"I'll be lucky to get forty head," he told Jude. "And that's only if Bill is feelin mighty generous. Pregnant heifers fetch top dollar, so I can't expect him to give em away."

Jude shook his head. "He's got to make a livin."

"I got to leave enough money for buildin the house. I don't know much about the price of lumber, and I expect them sheets of tin for the roof ain't cheap."

"I thought you said they's plenty of good cypress on the land."

"There is, but I got no clue how to saw boards from it. I ain't wantin no log house."

"Well, I know how you do it. You go to Ike Futch at the mill. You tell him you're willin to trade some of your trees for him to rip enough boards for the house. He'll come out there and cruise the stand, tell you how much he'll need for the trade. Course he's goan want a lot more wood than he gives, cause he's got to bring a crew in there to cut the trees and get em to the mill."

"He'll do that?"

"He did it for me, and I ain't had but the one little head there in the back."

John Morgan studied his figures. "Damn," he said. "I hadn't figured on cuttin more than it took to build a good house. Sarah loves them big cypress, and so do I."

"They'll leave the younger trees. The strand will come back eventually, course you'll never see it like it is now, slow as cypress grows. Your grandkids might, but you won't."

John Morgan again looked at his calculations. He tapped the table with his pencil. "I reckon it's the only way," he said. He looked at Jude. "How long does all this take? Did you have to wait for them to get around to cuttin your trees? I'd kind of like to get started soon as I can."

Jude shook his head. "They already got sawed cypress at the mill. You just have to sign a contract with Ike, give him a year or two to come in and cut, and he'll give you the lumber you need up front. You may get the house built fore they drop the first tree out there."

John Morgan removed his hat and set it on the table. He looked at his uncle. "Well, I reckon I've got a plan, then. I'm sure grateful for your help. You've likely saved me from makin a lot of mistakes."

"I know them mistakes, cause I done made most of em long before you was born."

John Morgan got his hat and set it on his head. He stood and began replacing the money in the sack.

Jude gestured to the sack. "You reckon you might ought to put that in the bank? They got a sound brick one in Kenansville now. The little I got is in there. They even give me this change purse here." He pulled a zippered envelope from his pants pocket, a canvas affair with the name of the bank on it.

John Morgan paid a glance at the small purse. "Maybe someday," he said, "I'm fixin to start spendin some of it right now."

"You're fixin to go see Bill."

"Yessir. I'm fixin to buy me some cows."

*

On the morning of April second, his eighteenth birthday, he and his cur dog met Barely and Frank at the juncture of Williams Road and the railway. It was cool with only a hint of the coming sun in the eastern sky yet an old turkey gobbler in the Tyson Creek swamp was already summoning his hens. The three mounted men paused briefly at the mouth of the sandy road, each with a hand cupped to an ear as to better hear the one sound of spring they all thought exciting.

"Would you listen to that music," said Barely. "That old tom sounds hornier than me."

"Now that's a stretch," Frank said. "Least he only carries on like that in the spring."

"Ha, ha, you're so funny."

They turned their horses and began following the sugar sand road running due west like a pale flaw in the otherwise seamless night. The cur dog a casting shadow ahead of them and the land soaked with dew and coming alive with the sounds of a new beginning. The horses' progress quiet in the sand save for their breathing and the soft creak and jingle of tack. They rode and brown thrashers began to flit among the palmettos, emitting subtle rustlings and the raspy calls that were proof positive of the dawn. Quail began to whistle. Barred owls and crows and redbirds called for the morning and soon the glistening world began to form.

"Rumor is we'll be in the war soon," said Barely, his voice out of tune with the natural sound already there.

"I won't be," said John Morgan. "I got too much to do."

"You ain't got to worry, boss" said Frank. "Them Yankee politicians is talkin bout a draft all right, but I heard it's only the fellers twenty-one to forty-five that's apt to get called up. Old Barely here's the one needs to be worried."

"Shit," said Barely. "We ain't gettin in that war. President Wilson done said it."

"Yeah, well, he's a Yankee ain't he."

Barely laughed. "You hear that, boss? You ever seen somebody hate Yankees the way he do? You just mention the word and he's got his knife out. Just the other day he told me he wouldn't be caught dead in St. Cloud, just cause the place has got a few Yankees."

"A few? The damn place is full of old Yankees. They's probably some of them sons of bitches the ones I fought in the real war."

It was good daylight when they got to the Williams place where Bill, together with his son and two nephews, stood waiting next to their saddled horses. From there the seven riders rode northwest with the two cur dogs ranging ahead, the dogs' noses reading the air for news of interest and then suddenly streaking westward when they'd found it.

"They're in the palmetto flats," shouted Bill. "Right where I figured they'd be."

They fell in behind the dogs at a canter and by noon had driven more than sixty head to the trap next to the Williams barn. While John Morgan, Frank, and Barely got a fire going outside the pens,

Bill and his boys cut out thirty-four yearling heifers that Bill thought to be pregnant with their first calves, hazing them one by one through a gate and into the section of the trap where John Morgan sat his horse ready with his catch rope. The heifers too big to throw, he and Barely worked as a team to catch and hold them for the branding. When he had one caught and his horse backing, Barely'd run in and grab its tail. Together they'd stretch her until Frank could step in with the iron, burn a backwards R next to the rocking W already on her hip and slather it with blue ointment. The cow walleyed and bawling, the smell of burning flesh and hair, and the men all working frantically as to stress the animal as little as possible. Then, amid the choking dust they'd raised, they'd release her by opening a gate and hazing her through to the open flatwoods beyond. They worked, repeating the process until all the yearling heifers had been branded, whereupon Bill began sending in heifer calves that were from four to five months old. They branded and released a total of fourteen calves, turned them out to rejoin their mamas who still belonged to Bill. Then, tired, dirty, and soaked with sweat, they all walked to the front porch to unwind with some of Mrs. Williams' scuppernong wine.

"I never been kicked so many times in my life," said Barely. "That old bald-faced one with the droopy horns got me three times, the last one right in my family jewels. Like to of knocked the wind right out of me."

"Now that's sayin something," said Frank.

Everyone laughed, and when it was again quiet: "If you wasn't so slow, old man, she might of only got me once."

They laughed again and drank from their tumblers and the stories of the day seemed to have no end until Bill Williams thought to shift the conversation to more serious matters.

He looked at John Morgan. "Sorry we ain't caught more pregnant heifers than we did. If you want more, we can hunt again tomorrow."

John Morgan looked at his crossed boots and looked at Bill. "Have you come up with a total?"

Bill nodded. "How's nine hundred sound?"

"Sounds more than fair to me. You sure?"

Bill cast the boy a sideways glance. "You questionin my arithmetic?"

"No, sir. I'd never do that."

"Well, we're settled then," said Bill. He reached and tapped the arm of the boy's rocker. "And looky here. It'll be several years fore them few cows will do you any good. And that's if you're lucky. You best hold tight to any money you got cause the tax man won't wait for you to build a profitable herd. Your next few years goan be tough, mighty tough." Bill Williams paused to sip his wine. He looked at John Morgan. "People think all this is mine," he said, waving his free hand in the air in a grand sweeping arc. "But it ain't mine. I'm just rentin it, is all. I thank God every day for Him lettin me use it while I'm on this earth. But if I don't pay the rent, then I won't get to keep usin it. It's that simple. What I'm tryin to say is, it's hard to buy property, but even harder to hold it."

"Yessir," said John Morgan. "Reckon I'm about to find that out."

"Yes, you are, son. You surely are."

*

Early in May he began to accumulate the materials for building the home, working from a list of items his uncle had helped him create. Over the span of two weeks he and Barely and Frank made multiple trips with the wagon to Kenansville, returning each time with a heavy load of lumber which they sorted and stacked in close proximity to the staked-out floor plan of his future home. With all of the lumber on site, they made several trips to Kissimmee for hardware, purchasing several kegs of assorted nails and hand tools his Uncle Jude had not already provided, the ten-foot sheets of tin needed for the roof along with bricks and mortar for the footers. He bought pipe, a new pitcher pump, and a well tip, estimating what he'd need and confirming he could return what was not used in sinking a well. And when the trips were done he stood beneath the oaks, pondering all that he'd procured and feeling a bit overwhelmed by the enormity of the work to come. He was actually fearful, yet anxious to begin.

After first sinking a well, they were almost two months building the house, working from plans Jude had once used to build his own sturdy home. John Morgan and Barely and Frank labored six days a week while Jude and a carpenter friend named Canada were available every Saturday to instruct and insure the work was headed in the right direction. They did not work on Sundays. On Sundays they went their separate ways to rest and tend to matters uniquely their own.

As the work progressed the womenfolk came often to the hammock bearing food and encouragement. Sarah and Betty and Etta. They'd noon with the men in the shade of the oaks against the oppressive heat, after which Sarah would invariably seek the sun. Her face and arms now deeply tanned and paired with her raven hair and dark eyes she could have passed for a Seminole. At least, that's what John Morgan claimed. She was his "Indian princess" and seeing her and holding her on these visits restored him, strengthened his resolve to finish their home.

Deep into July they labored through the sweltering heat, their hands becoming calloused, their fingernails blackened and lost to errant blows of a hammer. Their bedrolls cast beneath a stretched tarp, the nights too warm for a fire yet they were never without one, fat lighter heaped with wet Spanish moss to deter the ravenous mosquito hoards always unleashed by the setting sun. Thunder and lightning and strong winds virtually every afternoon, rain so heavy in some of these storms as to cause grown men to shudder and voice nervous jokes about Noah as they stripped off their clothes to bathe amid the deluge. They worked and they suffered and by late July they stood in what now could be called a yard, stood with their shoulders thrown back and their heads high as the sun blessed the new tin roof of a handsome home.

"Now all it needs is some furniture," said Barely, elbowing the boy's arm. "Some furniture and a passel of young'uns playin out in the yard here."

Frank Finney bumped back his hat and shook his head. "I ain't never built a house before. Makes you feel right proud. It surely does."

"Listen to that," said Barely, again elbowing the boy. "Old cuss is gettin sentimental on us."

John Morgan smiled. "He's got a right to. He's earned it, same as you."

Barely grinned and scuffed the ground with his boot. "Shoot," he said. "It was fun, I reckon, but I wouldn't want to do it for a livin. I ain't no carpenter."

"You can say that again," muttered Frank.

John Morgan looked at both men. "Well, it's good that we got our hammerin arms in shape, cause we still got cowpens to build."

Both men's eyebrows arched.

"Not for a while, though. Not till Sarah and me get moved in and all." John Morgan paused and turned and seemed to study something in the flatwoods beyond the hammock. "Y'all want to foller me to Uncle Jude's, I'll get you paid. Maybe Aunt Betty and Etta will have somethin good on the stove. We can actually have us a sit-down meal for a change."

"Now you're talkin," said Barely.

*

By September's end they were in the new home, his having purchased enough used furniture in St. Cloud to provide some semblance of comfort for the time being. He got a woodstove from Kissimmee which his uncle helped him connect to the pipe installed during construction of the house. He was two days gathering and splitting oak and fat lighter to feed the stove, stacking the cut wood along the east side of the house in hopes that the roof's overhang might help to keep it somewhat dry. Next he fashioned an outhouse to the rear and west of the house, a pole barn to house the mules and horses as well as the Jersey cow and its new calf. In early October he summoned Barely and Frank and, with their help, built a partitioned trap off the pole barn using cypress boards nailed to lighter posts. Last, he built a smokehouse among a cluster of young cabbage palms east of the home, fully aware that feeding his family was the most pressing matter he faced. Butchering one of his cows was the last thing he would do. The cows were untouchable for food or sale, for at least three years. For the next three years hunting and fishing and trapping had to sustain them, otherwise the future he'd envisioned would never be possible.

*

Now come days of worry. He's counted his dwindling money and set aside an amount to purchase staples. He's not at all sure it will be enough. On a cool morning in October he hitches the mules to the wagon and goes with his family to the small store in Kenansville. Within the aisles of the store Etta is his compass. She relates to him and Sarah all that will be needed for a functional household. They purchase salt and flour, a hundred pounds each, a ten pound sack of coffee beans. Etta insists on several packets of seed and a bushel of sweet potatoes, saying that growing their own greens and potatoes come spring made more sense than trying to buy such things. She goes on to select a variety of dried beans, a small sack of sugar, a box of yeast, and a tin of pepper. They've no thought to splurge, yet Etta then insists on some of the vegetables only recently arrived from Okeechobee. She tells him in her deadpan way that a woman with child must have vegetables, tells him as if commenting on the weather.

John Morgan is slow to comprehend. He stares blankly into Etta's dark eyes, his mouth slightly agape. He looks at Sarah, who is smiling, yet says nothing. He cuts his eyes back to Etta. He shakes his head as if to ward off an annoying insect.

"What?"

Etta smiles and nods her head. "You goan be a daddy."

He is speechless. He steps and stands, his eyes shifting repeatedly from one woman to the other.

"I spect she's about six weeks along."

He reaches and draws Sarah to him. He hugs her and peppers her hair with kisses. "Oh, boy," he says. He reaches with his left arm and gathers in Etta, hugging her neck and planting a kiss on her graying temple.

When finally he releases the women and steps back, the color drains from his face. His forehead wrinkles and his eyes narrow. "We got to get home," he blurts. "I got a lot to do."

*

Jude and Aunt Betty were waiting at the hammock when they got back, Betty sitting at the top of the new porch steps while Jude stood with hammer in hand next to the pole barn, a crude wire cage holding chickens on the ground beside him.

John Morgan smiled upon seeing his aunt and uncle. He raised a welcoming hand and halted the mules before the porch. He set the brake and hopped down and turned to help the women from the wagon, noticing as he did that Jude had stopped what he was doing and was striding purposefully toward him. He then noticed the look of concern on his aunt's face.

"Hey," he said to Betty. "Boy, have we got good news."

Betty unseated herself from the stoop, reaching and grasping a support post to maintain her balance as she rose. She smoothed the folds of her dress and looked at her nephew.

"Well, that's good," she said, her tenor restrained. "What kind of news?"

John Morgan, having helped both Etta and Sarah to the ground, stood with his arm around Sarah's shoulders. He waited until Jude reached them before saying: "We're going to have a baby."

His words stopped Jude in his tracks. Aunt Betty's mouth opened, and then she began to cry.

John Morgan cocked his head in puzzlement. He looked at his uncle, too befuddled to say anything.

Jude stepped to him and Sarah. He extended his hands and grasped each of their shoulders. "Congratulations," he said, yet there was no joy in his voice.

John Morgan looked at his sobbing aunt and looked at his uncle. "What's wrong?" he said. "We thought you'd be happy for us."

Jude nodded that he was happy. "We are, boy. It's just that we got news as well." He reached into his breast pocket and retrieved a folded slip of paper. He handed it to John Morgan. "It's a telegram," he said. "Tim Edwards brung it to me late yesterday. But it was sent almost a week ago. Said they couldn't figure out who Florida Boy was. When he let me read it, and I seen it was from Missouri, I figured it was for you." Jude paused to look at the boy. "I'm hoping you'll tell me I'm wrong."

John Morgan studied the words on the paper: HE IS COMING. SORRY, I HAD NO CHOICE . . . . BOB.

"Shit," said John Morgan.

"Reckon that means it *is* for you."

John Morgan exhaled a deep sigh. "Yessir, I'm afraid so."

"You want to talk about it? Sounds like somethin I might need to know, since I'm the one right next to the train tracks."

John Morgan nodded. He looked at Etta and looked at Sarah. "Why don't you all go on in the house. We'll be in directly."

When all three women were inside, he waved the telegram at Jude. "It's from Bob Crawford, the man I worked for out there."

"Well, who's he talkin about? Who's comin?"

"It's got to be a feller named Andre," said John Morgan, looking his uncle in the eye. "He's a bad man, Uncle Jude. I didn't think he'd bother tryin to find us. But apparently I was wrong."

Jude's eyes panned the hammock. He looked at the boy. "You obviously didn't tell this Bob feller your name. Does the Andre feller know it?"

John Morgan shook his head. "I was careful not to tell anybody. I tried to let on that I was from Texas, ceptin I did tell Bob I was from Florida. And I must of mentioned Nittaw, cause it's right here on the telegram."

Jude leaned and spat. "Well, how are we goin to handle this? You want to let the law know? I know Sheriff Barber, known him since we was kids."

John Morgan shook his head. "No, sir. I can't bring the law in on this. For all I know, the law may be lookin for me too, the law out there anyways."

"Damn, boy. This is soundin worse all the time."

"Yessir, it's a mess all right."

Jude stepped and stood. He leaned down and plucked an acorn from the ground and briefly studied it before tossing it away. "Well, how am I goin to know this Andre? If he's thinkin you live in Nittaw, my house is the only one he's goin to see when he steps off the train. He's bound to come to my house."

John Morgan nodded. "You'll know him. He's big and muscular, dark hair with eyes like a polecat. That's what he reminded me of: a polecat with no sense of humor."

Jude emitted a little chuckle. "Polecat, you say." He chuckled again then looked at the boy. "Well, what are we goin to do? I'll be afraid to go off and leave Betty at the house alone. I cain't take her to work with me."

"Bring her out here until this is settled. I'll come stay with you, handle it right there when he gets off the train." The boy paused and leaned and spat. "How often is the southbound train runnin these days? Is there one every day?"

"Every other day. The next one's tomorrow afternoon, should be about four o'clock."

"Tomorrow," John Morgan said. "Then I best get to your place. If this telegram is a week old, he could be on it." He sighed. He looked at the ground and looked at his uncle. "This would have to happen now," he said, gesturing to his new smokehouse. "I was plannin on huntin this evening. That ham y'all give us is the only meat on the place."

Jude turned and pointed to the caged chickens by the pole barn. "We brung you four layin hens, and that old leghorn rooster. That's what I was doin over there. I took it on myself to build em a roostin box, so the varmints don't get em their first night here."

John Morgan managed a smile. He shook his head. "I don't know what to say."

"You don't need to say nothin."

John Morgan nodded. He gestured to the house. "Do we need to go fetch anything for Aunt Betty?"

"I spect she'll be just fine. One night without her comforts won't bother my Betty. I can bring her stuff tomorrow if need be."

"Well, let's go in and tell em what's goin on. I'd like to reach your place before dark, so I can study the lay of things in the daylight."

*

The sun was yet an hour high when they quit the Williams' road and took to the old cattle run leading to Jude's place. Jude in his buggy and Old Trotter locked in its customary gait while John Morgan on Shorty rode alongside in order that they might converse as they traveled.

"We're bout to have us a road here," commented Jude, gesturing with the reins to the rutted evidence of their repeated trips through the scrub country.

John Morgan nodded, his head all awobble due to the pace set by the mule. "Damn, I wish you'd learn that mule to walk. I ain't too fond of trottin everywhere."

Jude grinned. "He's somethin, ain't he?"

"Shit," breathed John Morgan. "He's somethin all right."

They traveled and as they rounded the cypress head behind the house a flash of reflected light near the railroad caused them to halt simultaneously. They studied the gleaming light, while the horse and mule stood with heads high and ears pricked forward as if they too were wondering how a second sun came to be there.

"Is that an automobile?" said John Morgan.

"Has to be, shiny as it is."

"You ever seen one out here before?"

"A couple times. It's probably railroad people. I heard a while back they was startin to use em."

"Well, I don't see nobody movin around. They must be inside the depot."

"Probably," said Jude. "Let's ease on up to the house. We can see better from there." He paused and shifted his gaze from the distant motor car to his nephew. "You got them guns loaded?"

"Yessir." He shifted the reins to his left hand and pulled the forty-four revolver from his saddlebag. "Here," he said, "you take the pistol. The rifle's all I need."

Jude reached and took the weapon and they put the animals forward at a trot. They halted behind the pole barn and stepped down and momentarily stood peering at the automobile over the stalls within the barn. John Morgan pulled the Winchester from its scabbard and levered a cartridge into the chamber and eased the hammer to half-cock. He looked at his uncle.

"You reckon I should ease over there and see who it is?"

Jude looked at the car. "I reckon one of us needs to. It'll be dark soon. I won't be able to sleep a wink not knowin what's goin on."

"All right. You stay here. It's probably just railroad men like you said, so I'll be back directly."

Jude nodded. "I'm gonna get my shotgun. I ain't shot pistols much."

"Me neither."

"You be careful."

"I will."

Rather than take the path to the depot, he circled south where palmettos and wax myrtles offered better concealment. With about fifty yards to go and him focused on the rear of the windowless structure, a muffled shot rang out, followed by another in quick succession. The second shot gave him a direction, as well as a sick feeling in the pit of his stomach. He turned and sprinted for Jude's house, straining to see anything that would explain what was happening.

He ran with the rifle ready at port arms. When able to see the rear of the house, he stopped suddenly and dropped to one knee. Some sixty yards away, Jude lay on his back at the foot of the porch steps, his arms raised in surrender while a man on the porch stood aiming a pistol. John Morgan breathed. He rested his elbow on his raised knee, took aim and fired. The man on the porch lurched sideways but did not go down. Another cartridge already chambered, the boy fired again and the man dropped to his knees as if suddenly having the notion to pray. John Morgan aimed again, but before he could touch the trigger the man fell forward with a thud. He lay face down and did not move.

Jude had rolled to his hands and knees and was crabbing sideways toward his nephew. "They's another one," he called. "They's another one in the house."

John Morgan came forward with the rifle cocked and ready, his eyes darting between the backdoor and the lone window on his side of the house. No movement. Nothing. He called to Jude: "You all right?"

"Hell, no, I ain't all right. That son of a bitch put a new part in my hair."

He got to his uncle and helped him to his feet, all the while watching the back door, the field in front of the house should the man go out that way. Blood trickling down Jude's face and the sight of it causing his heart to beat even faster.

"You sure there's another one?"

"Positive. I seen em both when I opened the door. They was settin at the table like they owned the place."

Then from within the house: "I'm coming out. I'm unarmed, so don't shoot."

John Morgan stepped around his uncle. "Come out with your hands up," he shouted.

Movement at the doorway, a pair of upraised hands then a man's face easing into view. "Don't shoot," the fellow said.

"I ain't goin to shoot unless you make me. Come on out so we can see you."

Like the man on the porch floor, the fellow exiting the house was dressed in a suit. Tall and lanky, he stepped out with his hands high and his eyes wide. He scarcely looked at the body on the floor, just a glance to avoid stepping on it and the blood that had ebbed from beneath it, the pistol that lay next to the dead man's right leg.

"The bartender," John Morgan said.

"Bartender?"

"Yeah. It's him all right," he said to Jude. "Just stand right there," he called to the man.

He began walking to the man, the rifle at the ready, Jude a step behind and wiping blood from his forehead. Reaching the porch, John Morgan halted and looked up at the man.

"Have a seat," he said, "there on the stoop."

"Anything you say, Tex," the man said, then did as told. He sat with his arms resting on his knees, his hands extended in the air beyond. "None of this is my doing. Andre made me come with him."

John Morgan studied the man. "But why," he said, "what's Sarah to him?"

"Sarah," said the man. "He couldn't care less about that girl. He came to kill you. You took his pride and his joy. That rifle you're holding. The man was obsessed with it."

John Morgan glanced at the Winchester and looked at the man. "He come all this way for a rifle."

The man nodded. "That, and to kill you. Russians are a prideful lot, stubborn as hell they are."

Jude quit mopping his brow and pointed a bloody finger at the man. "And you come to help him do it."

The man shook his head. "I came because he'd have cut my throat if I didn't. I despised the man. The way I see it, you've done the world a favor. I'm glad he's gone."

John Morgan shifted the position of the rifle. "What about the law, there in Missouri? Do they know about me?"

The man again shook his head. "I don't think so. Everyone figured the girl and old Etta killed King, figured he had it coming. To my knowledge, they haven't even bothered to work the case. But Andre did. Not because of King. He didn't care about King. He only cared about his rifle. He knew a kid had tried to cash in a gold chip. He remembered seeing you the night you tried. So when he counted the money, he had a pretty good idea who had bopped him on the head and taken his rifle. He just didn't have a clue how to find you."

"So how did he? Find me I mean."

"He beat it out of one of the whores. You never should have told that Sarah who you worked for, cause that Crawford fellow wasn't going to lose his wife to save you. And can you blame him? I'd have done the same thing in his shoes."

"I don't blame him."

"No. You shouldn't. And you shouldn't blame me. Like I said, he'd have killed me if I had refused to come with him."

"So you think we should let you go?"

"That would be nice. I promise you it will be the last you ever see or hear of me. And rest assured, I'll tell no one what happened here. Why would I? It would only implicate me in an attempted murder." The bartender pointed to Jude. "He tried to kill you in your own home. How will that play in the courts around here? Believe me, I don't want to find out. I just want to go home. I've got a wife and child that need me, if that makes any difference to you."

John Morgan gestured to the body with the rifle. "What about him? There anybody out there goin to care about him not comin back?"

The bartender glanced at the body behind him and looked at John Morgan. "He's got a younger brother. Andre left him in charge of the house." He paused as if weighing his next statement. "He's cut from the same mold as Andre, so he might be a problem for you. I don't know what Andre told him, about where we were going and all."

"And I don't know what you'll tell him."

"No. You don't. I can't promise you that I'll tell him nothing, because, like I said, he's as ruthless as Andre. If he puts a knife to my throat, I'll tell him anything he wants to know."

John Morgan nodded. He looked at his uncle and looked at the bartender. The rifle in his right hand, he reached with his left and grabbed hold of the support post at the end of the porch. He bounded up and onto the porch. He eased along the wall until next to the face-down body then hunkered down and picked up the pistol. He tossed the weapon on the ground at Jude's feet then reached and felt Andre's neck. He shook his head and stood tall. He looked at the bartender.

"Where's your gun?" he said.

"I don't have one, never did."

"Stand up," said John Morgan.

The man rocked forward and stood, his hands hovering all the while in air before him.

The boy looked at Jude. "You want to make sure while I watch him?"

Jude stepped to the man and reached out to do as asked but stopped short and stood looking at his own blood-soaked hands. He looked at the man. "Sorry," he said, then fell to frisking him without further comment. When satisfied, he looked up at his nephew. "If he's got one, it's in a place I ain't goin."

John Morgan hopped down from the porch. He eased the hammer down on the rifle and lowered it to trail by his leg. "You ain't drove that motor car all the way from Joplin. Where'd you get it?"

"A place called Titusville," the bartender said. "Andre paid a man for the loan of it when he learned there were no passenger cars bound for Okeechobee. Like I said, he was a prideful man."

John Morgan nodded. "And you'll return it?"

The man looked at him, lowering his hands for the first time. "Of course," he said. "I'll catch the train there."

"Well, you best get movin, fore I change my mind."

The man started walking for the depot but suddenly stopped and turned to look at the boy and his uncle. "Thank you," he said. "You have my word that I'll do my best to keep my mouth shut. I won't say a word unless I'm left no other choice." He turned and began walking and this time he did not stop until reaching the automobile.

"You reckon his word is any good?" said Jude.

"I think so. I never saw any meanness in him out there or here either."

John Morgan and Jude stood watching him go and did not avert their gaze until the northbound car had chugged from sight, whereupon the boy stepped close to his uncle and reached to examine his wound.

"That's goan leave a scar," he said.

Jude nodded that it would. He gestured to the body on the porch. "How bout you?" he said. "You goan be all right?"

John Morgan nodded. "That man was tryin to kill you. Wasn't nothin else for me to do."

Jude nodded. "I'm sure thankful you tend to hit what your shootin at."

"Speakin of shootin, where's my pistol?"

Jude scratched his head. "Think I dropped it when that feller fired the first shot. It's got to be on the porch. It all happened so fast, ain't no tellin where it is."

*

As the sun sagged below the horizon they loaded the body into Jude's buggy, solving a mystery as they did. The boy's pistol was under the body, along with a whole lot of blood. Jude tried for almost an hour to scrub the blood from the porch floor. But his efforts were futile. The stain composed that day would remain for as long as the house would stand, as it would in the minds of the men there to witness how it came to be.

They buried the body next to the Indian grave in Orange Hammock, raking leaves and debris over their work so that to the unschooled eye there was no difference between the two mounds. All evidence of Andre was given back to the earth, save for his pistol which Jude kept as a reminder of just how close "old death" had come to him that day. And when done, they proceeded to John Morgan's new home where they told their loved ones there was no longer any need to worry. Yet the wound on Jude's head left the women skeptical and full of questions, questions for which answers would never be forthcoming.

And when all had bedded down for the night he led Sarah from the quiet house. He brought a quilt and spread it on the ground beneath an opening in the canopy above so that they might view the heavens. They stripped naked and lay entwined on their backs, him caressing her still flat belly and her speculating on the future of the child growing therein. They spoke of the constellations, assigning them names they vowed to share only with their children, haughty names that would one day die with them and never again be thought of or spoken. They lay, him marveling at her starlit beauty and her loving him more than life itself while the night creatures invisible about them halted their business to watch in awe with great pupiled eyes these pale beings come into their night. The chorus of peepers also fell curiously silent as if perhaps out of respect, or maybe them having been shushed by God so that all might hear the purest sound gifted by Him. They loved and they slept until their new leghorn rooster announced the coming sun whereupon they dressed and crept back into the house.

6

Curlew

In the days following the incident with the men from Joplin he focused mostly on food. November brought cooler weather and with it the urge to hunt. Though Sarah always wanted to accompany him, he would allow her along only if he was hunting close by the house. She was pregnant; therefore, he did not want her anywhere near a horse. There'd be plenty of time for riding after the baby was born. Until then, he would go alone on any venture requiring him to use a horse, whether it be hunting game or just checking on their cattle.

He taught her to use the twenty-two pump gun and, much to his amazement, she soon was his equal with the little rifle. They often bagged squirrels with the weapon in the hammock behind the house. The gray squirrels turned out to be Etta's favorite meat. The woman was a wizard at turning the tough, rubbery meat into a melt-in-your-mouth delicacy that all truly loved.

"You got to boil the meanness out of em," she'd say. "Boil em and then dice em up in chunks, simmer them chunks all day in rice and gravy. Unless they be specially young you don't never want to flour and fry em. Old squirrel be tough as shoe leather if you fry it."

The squirrels were good yet each one cost a precious bullet. The return in protein simply wasn't enough to sustain a household of three hungry people. And it soon became difficult to bag enough for a meal on a single hunt, the bushy-tailed rodents being quick to adapt to the pressure presented by the new two-legged predators come into their world. John Morgan knew it was larger game that he needed, larger and less costly in both time and money to acquire. He knew the answer was to go it alone, leave Sarah with Etta and broaden his search in order to meet their needs. So the second week of November he saddled his horse before dawn and rode west toward Lake Kissimmee.

He rode with the Winchester secure in its scabbard and his father's twelve gauge yoked across his lap. As the day dawned quail began whistling at numerous points in the flatwoods yet he paid them little mind. Quail were excellent eating but he would not go out of his way to hunt them. They were for him a target of opportunity. If he'd chance to ground shoot an entire covey he'd take it, but otherwise he'd leave them alone. They were simply too small and too difficult to bag in the numbers he needed. He rode and he watched the sunrise in reverse as the bone-gray cypress ahead slowly turned gold, the transformation beginning at the peak of the crowns and creeping downward as the coming sun rose behind him. He noticed flight after V-shaped flight of curlews passing overhead on their way to the flats along the lake. His eyes those of a hunter and never still, taking note of every detail, searching not for an entire animal but for an eye or an ear, for a horizontal line too precise to have been drawn by the random hand of nature. When coming to bare, sandy openings in the palmettos and wire-grass, he'd lean right and left in the saddle to study the ground for sign. At the muddy edge of the cypress strand, he found what he was looking for.

The broom sage at the water's edge looked as though it had been turned by a single-bit plow. He rode a short distance north follow-ing the hog rooting, then turned back and measured its existence to the south. He briefly sat the horse, studying the sign, then put the horse forward, westward into the cypress strand, the horse sloshing and high- stepping through the shallow water. On the far side of the strand there was even more rooting sign. He halted the horse and sat looking and listening. He reached and slid the rifle from its boot scabbard, stowing the shotgun as the rifle had been and then checking to confirm he had a cartridge chambered before standing the rifle on his right leg. He sat looking and listening. He cupped his left ear with the reins still in that hand. Subtle grunting, the sound of hogs busily feeding. He clucked the horse northward up the edge of cypress, traveling only a short distance before halting to again listen. He spoke in a whisper to the horse. "They're in those myrtles," he said. "You be good now."

He dropped the reins and eased down to the ground, patted the horse's neck before leaving it to begin his stalk. He stepped slowly, the mud sucking at his boots. A few feet on, he squatted on his haunches to peer beneath the clump of wax myrtles from which the grunting seemed to emanate. Movement, yet it so dark beneath the leafy trees he couldn't make out detail. He eased the hammer back on the rifle and shouldered it, his elbows pressed to his knees, him squatting and straining to make heads or tails of the animals foraging in the gloom. Confirming an eye, he aimed and fired, setting off an explosion of squealing and crashing in the thicket as hogs and pigs sought to make their escape. His horse behind him issuing a startled snort and shake of its head but standing its ground as all hell broke loose around it. A large sow blinded by terror barreled straight at John Morgan, knocking him on his ass before he'd chance to lever in another cartridge. He rolled to try and get a shot with the hog past him but it was headed straight for his horse. Rather than bolt itself, the horse squatted, lowering its head as if to meet the hog head on, the horse's eyes walled and its mouth contorted in an angry snarl as it tried to bite the hog as it streaked past. And then, as sudden as the report of the rifle, all was quiet. The hogs were gone as of they'd never existed. John Morgan struggled to his feet, the seat of his pants soaked and him splattered with mud. He laughed out loud as he bent down to retrieve his hat. The horse shook its head and whinnied, as if it too had found humor in those frantic few seconds. John Morgan looked at his horse. "Old hog don't scare you, does it," he said. "Did you get a mouthful of that sow?"

He futilely tried to wipe some of the mud from his pants then turned to see what his shot had done. He dipped low and duck-walked beneath the myrtles, finding that a fair-sized pig lay dead a few feet in. He grabbed hold of a hind leg and dragged the coal-black animal out into the open. Fifty to sixty pounds he estimated, a fine black sow in good condition. He propped the rifle against the animal and fished his knife and some string from his pants pocket. He cut slits between tendon and bone on each of the hog's hind legs, then threaded the pigging string through these slits and tied it off. Picking up his rifle, he got hold of the string with his other hand and dragged the pig to his horse. The horse stiffened and tried to bite the carcass as he hoisted the animal up and looped the string over the pommel horn. "Quit that," he told the horse. He climbed into the saddle and laid the rifle across his lap. "Why are you hatin hogs all of a sudden? That old sow scare you that bad?"

He rode out to the lakeshore, to the lone oak where he and Sarah had spent the night not long ago. Approaching the oak, he smelled smoke and immediately after located its source a short distance up the shore. He could see a figure crouched next to a small fire, a wooden skiff beached a few feet west, the long barrel of a shotgun protruding from its bow while the lake lapped at the boat's stern. He rode to investigate, the man at the fire not noticing him until he was a few feet away.

"What the . . . ?" said the man, jerking his head to see what had come upon him. "Oh," he said. "Howdy. Climb down and set a spell. I was just about to have some breakfast. I got more in the boat iffen you ain't opposed to pluckin another'n."

"Howdy," said John Morgan. The man was old, having white hair and a beard equally white save for at the corners of the man's mouth where the hair had a yellowish hue. He studied a pile of white feathers next to the man, a speckled coffeepot set in the coals and a naked bird roasting on a makeshift spit over the flames. "That a egret you're fixin?"

The man looked. "Egret," he said. "Hell, no. Egret's a fish eater." He held a long knife in his hand and he waved it at the skewered bird. "This here's a curlew, tastes a heap better than any egret. You ain't never tried it?"

"No, sir, I ain't." He dropped the reins and stepped down from his horse. He laid his rifle on a clump of switch grass that had been flattened when the lake had been higher. He looked at the man. "I've heard they're good eatin."

The man nodded that they were. He leaned in and captured a spindly leg bone and pulled drumstick and thigh off the roasted bird. "Here ye go. See what ye think."

John Morgan hesitated to take the offering. "You sure I won't be shortin ya?"

"You ain't shortin me. The breast has got all the meat. This is just a taste."

John Morgan stepped forward and took the meat. He sampled the thigh meat. "Damn," he said. "That's really good. Tastes just like chicken."

The old man chuckled. "Don't everything?"

John Morgan ate, nodding his head that many things did.

"I hunt em cause there're easy." He gestured toward the boat. "I usually can get three or four with one shot from the old long tom there. This mornin I was real lucky. This mornin I got seven. Number eight shot works best—more shot, more birds, you see."

"Yessir. I know that to be true. Do you get em right here on the lakeshore?"

"Any place the water has receded. Curlews ain't wadin birds. They's worm eaters. They use that long curved beak of theirs like a probe to get at their dinner."

John Morgan nodded. He sucked the last of the meat from the bones and tossed the bones in the grass. "Boy, that was good. I'm goan remember this."

"They even better smoked. Just salt em down and smoke em for bout ten hours. The blame things will keep for days; that is, if you let em. Round my place they disappear pretty quick."

"That's good to know."

The old man nodded that it was. "I see you got you a pig."

"Yessir. I come down here to the lake to dress it in the shade of the oak over there, so I could wash up and all."

"You live round here?"

"Yessir. My place is back east there a piece. I own this here land we're standin on."

"You don't say. I been messin round out here for years. Never realized I was tresspassin."

John Morgan shook his head. "You ain't tresspassin unless I say you are. And you've given me no reason to say it. You're welcome to go on about your business like you always have."

"Well, I appreciate it." The old man looked at his brogans and looked at the boy. His blue eyes dimmed with age and them beginning to swim. "It ain't often I meet someone I care to be around. You mind tellin me your name?"

"No, sir. I don't mind at all. It's Rawlerson, John Morgan Rawlerson."

The old man nodded. "Well, Mr. Rawlerson, I'm Jim True. But the characters I know usually call me Ain't."

John Morgan looked at the man. "Ain't True?"

"Yeah, crackers got a warped sense of humor. They don't never miss a chance to take you down a notch." True reached and rotated the stick he used as a spit. He fanned the coals then looked at the boy. "Actually it was my sister that started it, so reckon I had it comin. I developed the habit of fibbin to her at an early age."

John Morgan grinned. He scuffed the ground with his boot. "Well, I like it," he said. "It's a name I ain't likely to forget."

*

It was almost noon when he returned from his hunt so he expected that Sarah would be sitting in the sun as had been her custom of late. But Sarah was not in the yard. It was warm so after tying his horse at the pole barn he carried the dressed pig to the smokehouse and hurried to the house for salt and the utensils he'd need to butcher the meat for hanging. Upon entering the house he instantly sensed that something was wrong. A pall of silence within the great room, no one to be seen.

"Sarah," he called.

"We back here." Etta, her voice emanating from his and Sarah's bedroom.

He hurried into the room and found that Sarah was in bed. Etta seated in a chair brought from the kitchen and holding his wife's hand.

He stepped close, his eyes fixed on those of his wife, eyes displaying a look of sadness he recognized immediately. He knew, with nary a word having been spoken. Yet he held hope that it not be so as he circled to the opposite side of the bed from Etta and reached and gently touched Sarah's cheek. "I'm here," he said, to which Sarah managed a weak smile. He looked at Etta.

Etta nodded. "She weak, but she goan be all right."

"What happened?"

"Only God knows. It wasn't nothin she done. You know she been extra careful."

He sighed. He bent down and smoothed hair back that he might better see the eyes that had bewitched him, the eyes that for him held life itself. "I'm sorry," he said.

Etta let go of Sarah's hand and stood. She looked at John Morgan. "Now don't go thinkin you caused this. Ain't nothing either of you done caused it. It just happens. Don't nobody but God know why. It just wasn't time yet. Your young'uns will come, young as y'all be."

Sarah lifted a hand to him and he took it and she smiled. "I'm all right," she said. "I'm a little tired but Etta says that is to be expected." She squeezed his hand. "Did you ride far and see many wonders? Did you see the lake? Tomorrow I would like you to sit in the sun with me. I would like you to tell me everything."

John Morgan nodded. "I'll sit with you forever, if you want."

Etta turned and headed for the door. She motioned with a hand for him to follow. "Sleep is what she need now. Y'all can talk all you want tomorrow. Right now you need to hush and do what I say."

*

Sarah would be fine. In only a few days she was back riding with John Morgan. They rode one day far to the north, to a distinct point where the open palmetto flats transitioned to a mature pine forest. The big pines, he thought, marked the north boundary of their property. They turned westward, following an old cattle trail clear to Lake Kissimmee where they watered the horses before striking southeast and into the deep shade of Orange Hammock. Seeking the one tree that produced sweet oranges, John Morgan had no choice but to take Sarah to the Indian gravesite, the site which now harbored two graves. They nooned next to the graves, eating several of the sweet oranges picked from the nearby tree and Sarah seemingly unaware that there was now an extra grave until she suddenly posed a question that left John Morgan unable to swallow his last plug of orange.

Sarah broached the question by gesturing to the newest mound. "That's Andre, is it not?"

"Andre?"

Sarah nodded. "We women are not as easily fooled as you may think."

John Morgan swallowed. He stood and dusted the seat of his breeches. "I reckon you're not," he said. "Let's saddle up and see some more of our land."

They rode from the hammock heading eastward. On a little rise between two cypress heads they came to a solitary live oak which Sarah thought particularly beautiful, the tree far from any others of its kind and the ground surrounding it void of palmettos as though having once been cleared by the hand of man.

"I believe this was an old homeplace," said John Morgan.

Sarah sat her paint horse, her eyes panning the tree and the surrounding land. "It is a lovely spot," she said, her hair lifting and falling to a cool breeze that strangely seemed to reside only in the shade of the oak. "I could stay here forever."

"Forever is a long time," John Morgan said. "It's pretty, but I reckon it might get old after a day or two."

"You make fun of me."

John Morgan looked at his wife. "Only because I love you," he said. "If you want to stay here forever, I do, too."

The day following, they rode to the southern reaches of the property where he killed another hog, this one a large sow weighing close to two hundred pounds. He'd worried that perhaps the sight of him killing a large animal might upset Sarah, knowing that the larger the animal the greater the trauma felt by anyone, even himself. Yet he needn't have worried. Through sharing the experience with her, he learned she was even more philosophical than he'd realized. "Death does not bother me," she told him as they stood over the fallen hog. "Death is the destiny of all living things. Without death there can be no life."

As Thanksgiving approached, they tried without success on several occasions to bag a turkey. The big birds seemed to have gotten the word and changed their habits. So, with only one day left to succeed, John Morgan chose instead to go after curlews out on the lake. It was a good choice. Using only three shells he and Sarah bagged enough of the white ibis to feed not only the three in their household, but his aunt and uncle as well. As they gave thanks and dined beneath the oaks the next day, his uncle planted a notion in John Morgan's head that caused him to make a declaration that would resonate in those parts for years to come.

"That's about as good a bird as I ever et," said Jude, leaning back from the makeshift table and mopping his chin with a cloth napkin. "You sure them was curlews?"

John Morgan smiled. "Yessir. I promise they were."

Jude shook his head. "Well, you wouldn't think it to look at em, and I been seein em my whole life." He looked at John Morgan. "You don't never have to worry bout starvin, many as they is on this place. Hell, you could name it after em, thank em for tastin so good."

Everyone laughed, but when it was again quiet, John Morgan, in all seriousness, said: "I just might do that."

*

Now come days of joy, days of reflection. After the hard frosts of January and February, March arrived truly pleasant, the mornings cool and the afternoons warm enough for swimming. The older heifers had dropped their calves with all but one accounted for and them doctored against screwworms and now with their mamas ranging close to home and their presence there a comfort, a source of pride for all within. The younger calves he'd bought were also there, having been weaned from the Williams' cattle and driven to the trap at the homeplace with the help of Barely and Frank. They'd held the newly orphaned calves penned for two days in an attempt to imprint their new surroundings before releasing them to join the already free cattle wearing the Rawlerson brand. Now, at least for the time being, all of their cattle could be seen together.

This spring, more than any other John Morgan could remember, portended a new beginning for cattle and man alike. All one had to do was look, he mused, the lush new growth with its brilliant greens and his heifers nursing calves, God's miracle of rebirth there for all with eyes to see. The sights and sounds and smells, the very air he breathed caused him to revel in his good fortune, yet the fear that it may be temporary always there to temper his enthusiasm, to render him serious beyond his years.

*

He has positioned the wagon alongside the end of the depot's loading dock and is waiting with Sarah for the northbound train to come to a halt. Tim Edwards hops from the caboose just as the cars are at dead stop. He strides to the dock and ascends the steps and raises a hand in greeting.

"Howdy, Tim. You bring us our feed?"

Tim nodded that he did. "Got the bill of lading right here." He reaches to unlatch the door on the car adjacent to the dock. When he slides the door open, he is the picture of a man surprised. "Jesus . . . " he says. "How the hell did you get in there?"

"This car ain't fit for Jesus," replies a voice within the car, it raspy, scarcely above a whisper. "You promise not to club me, I'll tell ye how I come to get here."

Hearing the voice, John Morgan leaps onto the dock and steps to see inside. "Pick," he says. He turns to Sarah. "It's Pick." Seeing the old man is trying to unseat himself from the floor, he steps on into the car and grabs both of his gnarled hands and pulls him to his feet.

"I know that voice," says Pick, him still in his rags with the fruit-picker's bag slung over his shoulder. "You ain't a ghost, are ye, Florida Boy? I thought maybe you was dead."

"I thought the same about you. Step on out here and get you some air. It's hot as hell in here."

"It is that. Reckon my jar of water is the only thing saved me."

Tim Edwards is standing back, as if fearful the man may try and touch him. "You old fool," he says, "lucky for you we had to stop here. You'd of been dead for sure by Jacksonville."

"Here, Pick," says John Morgan, "step over here and meet my wife."

"Your wife? Where we at?"

"Nittaw."

"That don't tell me much."

"It's where I live. I'm back home now. Come meet my wife."

"All right." Pick shuffles forward, exhibiting great caution with his free hand pawing the air for danger. "We there yet?"

John Morgan halts him a few feet from the wagon. "Sarah, this is Pick. He helped me get to Joplin. I'd have been lost without him."

Pick seems to be studying his wrecked shoes. "Gettin pretty deep round here."

Sarah is smiling broadly. "I'm happy to meet you, Mr. Pick."

Pick leans to the boy. "Sounds pretty," he says.

"She's beautiful."

"I'm proud to make your acquaintance, young lady. You've got you a fine young man, here."

"Yes, I do."

"John Morgan," Tim Edwards injects. "I've got a schedule to keep."

The boy throws up a hand to signal that he heard. "Come have supper with us," he says, glancing at Sarah to see if she is still smiling.

Pick shakes his head. "I thank ye, but I got to be movin on. Got to get north fore the summer catches me."

Tim Edwards steps to John Morgan. "I'll put him on one of the flat cars. He'll be all right there. You want this horse feed, you better get it off my train."

The boy nods that he will and looks to Sarah. "Run to Aunt Betty. See if she's got any food Pick can take with him."

As Sarah climbs down and heads to Jude's place, John Morgan turns to Pick. "It's so good to see you, my friend."

Pick pats his arm but says nothing. He steps and stands as if mortally embarrassed. "Where do you want me, Mr. Brakeman? I need to set down."

John Morgan watches Tim Edwards lead the old man to the steps and then help him down them. He calls out that he'll bring him the food then shakes his head and turns to unload the sacks of feed. He's just loaded the fourth and last bag in the wagon when Tim Edwards returns to the dock.

"He's situated," he says.

"Thanks, Tim. He's a good old man."

Tim nods. He looks as if he's something more to say but is not exactly sure how to say it.

"Is somethin wrong?" says John Morgan.

"I hope not," says Tim. "I seen your brother day before yesterday."

"You seen Archie?"

Tim nods. "In Jacksonville. Him and another feller was hangin round the depot. Archie recognized me and come over. I figured he wanted news about you and all. But that wasn't his motive at all. He starts in tellin me how rich he is, how he's wanted by the law up in Georgia." Tim pauses to study the look on John Morgan's face. "Yeah," he continues. "Well, I say, whoa there, Arch. That's something I probably don't need to know. He acts like he ain't even heard me, goes on to say he killed two men for tryin to rob him."

"Shit," says John Morgan. "You know Archie was always given to lyin. I reckon he still is."

Tim shakes his head. "I hope you don't take offense at me sayin this, but I think your brother's got a screw loose. You should of seen the look in his eye when he told me about cuttin those fellers' throats. If he was lyin, he fooled me. I couldn't wait to get clear of him."

John Morgan turns and looks to see if Sarah is coming. He looks at Tim. "Did he say if he was headed here? Did you tell him about me ownin land and all?"

Tim shakes his head. "I ain't hardly got a word in edgewise with him. He done all the talkin. Said he was goin to South Carolina to sell some dogs. They had a crate full of hounds in the motorcar they had."

"They had a car?"

Tim nods. "I think you're lucky he ain't headed here, the way he was actin. I think Archie's done gone bad. I hate to say it, but that's how he struck me."

John Morgan again looks toward his Uncle's house. "I been afraid for him ever since Jude told me he run off. Reckon I should've never left him the way I did."

Tim shakes his head. "Well, I hope me tellin you this don't mess up our friendship. I just thought it was somethin you ought to know."

"You done the right thing. He's my brother. If you see him again, tell him to come home. Tell him we got that place we always wanted."

*

A week after his nineteenth birthday he sat Indian-fashion by a fatwood fire in Bill Williams' front yard. Barely and Frank also there, along with Bill's boy, Will. The evening chilly for April, so the fire and the shine they sipped were a comfort to their tired bones. They'd all spent the day mammying-up Bill's calves that he might brand and mark them the next day, with a reasonably clear conscience that they all belonged to him. The talk around the fire began about their day, but quickly shifted to the war in Europe.

"They done it day before yesterday," said Frank, leaning a bit trying to avoid the dark smoke swung to him by a shifting breeze. "The damn Yankees got us fightin the Germans now. I read it with my own eyes at the post office in Kenansville."

Bill Williams was nodding his head that he'd heard it too.

"Shit," said Barely. "I ain't fightin no Germans less they come to Osceola County. They come here I'll damn sure fight em. But I ain't goin over there to do it."

"You'll go if you get drafted," said Bill. "You don't go they'll lock you up."

John Morgan sipped his shine and watched the occasional glowing ember drift skyward amid the column of dark smoke.

"Drafted?" said Barely.

"Yeah, drafted," said Frank. "It's where they pick your name out of a hat to go do their fightin for em."

"They? Who's they?"

Frank winked at John Morgan. "The government, you ignoramus. Who do you think they is?"

Bill Williams raised his jar to indicate he was about to comment. "They make you sign up, Barely. If you're of the age they're lookin for. I heard that every man between twenty-one and thirty-one has got to sign up. Heard it's to be on June fifth that you got to do it." Bill paused and looked at the men around the fire, then focused on Barely. "I reckon you're the only one of us here has got to worry."

"Shit," said Barely. "I ain't worried. I ain't signin nothin. They'll have to come catch me."

Frank slapped his leg. "Listen to that big talk. You'll get to thinkin bout it and be the first one in line. I know how you are."

John Morgan reached and slapped Barely on the back. "Don't worry, Barely. The law comes lookin, won't none of us admit to knowin you." He sipped his shine and looked at Bill. "You reckon us bein in a war will help the price of beef?"

"It's apt to. The army'll probably want all it can get. This war may turn out to be a blessin for us cowmen. Ceptin of course for old Barely here."

Barely struggled to his feet and dusted his breeches and chugged the last of his shine. "Y'all keep it up," he said. "They'll be a fistfight break out here directly."

Bill waved his cup at Barely. "Come on now, you know we're just joshin. A group gets together, there's always got to be somebody gets picked on. It just shows how much we like you. We picked you tonight cause we know you can take it."

Barely scuffed the ground and leaned and spat. He looked at Bill. "Well, tomorrow night it's somebody else's turn. Tomorrow night let's pick on Frank. He's so deaf he won't even know we're doin it."

"There you go," said John Morgan. "You done fired the first shot."

"Shot who?" quipped Frank.

7

A Dibbler's Moon

The tolerable weather of May came and went and by the first week of June the mercury approached one hundred degrees virtually every day. The unusually hot weather lasted for almost two weeks, with the humidity oppressive beyond anything John Morgan could recall. There were thunderstorms most afternoons which, though frightfully violent at times, caused a welcome drop in temperature that made for more comfortable evenings. On days with no storms comfort would not come until well after midnight, the day's heat hanging on like an unwanted guest. The two-week stretch so hot, he rode every morning to check the hog trap south of the house, knowing no animal caught would survive a full day without shade and water. It too hot to hunt, the trap was his only source of fresh meat, other than fishing. Fishing was their savior during the heat wave, it and swimming in the lake to cool off.

One evening after the storms dissipated they rode to the lone oak out on the lake. They brought with them a stout cane pole he'd cut months before from Uncle Jude's stand of bamboo, the pole now dried and varnished against rot, rigged with braided cord sufficiently strong to heft a gator, let alone a big bass. The cord tied about four feet from the butt of the pole and then wound lengthwise to the smaller tip where he half-hitched it so that only about three feet dangled free. To this bitter end were tied a succession of two, eight-ought hooks, the big pair about three inches apart, and on each was impaled a four-inch strip of white pork rind that was supple yet tough as any leather, the idea being that the rind might simulate an escaping frog or shiner when dragged across the water's surface. He called the rig a dibbling pole as had his father and knew it as a lethal tool for catching big bass at night.

The sun's slow sink into the lake almost complete, they hobbled the horses and walked to the skiff grounded on the shore, Jim True's skiff, purposely left there for John Morgan's use. The sun now but a golden arch far across the lake, the lake itself still as pooled mercury and stretching to the limit of their vision where it appeared the sun had set it afire. In their bare feet they dragged the skiff into the water and loaded the pole and a sack of eats, a canning jar of extra pork rinds immersed in a salty brine, a gallon jug of potable water and a length of coiled pigging string to be used as a stringer should they have the good fortune to boat some bass.

John Morgan first got Sarah settled on the bow seat then moved to the center seat where he unshipped the oars and sat facing forward as to be able to instruct his wife. With the left oar he brought the skiff about and slowly rowed a short distance into the lake, halting just outside the pickerel weed that defined the shallows along the shore. The sun now gone and a slice of moon against the firmament almost straight overhead, stars already beyond counting and their numbers growing still while the lake and the dry land from whence they'd come was fast being reduced to mystery and hearsay. A steady drone of mosquitos. An explosion of water somewhere down shore sounded as if a sizeable boulder had been dropped in the lake.

"They're feedin," said John Morgan. "Course with it southmoon, they're bound to be."

"Southmoon?" said Sarah.

"When it's straight overhead like it is now. Southmoon to a bass is like a dinner bell to us. Deer, too, you always want to hunt and fish when the moon is straight up or straight down. Southmoon or southmoon under, either one is good. When it's southmoon just after sunset, like it is today, we call it the dibbler's moon. No better time to be dibbling for bass than on a dibbler's moon. Heck, my daddy said I was born on a dibbler's moon, said that's why he knew I'd amount to somethin, said a dibbler's moon promises good luck for all sorts of things."

Sarah scarcely heard a word he'd said, so distracted was she trying to fan mosquitos away from her face and neck, her bare feet. "It must be the dinner bell for mosquitos, too. I've never seen so many."

"They're bad all right, but they'll let up here directly. They're always bad at sunset and sunrise, so thick you can hardly breathe for about twenty minutes, then hardly any at all. I don't know why, it's just the way it is around water."

When dark as the moon and stars would permit, he shipped the oars and began to teach Sarah how to use the pole, how to dibble for bass though nearly blind as old Pick while doing it. As he'd predicted, the mosquitos had vanished, with just the occasional loner left to annoy.

"You hold it like this," he told her, his right hand gripping the pole about a foot from its butt and his left about two feet closer to the tip. "See how I've got it?"

Sarah leaned forward, straining to see the positioning of his hands. "I see," she said.

"You've got to hold it pretty tight," he continued. "A big one hits it, she might take the pole if you ain't got a good grip. I had that happen to me one time."

Sarah gave an unseen nod.

"Now, you work the bait like this," he said, dragging the pork rinds slowly across the water while imparting a jiggle to the pole so the baits skipped and dove like some sort of panicked or crippled creature, the gurgling sound produced part of the ruse and making it easier to keep track of the baits' location. "You get the idea?"

"I think so," said Sarah. "What do I do if a fish grabs the bait? The line is so short. When Etta fishes, her line is as long as the pole. She just lifts the pole and the fish swings to her."

"Etta's fishin for bluegills and shellcrackers. We're fishin for bass, big bass. With a dibblin pole like this, you don't pull em in. You haul em in, like this." John Morgan demonstrated, drawing the pole in, hand over hand, as if pulling in a rope. "At night like this, it's always a surprise when one strikes. You'll set the hook without even thinkin—long as you hang on to the pole."

"And when I get to the end of the pole?"

"You get the fish to the side of the boat, and I'll be ready to lip it. You won't even have to touch it." John Morgan stood, his bare feet wide apart to accommodate the tipsy skiff. He handed the pole to Sarah and settled back on his seat. "Practice a little out here in the open water, get the hang of it before I ease us in close to the weeds where we'll really start fishin. Back in the pickerel weed is where they'll be. They lay in there waitin for a frog or shiner or somethin to come along."

Sarah extended the pole and began to drag the baits through the water, shaking the pole, doing her best imitation of what she'd seen her husband do.

"That's it," John Morgan said, the words scarcely out of his mouth when something walloped the pork rinds. "Holy shit," he blurted.

Sarah squealed, holding to the pole as it bowed deep into the water.

"Hand over hand," he shouted. "Haul her straight in or the pole will break." He shipped the oars and stood and stepped toward Sarah, his arms groping the air for balance against the rocking boat.

Sarah hauled in the pole, hand over hand as told with the bamboo framing against the gunnel and whatever she'd hooked coming to the surface in a fit of flouncing and flipping that soaked her with water, short but powerful runs right and left and then back on the surface, airborne, gills rattling and slamming against the side of the boat.

John Morgan dropped to his knees and reached and grabbed the braided line and with a mighty heave boated the mayhem. "Yeehaw," he said, pinning a huge bass to the bottom of the boat and holding it thusly until it eventually calmed and lay still. He laughed aloud, looking at the pale oval that was his wife's face. "You beat everything," he said. "You done caught the biggest bass I ever seen."

Sarah sat gripping the skinny end of the pole, the rest of its length in the lake behind her. She giggled. "I did good?"

"Good! You done great. Nobody could of done better."

Sarah strained to see her catch, the lighter colored belly and throat about all she could make out. "Hold it up," she said. "Hold it up high, so I can see."

They fished only an hour and a half longer, a lull in action together with a glance at the moon's position telling John Morgan that the feed was over. Sarah had caught four fish in all, her first by far the largest yet the other three surely respectable, ranging from four to six pounds. After beaching the skiff, they carried the strung fish and the rest of their things to the oak. They shed their clothes and used a cake of lye soap to bathe in the lake and then returned to the tree. John Morgan spread his rain slicker on the ground and they sat naked beneath the oak while their horses cropped grass and the earth in its slow turn dragged stars in their billions ever eastward. They held to each other and they relived the adventure they'd only just shared. The intense excitement now and forever relegated to memory.

"Did you have fun?"

Sarah squeezed his hand. "My heart is still racing," she said. "You make me very happy. You show me things I could never have imagined."

"That big bass you caught is somethin really special. If you live to be a hundred and fish every day, you may never catch another one like it." He reached and stroked her hair. "Did I tell you my sisters loved to fish?"

"No. I did not know that."

"They truly loved it, especially Marcy. There was nothin my Marcy would rather do. I'd give anything if she could've been here with us."

Sarah again squeezed his hand. "I think she is," she said. "It is good that you keep your family in your heart."

"I sure miss them."

"Yes. I know you do, even though until now I never had family to miss. Now that you live in my heart, I know how it feels to miss someone you love. I think it must be the worst pain of all, to miss someone you love."

"I promise to never make you miss me too long."

Sarah patted his hand. "And I promise to give you a child, this time."

John Morgan was silent. He tried to make out her face. "Are you pregnant?"

"Yes. I think so."

He held her for a long time, her words crafting within him a gamut of emotions from joy to fear. "We'll go see the doctor tomorrow," he finally said. "We ain't takin no chances this time."

*

The day following they travelled by wagon to Kissimmee. Doc Lowery examined Sarah and pronounced her indeed pregnant, stating that she was in good health and he could find no reason why she wouldn't carry the baby to full term. During the ride home Etta broached the subject of a name for the expected child, saying: "You belong to name a child while it still in the womb. A name give it its personality. You don't want it layin in there for nine months thinkin it be a it."

"It Rawlerson," said John Morgan. "That don't sound half bad to me."

"Go on, now," Etta chided. "I ain't cuttin the fool bout this. Namin a child is serious business."

"But we don't know what it is," Sarah said.

Etta nodded, her great frame swaying to the sandy road's undu-lations, her seated firmly at the center of her surrogate family and willing to express loudly her convictions. "You name it now for a girl and that's what it'll be." She leaned into Sarah. "You want a girl or a boy?"

Sarah laughed, not sure if the woman was serious. "Either is fine with me," she said.

"I want a boy," said John Morgan. "A whole bunch of big strong boys to help me with the chores when I get old and feeble."

"Men always wantin boys," said Etta. "Y'all had your way, they'd soon be no more peoples, just a bunch of randy old men wanderin the earth lookin for what they be missin."

John Morgan smiled and winked at Etta. "Oh, I hope they's lots of girl babies born. I just don't need the worry of knowin they're my daughters."

"How about July?" Sarah said, her thoughts obviously having taken a more serious path. "Today is the first of July. If we name the baby July it can decide for itself what it wants to be."

John Morgan leaned forward to see past Etta. "So you reckon July would work either way?"

"I think so," said Sarah. "Don't you?"

"July Rawlerson," Etta said, her accentuating every syllable as though conducting a test of the proposed name. "Sounds like a man to me. Cain't picture no girl what looks like a July."

Sarah looked at Etta and looked at John Morgan. "How about June, then? June if it's a girl and July if it's a boy."

Etta gave a "why not?" gesture with her hands. "You the one goan be dealin with the misery. You got the right to name the child what you want."

Sarah cocked her head to look at Etta. "You don't like my reason-ing?"

"I ain't said that. I like names from the Bible, is all. Names like y'all two has."

John Morgan gave the reins a little shake to let the mules know he'd not forgotten them. "I like July," he said. "It's a name got some strength to it. July's a tough month. May be our son will be just as tough."

Etta shook her head. "Oh, Lord," she said, "sounds like the man done made his mind up." She reached and pinched the back of Sarah's hand. "Talkin bout tough. Men only thinks they know about tough. They had to do what you got to do, they'd know what tough is."

*

He was almost finished with the milking when the horses in the trap let him know he had company. Setting the pail to his right, he stood and gazed over Queenie's back to see what had the horses blowing and pacing the south side of the trap. The sun not yet up, the rider coming into his yard was but a shadow, yet the cream horse he rode was unmistakable.

"Mornin, Frank. You're just in time for breakfast."

Frank Finney halted his horse next to the pole barn and eased down and looped the reins about a support post. He adjusted his cap and stretched, bending as if to touch his toes but scarcely reaching his knees. "If that's an invite, I'll not be so rude as to turn you down."

"It's an invite. What brings you all the way out here so early of a mornin? Barely ain't gone and got himself throwed in jail again?"

Frank shook his head. "Naw, worse than that. He got himself drafted."

"Drafted," said John Morgan. "I thought he wasn't gonna register for the draft."

"Yeah, well, he did. He's on his way to basic trainin right now. Left yesterday for Fort Jackson, South Carolina."

"Damn," said John Morgan. "I have a hard time picturing old Barely as a soldier."

Frank nodded his agreement. "His mama sure didn't want him to go. She wrote Governor Trammel tryin to get him out of goin, course I could've told her that was a waste of time. Park Trammel don't know Barely Thompson from Adam. You got to be somebody to dodge the draft."

"Well, I hope he keeps his big head down over there."

"You and me both. I've grown kind of fond of old Barely."

John Morgan smiled and opened the stall gate to let Queenie go back to pasture. He reached and picked up the pail of milk and motioned to the house. "Well, let's see what the ladies have fixed for breakfast. Now that you're here, if you ain't got anything better to do, why don't you ride with me to see about introducin some new blood into my herd."

"You goan buy you a bull?"

John Morgan shook his head. "I cain't afford to buy one yet. I'm gonna have a look at Ted Smith's. If he don't mind me runnin my cows with his for a while, that bull of his is no relation to Bill Williams' Mixey."

"I get ya. You don't want Mixey breedin his own offspring."

"That's right. Near bout all my cows and calves come from Mixey, so I got no choice but to look elsewhere now. I can't have no inbreedin goin on."

"No, sir. You don't want that." Frank cupped his chin pensively. "Speakin of old Bill, have ye seen his new automobile?"

John Morgan began walking to the house. "I ain't never seen his old one."

Frank fell in beside him. "You a regular jokester this morning, ain't ya?"

*

By the end of August Sarah was beginning to show. While she saw no reason to deviate from her normal routine, John Morgan seemed to loathe having her out of his sight. Anytime she thought it necessary for her to leave the house, a minor argument was sure to ensue.

"I'm just going to collect the eggs," she pleaded. "You don't have to come with me. I promise not to get lost."

"I ain't worried bout you gettin lost. I'm worried bout you gettin snakebit. You seen them two ground rattlers I killed yesterday. Just give me the basket and I'll collect the eggs."

Sarah swung the basket out of his reach. "No, you might get snakebit." John Morgan sighed. "Sarah," he said, "just give me the basket."

"You always have to be right, don't you?" She tried to circle him and squeeze through the doorway but he caught her and lifted her in his arms. "Put me down," she said. She looked beyond his shoulder to locate Etta. "Would you please tell him I am right?"

Etta set her sewing aside and unseated herself from her rocker. She strolled over and stood glaring at the couple, her eyes narrowed and her lips pursed. "Ain't neither of y'all right. Y'all both bout to drive me stupid." She reached and snatched the basket from Sarah's hand. "I'll go hunt the damn eggs. Scared as I is of snakes, I'd rather wrestle a big ol cottonmouth than listen to any more of y'all's bickerin. Y'all mind me of my young'uns when they was little. I got a good mind to go cut me a switch right now. A good switchin's what y'all need." She continued to glare a few seconds longer, then reached and brushed John Morgan aside. "Now get on out the way so I can find me some eggs, find me some place where there ain't all this arguin goin on."

Later, when Sarah was taking her afternoon nap, John Morgan joined Etta as she sat rocking on the front porch.

"Sorry we been gettin on your nerves," he told her. "I reckon it's my fault. I've been a sure enough worrywart, here lately."

"Shoot," said Etta. "It ain't y'all that's got me frettin. With the baby comin, I got to thinkin bout my own young'uns, got myself homesick to see how they doin."

"You ain't wantin to go back to Missouri, are you?"

Etta stopped rocking. "I would like to see my kids, see how many grands I got me now."

John Morgan sat with his elbows propped on his knees. He dipped his head as if noticing something on the floor.

Etta reached and touched his shoulder. "Now don't you worry. I ain't goin nowhere till after the baby is born. I wouldn't miss deliverin your baby for nothin. Sarah in there is my child, has been her whole life."

He took hold of her hand and held it between both of his. "You are God's own gift to me. I'd be lost without you."

"Go on now. You get me to bawlin like a baby with talk like that."

*

Early in October Ike Futch came with his crew and began cutting his promised cypress, a dozen men with twice that many mules harnessed and pulling sleds to extract the sectioned logs. A steam-powered ripping saw to bark the logs, to square them into beams that were then loaded onto freight wagons pulled by eight-mule teams. The men doing the heavy labor mostly blacks, men shirtless with ebony skin agleam with sweat and them heavily muscled like gladiators from a different time and them raising baritone voices in rhythmic song so that for days the woods hummed from dawn to dusk with a sound foreign yet pleasing to any ear. The crew worked four weeks until the flagged trees had all been felled and sawed and hauled away. And then one morning they simply were not there, vanished, like a thing gone extinct and leaving a wrecked forest of stumps, tops, and a profound silence in its wake.

*

Already it is hot on this November morning when Etta and Sarah halt the wagon before a small café in St. Cloud. They've been to see Doctor Lowery and are hoping to get a bite to eat before attempting the long ride home. The proprietor looks up from behind his counter when they walk through the door, his look not amicable as he peers above wire rimmed glasses all cockeyed from some past mishap. "No colored in here," he says, his eyes focused on Etta. "You want food, you got to go round back. We got a room back there for you people."

Sarah, now heavy with child, glares at the man.

Etta turns for the door. "You go on and set down. I don't mind goin round back."

Sarah looks at her and looks at the man. "No," she says, "now that I see who's in here, I'm coming with you."

*

It so early in the morning there were few people about the Charleston railyard when Tim Edwards hopped from the caboose and strode toward the depot. His light dungaree jacket impotent against the January cold, he walked briskly, his thoughts so focused on hot coffee awaiting him inside the ticket office that the sound of his name being called did not immediately register. Two steps on he stopped and looked to his left, his breath pluming and his eyes searching for the source of the voice.

"Over here," the voice familiar.

Tim squinted to see beneath the raised floor of the loading dock across the tracks, the wretched figure there and returning his gaze not at all familiar. "Who's there?" he said.

The man crawled from beneath the dock and stood beating about his person as if he may have thought the rags he wore for clothes on fire. "It's me, Tim."

Tim Edwards studied the unshaven face, the filthy shoulder length hair and the feckless grin. "Crap," he muttered to himself. He sighed and begrudgingly turned to face the man that was now coming to him. "Hell, Archie, you look like shit. What are you doin layin in the dirt like that?"

Archie came on, halting before Tim and standing like a man reporting for some sort of inspection. "You ain't got a dollar I could borry, have ye?"

"No, I ain't," said Tim. "Ever one I got is done spoken for." He pointed to the knife stuffed in Archie's waistband. "Why don't you sell that pig-sticker. You ought to get at least a dollar for it."

Archie looked at the knife. He seemed startled by it, as if just now realizing it was there. "My knife," he said. He looked at Tim, grinning broadly. "They had to give it back to me," he said.

Tim's eyebrows arched. He shook his head. "I don't know what the hell you're talkin about."

"The cops. They took it from me when they locked me up."

"You been locked up, have ye?"

Archie nodded that he had. "I ain't now though."

"I can see that."

"How bout fifty cents? That'll get me a loaf of bread at least."

"Aw, hell," said Tim. He dug in his pants pocket and came out with a handful of assorted coins. "Here," he said. "Now you and me both are broke."

Archie took the coins and turned to go.

"You're welcome," said Tim. He shook his head and called: "Archie."

Archie stopped and looked over his shoulder. "What?"

"John Morgan said if I saw you to tell you y'all got a place now. Said to tell you to come home."

"We got a place of our own?"

Tim nodded. "A big place out on Lake Kissimmee. He's already runnin cattle on it."

Archie stood. "All right," he said, then turned and began striding for the commissary down the tracks.

Tim watched him go. "All right?" he questioned himself. He shook his head. "That's one crazy sumbitch goin there."

*

Sarah's pains began in late February, it cold outside and a cruel wind from the north pummeling the trees within the hammock. She was helping Etta with breakfast when she suddenly grabbed her stomach and groaned.

Etta quickly escorted her to the bed and had her lie down. "Draw them knees up," she said. She leaned in and felt Sarah's distended belly. "It wantin to come out," she said. "We got to keep track of your pains, now. You let me know soon as you get the next one."

Sarah nodded, her eyes wide and watching Etta's every move. "Are you going to call John Morgan?"

Etta shook her head. "He's right outside if I need him. He's plantin them two cedars is all. He'll be in directly."

The pains continued to come, becoming much more regular toward late afternoon. John Morgan paced about the bed while Etta sat stoically reading Sarah's facial expressions, each successive pain's coming and going etched clearly there so that no word need be spoken. Sarah writhed and groaned and breathed and just after sunset her water broke, causing Etta to shoo John Morgan from the room.

"Boil me some water," she told him. "It won't be long now."

John Morgan hurried to the great room, to the kitchen stove where he loaded in kindling and lit it and then stood near panic when noticing he'd not fetched in oak for a proper fire. He bolted from the house and into the now full-grown night. He circled to the east end and began loading his arm with sawn oak. Having all that he could carry he turned, noticing as he did the sliver of moon almost straight overhead, the dibbler's moon which to him was a good omen and he felt adrenalin go through him as if he might have been touched by God, a touch of reassurance, he prayed, yet panic still gripped him and he leaped the steps and bounded into the house not at all certain of anything save for the need to stoke the fire.

A good fire going and the kettle of water beginning to steam, he heard Sarah scream, a long, wailing plea that cut him like a knife. He ran to the bedroom, arriving just in time to see Etta hoist aloft something resembling a skinned rabbit, to see her smack the bloody creature's bottom and hear it give forth a pronouncement of life again and again. He stood frozen, then he lunged to Sarah's side, tears streaming form his eyes as he saw her lying there wearing a tortured smile of relief.

"Where's that water?" said Etta. "You all's boy here needs a bath."

John Morgan leaned in and kissed Sarah. "It's a boy," he said. He kissed her again. "I need to fetch the water." He started to go but stopped and leaned in to kiss her again.

Sarah smiled. "Go ahead. I'm all right. You heard Etta. July needs a bath."

"July," he said. He looked at the bawling baby and looked at Sarah. He nodded and ran from the room.

Etta laughed out loud. "That man excited," she said. "Ain't no tellin what he goan bring back in here."

8

And Then He Was Old

The day following he sent word by Frank Finney to his aunt and uncle. Jude and Betty came that very day, their buggy careening into the yard with Betty holding to her hat and Jude hauling on the reins to slow his stubborn mule while paradoxically whooping and hollering as if to urge the trotting animal on. They brought with them prepared food and tiny blue articles of clothing darned and sewn by Betty's own hand. When asked how she'd known it would be a boy, Betty simply shrugged and said that she'd an identical set in pink at home, that the next baby should be a girl that her labor not be wasted.

In mid-July he rode to Bill Williams' with his six-month-old son perched in his lap, his hand so large cupping the baby to him and the horse's rocking gait causing the boy's head to bob as he slept the good sleep known only to innocents. The Williams doting over the child, saying repeatedly that he had his mother's eyes, eyes so dark and depthless that in years to come every woman in Florida would be in danger of falling prey to his charms.

As for John Morgan, he fell into the habit of wanting the boy with him, even when he had no particular place to go, nothing pressing to do. He'd ride talking to his son, explaining to him every detail of the land, the taxonomy of every plant and tree, every bird, snake, and animal they might encounter. They'd ride and he'd talk and the baby with his dark eyes wandering about, appearing to be keenly interested in all of which his father spoke. Whether this was true or not mattered little to John Morgan. In the sound of his own voice he found a contentment he'd never known. He felt suddenly whole with his son there pressed against him, the boy so helpless yet so full of promise and wonder that nothing else in the world mattered during these rides to nowhere. Nothing save for Sarah, for she had given him this precious gift. She had given him, in more ways than one, life itself, and he could not have loved her more for it.

*

One evening in September, the four of them relaxing on the porch after supper, an automobile appeared in the flatwoods north of Rawlerson Hammock.

"That's Bill Williams," John Morgan observed. "Wonder what brings him out this late in the day?"

Etta sat with July perched on her lap. "It usually bad news come late like this. Hope it ain't bad news he bringin."

The Model T rolled into the yard and stopped, Bill behind the wheel, another man, hatless, hair touching his shoulders, in the passenger seat beside him.

"Jesus," said John Morgan, slowly rising from his rocker, his eyes fixed on the long-haired fellow. "I believe that's Archie." He looked at Sarah. "That's my brother, Archie."

As the men exited the idling car, John Morgan leaped from the porch to greet them. He headed straight for Archie, stunned by what he saw when able to see his brother clearly: Archie in his rags with mouth agape, a top front tooth gone and him filthy with a stench of old sweat and a yeasty odor of rancid beer. A ratty leather satchel in his left hand and a bloody rag tied around his right, some of the blood appearing to be fresh. The dog Roy suddenly there and obviously loath to approach this strange visitor, it turning and slinking back to the porch with hackles raised. John Morgan stepped and stood, a pang of pity in the pit of his stomach. He looked at Bill Williams.

Bill shrugged. "He knocked on our door bout a hour ago, asked how to get here to your place."

John Morgan nodded. "He's my brother, Archie."

Bill nodded. "I finally got that out of him." He looked at Archie. "You ain't the most talkative feller, are you, son?"

Archie shook his head. He raised a hand and gestured to the porch. "Who's them people? What are they doin here?"

John Morgan looked at Bill. "I sure thank you for bringin him all the way out here. Have you had your supper?"

Bill reached and grabbed the steering wheel to climb back in his car. He nodded that he'd eaten. "I got to get back. Just happy I could help."

John Morgan raised a hand goodbye as Bill backed the car around and pulled away. He looked at Archie. "Damn, Arch, you're a sight. The first thing we got to do is get you a bath, get you into some decent clothes. What have you done to your hand?"

"Cut it with my knife, tryin to fix my shoe." He gestured toward the house. "Heard you mention supper. I could use somethin to eat."

John Morgan glanced at what his brother had called shoes, thinking it a stretch to call them anything but trash. "We got plenty of leftovers, but you ain't goin in the house till we scrub the road off you."

"Who are them people? You know you got a nigger woman settin on the porch?"

John Morgan stepped close to his brother. He glared at him. "That lady is a better person than you and me both. She lives here. I ever hear you cuss her like that agin, I'll run you off before you can say scat. Her name is Etta, and you best treat her nice or you won't be here long. I promise you that."

Archie grinned. "I got big, ain't I?"

John Morgan shook his head. "You've grown all right, just not in the way I was hopin you would."

Archie pointed to the porch. "That your wife? That man said you had a wife and kid."

He nodded. He turned to face the porch. "Sarah, Etta," he called, "say hey to my brother, Archie. See if y'all can find him some clothes. I'm fixin to burn these soon as he gets out of em. And bring me a cake of soap, please. I'm goan need lots of soap."

*

Sometime in the night Sarah was awakened by the baby. She rose and plucked July from his crib and went to the great room to nurse him. As she sat in her rocker to sate the baby's hunger she could just make out the form by the fireplace, Archie lying on a bed of quilts and him still as stone. She listened for his breathing but could hear nothing save for the soft and rhythmic sucking of the baby at her breast. Light from a full moon in the room and soon her eyes adjusted to the point where she imagined she could see her brother-in-law was awake, his head up and supported by a hand and him watching her.

"Did we wake you?" she asked in a tone just above a whisper.

Silence, the sounds of contentment issued by her baby but nothing more.

She watched, her eyes playing tricks until suddenly the head lowered, the certainty of what she saw causing a chill to crawl the length of her spine.

The morning following at breakfast Archie scarcely uttered a word. His eyes met no others save John Morgan's, and then only when his brother addressed him. When done eating John Morgan asked him outside and together they walked to the pole barn where he invited his brother to sit and talk. They sat with their backs to the stall boards, the day breaking around them and the rooster on its perch and making an occasional plea while the world beyond the hammock lay cloaked in fog.

"Did you come by Jude and Betty's? Do they know you're back?"

Archie shook his head. "I ain't left nothin there."

A look of puzzlement on John Morgan's face. "How are you feelin?"

Archie stared straight ahead. "I'm all right."

"You ain't all right. People try to be nice to you, and you act like they ain't even there. What's happened to you?"

Archie uncrossed his outstretched legs then crossed them back, reversing their order. "You left me," he said.

"I told you I'd be back. Why didn't you trust me? I've never lied to you."

"I don't trust nobody."

John Morgan studied his brother's profile. "You can't live like that."

Archie gestured with a hand toward the house. "You left me to go get that girl in there."

John Morgan looked, a sadness creeping into his eyes. "Yes, I did. We ain't kids no more. I've got a family now. That's what people do, you know. You grow up, get married and have kids of your own."

"I seen the way you look at her."

"What do you mean by that? Are you jealous of my wife?"

Archie poked at something in the dirt beside his leg. "I like your baby."

John Morgan shook his head, his look of sadness turning to one of frustration. "Talkin to you is like talkin to that rooster over there."

Archie cocked his head to have a look at said rooster. "Where'd you get him at? Is that Mama's rooster?"

John Morgan sighed. He got to his feet and dusted his pants. "Come on," he said. "I promised Etta I'd cut her a cabbage for supper." He watched Archie struggle to his feet and stand looking at him with his usual feckless grin there to spoil his face. "How'd you lose that tooth, anyway?"

Archie shrugged. "I just woke up one day and it was gone. Somebody must've socked me, I reckon."

*

His first two days on the place Archie shadowed John Morgan as he'd done in the long ago. He kept such close company that neither

Sarah nor Etta had a chance to express their concerns about his odd behavior. It was only when they'd retired for the night that Sarah felt comfortable speaking her mind.

"Is he going to stay?"

"No. I just ain't figured out how to do it. He's my brother. I need to try and set him on the right path, help him get his life straightened out."

Sarah stroked his hair. "You are good, John Morgan. You will find the right way."

"He scares you, don't he?"

"Yes, and Etta too. She thinks there is something wrong with his spirit. She says his eyes are as empty as his head."

"Etta," he said, stifling a chuckle. "She calls it like she sees it, don't she?"

"Has he always been this way?"

"He's been peculiar for as long as I can remember. He fell off a horse when he was three or four, got knocked unconscious. I think Mama and Daddy always figured that's what done it, figured the blow to his head addled his brain or somethin. But they'd never talk about it, as if maybe they thought it was somethin that would go away long as they never mentioned it."

"I am sorry for him, and sorry for you, my love. You do not deserve the worry he causes you."

John Morgan was silent. He pulled her in and held her long into the night, beyond conscious thought and on into nothingness.

When morning came Archie professed to be sick. He refused all pleas that he get up and accompany his brother to check the hog trap.

"I don't like leavin y'all alone with him," John Morgan said, having ushered the ladies to the yard. "I've a mind to cart his ass out of here right now. See him gone so I don't have the worry."

"But he is sick," said Sarah. "I don't want him to leave not feeling well."

"Huh," said Etta, "I think the only sick he be is in the head. I think he playin possum to get outta work."

Sarah shifted July's weight to her other arm. She looked at her husband. "He is sleeping. Perhaps he won't even know you are gone."

John Morgan nodded. "That's probably right. He'll sleep all day if you let him."

Sarah smiled. "We shall be quiet as mice."

John Morgan smiled. He reached and patted the baby's head. "All right," he said. "Sounds like a plan. Y'all be quiet and I'll hurry."

When out of sight of the house he put Shorty forward at a canter. He reached the trap in less than ten minutes, and was not at all surprised to see the gate was down. "Figures," he muttered to himself, stepping down from his horse and grabbing his rifle from its boot scabbard. He studied the two shoats in the trap but briefly before shouldering the rifle and dispatching the larger of the two. With the shoat still kicking, he reached and pulled the slide gate up and tied the line off. He harried the unmolested pig until it finally got the message and bolted to freedom. He leaned the rifle against the rails and ducked in through the gate. Grabbing a hind leg, he dragged the shoat out of the trap and over to his horse. He quickly tied all four legs together and hefted the pig up and onto the pommel horn to hang there like a satchel. He fetched his rifle and mounted up and headed for home, an ember of panic smoldering within him he could not extinguish.

Reaching the house he reined the horse hard, the animal planting its hooves and sliding through sand and leaves while John Morgan bailed out of the saddle and ran to the steps. He burst through the door and stopped, the house so quiet he could hear his heart hammering inside his chest like something trapped and trying to escape.

Etta, who had whirled about at his sudden entry, stood by the stove with mouth open and eyes wide. "Lawd, you give me a fright," she said. "You come in like the devil chasin you."

He looked at Etta and looked to the far side of the room where Archie lay as he left him. He eased the door closed. "Where's Sarah?"

"She in the bedroom, changin July."

He nodded and smiled sheepishly. He gestured toward the yard. "I got a pig to butcher," he said.

"Well, get to butcherin. We all right in here."

He started out the door but hesitated to look once again at his sleeping brother. He thumbed back his hat to scratch at something on his forehead then turned and continued on out the door.

He led his horse to the pole barn and unloaded its burden of swine. He slipped off its bridle and replaced it with a halter before giving it oats as reward for its dutiful labor. A look of contentment in the animal's eyes as it stood and ate, its tail in perpetual motion to ward off a squadron of bloodsucking flies come with the sun's first rays to penetrate the hammock's canopy.

In a hurry, he elected to not scald the pig. Instead he hung the shoat head-up from a rafter and dragged a washtub beneath it. He found the sternum with the point of his pocket knife and with an upward heave split the young animal's ribcage clear to the brisket. He returned to his starting point and slipped the blade between hide and viscera and in one smooth motion opened the carcass from sternum to bunghole as if it'd come equipped with a zipper. Next he cut through the diaphragm and reached up into the ribcage and past the lungs to sever the windpipe and grasp it just above the bronchial branch and pull downward to release all of the animal's miraculous internal design in a slow fall to the tub below, the ropy intestines the last to exit and him freeing them with a few flicks of his knife that traced the rectum's path to the outer world. He worked, strip-skinning the animal before quartering it, carrying to the pitcher pump each ham or shoulder where he'd wash them before moving on to the smokehouse to salt and hang the portion on one of the hooks there. He'd made several trips when movement on the porch stopped him as if the very march of time had suddenly come to its end. Archie in one of the rockers on the porch, his hands and forearms painted crimson as if he too had found work as a butcher, little July nested in his lap and the baby staring beseechingly at his father.

Something close to an electric shock ran through John Morgan, a shout of no in his brain though he'd no breath with which to voice it. He strode deliberately to the steps and up onto the porch, glaring at his brother as to catch his slightest move.

Archie merely sat as if completely shameless, as if the blood on his hands were a mystery to him as well.

Without hesitation John Morgan reached and took possession of his son. He stepped back and turned the baby this way and that to appraise his condition, him shaking so hard he could scarcely maintain his balance. He looked at Archie. "What have you done?"

Archie began to rock. "I made things right," he said.

John Morgan backed toward the door, his breathing shallow and rapid, his heart pounding and resurrecting a pain long buried in his memory. At the door he heard a groan within the house, the sound prompting him to action. He sidled through the doorway and shut and barred the door behind him. When he turned Etta was there on the floor by the woodstove, her sitting but trying to rise to her feet, blood on her neck and on the floor at her back, her eyes wide and panning right and left as if searching for an explanation. The fireplace poker on the floor next to her and she reached and touched it, gingerly, as though puzzled by how it came to be there.

John Morgan hurried to her and offered her a hand so that she might stand, the baby in his arm and him seemingly reveling in all his father's quick movements and the sight of his Etta suddenly rising before him. When he thought her steady, John Morgan inspected the crown of her head, the graying hair matted with blood.

"I don't know what happened," said Etta.

"Archie," John Morgan said. "He hit you with the poker."

Etta looked at him, her eyes like saucers. "Sarah," she said.

John Morgan could but shake his head, the panic in his eyes explaining better than words the nature of his fear. He helped Etta to the table and had her sit. A trail of blood drops on the floor and his eyes tracking them against his will. He gave July to Etta to hold, knowing in his heart that he was about to step into hell. He turned and read the crimson story to the bedroom, his legs threatening to fail him yet him drawn forward by the knowledge that the task at hand was his and his alone. At the doorway he held to the frame and stood like a man turned to stone, the sight he beheld killing instantly the remnant of little boy within him. He loosed himself from the doorjamb and stumbled forward, dropping to this knees to hold the limp body lying on the blood-soaked bed. He wept, convulsed by the sight of his dead Sarah, by the pain of knowing his everything, his reason for living was gone.

*

Sometime later he became aware of a hand on his shoulder. Etta, her face tracked with tears and her patting his shoulder, her head wagging slowly from side to side.

"She gone," she said. "Our poor Sarah done gone to meet her folks."

John Morgan glanced at his dead wife, the sight causing his stomach to lurch. He rolled away from the body and sat up. "Where's July?"

"He sleeping in my room." Etta swung her left arm into view, the arm she had thus far kept behind the folds of her dress. In that hand was John Morgan's big revolver. "He still out there settin on the porch," she said.

He looked at the pistol and looked at Etta, exhaling a sigh of resignation. "He's mad," he said, speaking more to himself than to Etta. "My brother is completely mad."

Etta nodded. "I'd of killed him myself, but I ain't knowin how to work this thing."

He took the pistol from her and spun the cylinder to make sure it was loaded. He stood, glancing again at Sarah's body, at the gory smile below her chin. "How long have I been in here?"

Etta shrugged. "It the middle of the afternoon," she said.

"And he's still out there?"

"Settin there like he just waitin for you to come do it, he is."

He started for the door but stopped. "You reckon you can clean her up? I don't know as I can do it."

"You go on. I can do it. That ain't Sarah there. That be her earthly vessel is all. Sarah with God now." Etta paused and gestured vaguely toward the front of the house. "And don't go thinkin that's your brother out there. The devil done got your brother."

He nodded and walked from the room. He stuffed the pistol in his waistband as he strode to the front door. When he stepped out onto the porch Archie scarcely paid him a glance.

"I was wonderin where you were," said Archie. "You left your horse saddled, you know. Daddy'll whip you good if he finds out."

John Morgan studied his brother. "You won't tell him, will you?"

Archie looked. "You think I'm crazy, don't ya?"

"The thought has crossed my mind."

"Well, I ain't crazy. I heard y'all talkin this mornin, heard you say how you was gonna run me off on account of how them women don't want me here. Well, now you ain't got to, now that I took care of them bitches." Archie rocked. He parried the air with a hand. "I reckon you're happy I ain't hurt the baby. I like the baby. Me and him gonna have a good time round here."

"I doubt that."

Archie looked.

"Come on, let's saddle your horse. Maybe we'll do a little fishin. I hear the bluegills are beddin."

Archie unseated himself from the chair. He checked that his knife was in its sheath. "Where we goan find us some crickets?"

"We'll just dig some worms. I know a place got lots of worms."

*

An orange sun stood just above the treetops as they set out, John Morgan leading the way with the shovel balanced across his lap and rocking to Shorty's gait. They rode north, crossing the palmetto flats and on to Orange Hammock. When about to enter the oaks and palms, Archie thought of something they'd forgot.

"We ain't brought no poles," he said.

"I got poles at the lake. Got a boat we can use, too."

"We got us a boat now?"

"It ain't mine, but the feller that owns it lets me use it."

"It ain't Uncle Jude's, is it?"

"No. It belongs to a feller you don't know. Uncle Jude ain't never had a boat."

Archie looked up at the sky as if something there had drawn his attention. He shrugged. "Well, he could of got one. I been gone, you know." He gestured toward his brother. "Why'd you bring that pistol?"

"Snakes," said John Morgan.

Once in the hammock John Morgan wove his way to the citrus trees and halted his horse. He stepped down and stuck the shovel in the ground, the light fading beneath the trees and there no wind yet the day's heat beginning to wane. He turned and looked up at his brother.

"Why don't you pick us a couple of oranges while I see if I can find some worms."

Archie dismounted. "They any good?"

"That first tree there is real good. They ain't quite ripe but close enough."

As Archie walked to the tree John Morgan grabbed the shovel and stepped next to the two mounds already there. A yellow fly bit his neck and he swatted it dead, muttering to himself about the pain inflicted by such a small insect. He positioned a boot on the shovel's trailing edge and used his weight to drive its point deep into the ground. He dug, glancing at his brother's efforts to reach an orange.

"Why did you have to come back, Arch? Why didn't you just stay gone?"

Archie looked with his clueless grin but said nothing. He turned back and tried once again to reach the lowest orange. "I can't reach one, damn it. You're all the time tellin me to do somethin you know I can't do."

"Well, I promise to never do that again," said John Morgan, the pistol raised and him sighting down its barrel. The explosion that followed caused both horses to scream and bolt sideways as Archie dropped as if falling through a trap door, a nearly ripe orange clutched in his right hand and it still there even after he'd struck the ground. He lay without moving, nary a twitch or contraction of muscle.

John Morgan lowered the pistol and stood looking at what he'd done. "God help me," he said, "I've killed my brother."

*

Etta was on the porch when he rode into the yard with the paint horse following behind. A lamp lit and on the floor beside the chair where she sat rocking little July. The sun gone and the little night-hawks John Morgan called bullbats swooping and diving after mosquitos somewhere above the hammock's canopy, their forays announced by the sound of wind rushing past folded wings, a sound he usually enjoyed. But tonight he did not hear them. Tonight his senses were numb to all save the sight of Etta rocking his son, Sarah's son.

Once he'd cared for the horses he joined Etta inside. They sat at the kitchen table mum for the most part until Etta's common sense began to cultivate a field wherein she planted seeds of hope surely to produce a future, prospects seemingly glum at best but a future nonetheless.

"I tried to clean up best I could."

John Morgan nodded. "You done good. I really appreciate it." He sipped his coffee, his eyes set deep in his head by dark circles resembling lamp black. "How's your head? You may need stitches."

"It don't feel like it. Feel like my old mop of hair come in handy. Take more than that old poker to crack this skull." She sat with both hands grasping her mug, turning it on the table thoughtfully. "Why you reckon he ain't killed me?"

"He thought he did."

"God knows you done the right thing, you know. You did what you had to do."

John Morgan shook his head. "I should of never gone to Missouri. If Sarah was still there she'd still be alive."

Etta's eyes smoldered. "Alive?" she blurted. "You hush with that kind of talk. She ain't had no life till you come and got her. These years with you the only life she had." She shook a finger at him. "That kind of talk don't look like you."

John Morgan looked at her and looked at his cup, his tired eyes growing moist. "You're right," he said. "I'll build the coffin in the mornin. I got plenty of cypress left over from buildin the cowpens."

"You thought about where? The only graveyard I seen is that one in Kenansville."

"I've got the place. Sarah picked it herself." His eyes began to swim. He sighed and reached and took up his cup. He sipped coffee with his eyes closed.

"When? The weather too warm to wait too long."

"Tomorrow, if I can get the coffin done soon enough. I don't want to stretch it out like I had to do with Mama. I ain't goin through that again."

Etta's eyebrows arched. "What about the preacher? It the middle of the week."

John Morgan shook his head. "I wouldn't know where to even look for him. Besides, Uncle Jude'll do it. He knows the Bible better than most. We'll go by there tomorrow. It's out of the way but there ain't no help for it. I've got to let him and Betty know what's happened."

Etta nodded. "Who else we goan tell about this? Ain't nobody goan miss that fool Archie, but folks bound to wonder bout Sarah."

John Morgan stared into space. "I'll miss him," he said. "He was my brother. Bad as he turned out to be, I'll still miss him."

Etta dipped her head. "I know," she said. "I hadn't ought to talk like that."

"As for who I'm gonna tell, I'll tackle those problems when they get here." He captured Etta's eyes with his. "The one person that's never to be told is July. He's to never know about any of what's happened. His mama died givin birth."

Etta nodded. "Lord knows he don't need to know."

"Speakin of the boy, how are we going to feed him? You ever cared for a child with no mama?"

"Don't you worry bout that. Old Etta got her ways. That boy goan be all right."

Later that night, after Etta had bedded down with the baby, John Morgan sat with Sarah's body. He spoke to her until fatigue overtook him and he descended into dreams wherein she was once again whole and in which there were no such words as pain or sorrow or death, dreams in which there was only life and love as they had once known them. Dreams that would be his food for life during all his days to come.

*

The morning following he milked the cow and fell to building the coffin. While he worked in the pole barn, Etta wrapped the body in muslin. Around ten John Morgan declared himself done, though his finished product he thought crude compared to his uncle's work. Yet Etta seemed impressed when seeing it, saying that Sarah would be proud of his efforts.

Together they carried the box into the house and loaded in the body. They stood and prayed silently before nailing the lid shut, before their last glimpse of the woman they loved. He hitched the mules to the wagon and brought it around to the front steps where they loaded the coffin while little July watched from his bed of quilts on the porch floor, him on hands and knees and rocking in place, jabbering in tongues known only to him.

It almost noon when they left for his aunt and uncle's place, they didn't get far before having reason to stop: Bill Williams and son Will in their auto and obviously on their way to see them. The mules leery of the noisy machine approaching on the crude road and them balking with the Model T still a hundred yards out.

When a few yards away Bill made a hard right turn into the low palmettos where he parked the vehicle. He left the motor idling and strode quickly to the wagon. He looked up at John Morgan as if about to speak when he noticed the coffin.

Bill looked at the coffin and looked at his friend. He opened his mouth but only pointed at the coffin, his expression the picture of puzzlement.

John Morgan nodded. "It's Sarah," he said.

Bill removed his cap and shook his head. "Oh my God," he said. "I—I'm so sorry." He continued to shake his head in wonderment. "What's goin on around here? What happened? How did she die?"

John Morgan seemed scarcely able to look at the man. "She was murdered," he said.

Bill's eyes narrowed. "Your brother."

John Morgan nodded.

Bill gave a knowing nod of his own. "Well, I'm sorry to have to add to this misery, but that ain't all he's done. I was on my way to tell you about your aunt and uncle."

John Morgan sat up straight as Etta covered her mouth with her free hand.

"The sheriff come by this mornin, told me Jude and Betty were found dead by Jude's bossman. Jude hadn't showed for work the last two days, old Gus went by to see what was wrong. Found em dead in their bed. Somebody had cut their throats."

John Morgan hung his head, his hat slipping from his head but him catching it and saying: "Shit."

Etta simply said: "Betty," and then began to cry. She hugged little July to her, him waking and looking this way and that.

"Where is he now, son? I told the sheriff about him comin to my house and him all bloody and sayin he'd cut hisself."

John Morgan seemed dazed. He looked at Bill for a few seconds before answering him. "He's dead," he said. "I put him down."

Bill stood digesting what he'd heard. "Damn," he said. He stepped and stood. "You takin Sarah in to the funeral home? They already took Jude and Betty, took em to that one in Kissimmee."

John Morgan shook his head. "I'm goan handle it myself."

Bill looked. He scratched the back of his neck. "You know the law is goin to want to know about this. I'd hate to see you find yourself in a fix, on top of everything that's happened."

"Reckon I'll worry bout that when it happens. Right now I've got to bury my wife." John Morgan looked at Etta. "You goan be all right?"

Etta wiped at her cheeks with the back of her free hand. She nodded and patted little July's bottom. She looked at Bill. "There goan be a service for the Vickers?"

Bill shrugged. "Sheriff said he'd notify Betty's people. I reckon they'll handle everything. They live up around Orlando." He looked at John Morgan. "I don't know that Jude has anybody."

"He's got me," John Morgan said. "They've got plots already bought in the Kenansville cemetery. I know cause he told me when Mama died."

Bill nodded. He gestured to the coffin. "Well, where you fixin to bury Sarah, if you don't mind me knowin?"

John Morgan gestured to the north. "Under a big live oak up there aways. Her and me found it a while back, looks like somebody used to live there at one time."

Bill nodded. "That old oak on a rise between them two cypress heads."

"That's the place," John Morgan said. He pointed to Bill's auto. "You and Will are welcome to join us."

"I'd like that, but I ain't sure the motorcar will make it up there. We'll have to go fetch our horses."

"You'll have time. I ain't dug the grave yet."

"All right, we'll see you up there," said Bill. He turned to go but stopped and looked back. "You don't mind if I bring Diane, do you? She thought the world of Sarah."

"Course I don't mind," said John Morgan. "And bring your Bible, if you will. I come off without ours thinkin Jude would bring his."

"I'll bring it," Bill said, turning and striding for his car.

He had the grave almost dug when Bill and family arrived at the oak, them rocking and swaying about the seat of their old mule-drawn wagon when they circled the tree in order that they park in its shade. The late September day hot and John Morgan shirtless and glistening with sweat. Etta and the baby on a quilt next to the oak's trunk and watching him labor, watching a pair of crows put to flight by the wagon's noisy arrival.

The ceremony they held was brief, none in attendance being schooled in such matters to where they might be tempted to prolong the inevitable. After John Morgan and Will lowered the coffin into the grave, Bill read the Lord's Prayer from his Bible and took a step back as if inviting others to have a say. And they each in turn said their goodbyes, their personal pleas to God that He might accept this daughter into heaven, that if there be but room for one more He could make no better choice than to take His angelic Sarah. For she was surely the purest of heart and soul, the best human any of them had ever known. Then John Morgan began to cover the coffin, pitching in dirt as though gripped by trance or spell while Etta and Diane sang "Just as I Am," repeating the verses they knew by heart until all the dirt had been moved, until John Morgan stood tall and leaned heavily on his shovel as though without it he'd surely fall.

He vowed that she'd have a fine stone memorial and then he expressed his love a final time before uttering the "ashes to ashes" he'd heard said so often before.

*

Three days later he attended the funeral for Jude and Betty at the Vickers' plot just north of Kenansville. Etta and July with him and the day overcast and it drizzling rain. He met Betty's brother and sister and felt obligated to explain to them all that had happened. He explained not only to them but to the sheriff as well, the sheriff a portly bald fellow who stood in his dark suit listening with raised eyebrows and when done listening who warned that John Morgan may not have seen the last of him. The dead had to be accounted for, he'd stated while jotting down all the particulars, the names and ages, the vague locations of the deceased. "You'll be hearing from me," he'd called from his automobile, though John Morgan never would. It was the last time he'd ever see the man concerning the matter.

*

In the days following he rode to Kissimmee and commissioned a headstone for Sarah. Two weeks later he went and got it and positioned it at the west end of the grave, the head of the grave from which he imagined Sarah would witness every sunrise to come, every new dawn until the sun was no more and there no mind to grieve its passing. He wept long at this thought and then climbed aboard his wagon and urged the mules westward toward Orange Hammock.

He left the wagon in the flatwoods and entered the oaks and palms on foot. It early in October and a subtle change in the air, less humidity and a cooling breeze that eddied through the trees instigating soft rustlings and much movement to entertain the eye. When almost to the citrus trees he smelled smoke. He stopped and tested the air, stood listening and searching with his eyes the conflict of light and shadow so profound within the hammock. Definitely smoke. He moved on to discover two persons seated tailorwise before a small fire, an old man and a young boy who wore their hair long and had eyes dark as onyx, the two of them relaxed and watching him come as if perhaps expecting him. A great sadness living in the old man's eyes as he raised a hand of welcome.

"Come," he said, "sit with us and we will talk."

John Morgan stepped forward and settled on the ground across the fire from the pair. He gripped the toes of his boots and watched the bright eyes of the boy, the small replica of the fire dancing in each. "What are y'all up to?" he said.

The man waved a hand at the oldest of the three graves. "We have come to speak with my grandfather, to tell him how goes the world and ask of him his opinion."

"I figured that was a grave," said John Morgan.

The old man nodded. He gestured again to the mounds. "Are these your people?"

The boy plucked a branch from a small pile by his leg. He broke the oak in half and fed both pieces to the fire. He watched John Morgan with what appeared to be a keen interest.

"One of em is. That one on the right is my brother."

"And you have come to speak with him."

"Yessir, I reckon so."

The old man nodded, his gray hair lifting and falling to an errant breeze that found its way through the trees. "The sadness in your eyes tells me this is true. Was his a good death?"

"No. He wasn't a good person."

The old man looked but did not comment. "I am told that my grandfather was a fierce warrior, a man who died on this very spot when he met an even fiercer soldier who had come to take our people away. I do not know this soldier's name. I only know my grandfather died so that the people could run away and hide. If he did not die that day we would not know this land. We would be lost in a world not of our choosing."

John Morgan nodded. "Oklahoma," he said.

"Yes. That is how it is called. I am told I have relatives there, though I have never met them and never will."

John Morgan gestured to the graves. "You all right with this?"

The old man shrugged. "What does it matter what I think? You are the white man. You make the rules in this time. Our time is gone."

"I care what you think. I ain't lookin to offend nobody."

The old man looked at the boy. "What do you think? Do these graves offend us?"

The boy shook his head. He picked up a branch from his pile and used it to poke at the coals.

"Well, I'm glad," said John Morgan. He untangled his legs and stood and dusted his breeches. "I got to go. I got people probably wonderin where I am."

"But you have not spoken to your brother. We will go away for a while, so you can visit with him."

John Morgan raised his hands in protest. "Don't do that. I don't even know why I come here."

"You come because he was your brother. Good or bad, he is still your brother."

"Yessir, I reckon that's it."

The old man raised a hand farewell. "If this boy here wishes to visit his ancestor, will you permit him?"

John Morgan looked at the boy. "Long as you don't mess with my cows, you can come anytime you want."

The boy smiled. "Thank you," he said.

*

The third week in October he learned from Frank Finney that Barely had died in a trench somewhere in France. Hearing this news, he persuaded Frank to stay with Etta and the baby for a few days, giving no other reason save that he needed time to think.

He left before first light on a Monday morning, it an overcast and gloomy day with the threat of rain carried by a steady southwesterly breeze yet him going without hesitation. He rode south across trackless land until striking the Peavine Grade just west of the Kenansville town limit. He followed the grade several miles then quit it and headed southeast toward the railroad. Crossing the tracks near Lokosee, he began following the old Hungry Land Trail. He stopped for the night beside the small drain where he and his mama and his brother had once rested. In the morning he made a fire sufficient to make coffee and ate jerky and bread brought with him before setting out again. He rode without stopping and he passed through the land he once considered his own and he passed by his home now occupied by strangers, by orange groves stretching to the horizon where once had been only pine and palmetto. New houses and businesses as he reached Ft. Pierce, it getting dark and the town aglow with electric lights. He turned north on Delaware and rode to the cemetery. Quiet, with lights on in the parsonage but the grounds otherwise dark. He dismounted and stood by the graves of his father and mother, his two sisters. The headstones pleased him, the dates and spelling all correct. He sat on the ground and watched a full moon's slow rise in the east. Talking as though in a family meeting, he related all that had happened to him since the others had died. He talked and then he bowed his head and cried, sobbing long into the night before righting himself and walking to the pastor's door. He knocked and when the door opened he removed his hat and stepped back as not to alarm the man framed within.

"Sorry to bother you," he said. "I just wanted to thank you for taking care of my mother and father's gravestones."

The pastor leaned to better see who was thanking him. "Rawlerson," he said. He offered his hand and they shook and he stepped back to look at John Morgan. "My lord, you've grown." Then he must have read the eyes for his demeanor suddenly shifted. "You're not here to bury someone are you?"

"Nosir, not tonight."

"Well, come on in. We can warm some supper for you."

John Morgan shook his head. He put his hat on and half turned away. "I thank you for the offer, but I need to be goin."

"Well, may God bless you, son. It sure was good to see you are doing all right. You are all right, aren't you?"

"I've been better," John Morgan said. He turned to go but stopped and looked back at the pastor. "You were right," he said.

The pastor smiled. "How's that?"

"You told me life is like a sad song."

The pastor scratched his head. "Yes, I probably did. I've been known to use that metaphor. It's one that I truly believe."

"Yessir. I believe it too."

He rode all that night and was back on the Hungry Land Trail when the sun's first rays stretched over the land. He stopped to rest his horse in a stand of pines alongside the trail, removing the saddle and bridle and simply letting the animal roam free in search of palatable grass. He pulled the Winchester rifle from its scabbard and moved to a large pine. He sat with his back to the tree's shady side and laid the rifle in his lap and fished his knife from his pocket. Opening the blade, he began to carve on the stock, working tediously for a good long while and then raising the weapon to the sun's light to inspect his work. "JMR," he read, and then he put his knife away and tipped his hat forward on his head. He dozed until something woke him, a rambling voice that somehow seemed familiar. When he thumbed back his hat to look, he thought that perhaps he was dreaming.

A stooped figure was headed south on the trail, long white hair and flowing beard, staff in hand and walking a staggered gait so slow that it appeared his own shadow might overtake him.

"Hey," John Morgan called.

The man stopped in his tracks, leaning on his staff. He cocked his head to see who was calling. "Hey to you," he said. He pulled at the strap snaking over his shoulder to the bag holding his worldly possessions. "You know your horse has got loose? Seen him back aways."

"He knows where I am. Come over and I'll fix us some coffee."

"Don't mind if I do," said the man, him turning in small increments until facing east whereupon he began to close the distance between them, stabbing with his staff and stepping and stabbing again.

"Do you remember me?" John Morgan asked.

The man only a few feet away turned enough that he could see the questioner. "Can't say that I do," he said.

"It was three, four years ago. My mama and me met you on this very trail. You was headed to Miami, you said, runnin away from winter."

The man chuckled. "Reckon things don't change much, do they?"

John Morgan looked at the man's bare feet. A pang of pity coursing through him. "Well, have a seat," he said. "I'll get a fire goin, fix us some coffee."

He built the fire and fetched water from the drain that was just up the way. When the coffee had boiled he poured his cup to the brim and handed it to the man, along with a slice of salt pork and a hard biscuit.

The man watched him. "You've only the one cup, ain't ye?"

"That's all right. I'll have some after you're done."

"That's uncommonly kind of ye, my boy. It's not often I run into somebody willin to drink after the likes of me."

"Yeah, well, I got a question for you. What keeps you goin? I mean, do you have family?"

The man chewed his pork. "I did once. They all dead. Been dead for years. That's how come me to take up the road. See the sights, ye know. Figure long as I keep movin, old death can't get me. I owe it to God to keep livin, you see. If He'd wanted me, he'd of taken me long ago. I reckon He's kept me here for a purpose. I believe everybody's got their purpose. Mine, I suspect, is to show other folks how good they got it." He laughed and took another bite of the meat.

John Morgan watched the man, thinking about what he'd said. "Don't you miss your family?"

"Sure I do, but where does that get me? I try not to look back too much. There ain't nothin back there I can change, so what's the use. Remember the good, is what I say. The good will sustain ye." He paused to swallow then pointed to John Morgan. "If you've lost family, ask yourself what they'd want you to do, then go on and do it. It's as simple as that, I think. Just go on and do what will make them happy."

John Morgan slowly nodded his head. He stood and whistled sharply, then bent to packing away his things. "I'm sorry to hurry you, but I got to get goin. You just convinced me I got work to do, and plenty of reason to do it."

The old man passed him the cup and reached for his staff. "Me, too," he said. "Winter's comin and I'm too far north."

The horse Shorty trotted into the stand of pines and stood obligingly waiting. As John Morgan saddled the animal he posed a question to the man. "If I give you some money, will you use it to buy you some shoes?"

The man was on his feet but not yet at his former height. He looked at John Morgan. "Keep your money. I ain't never liked shoes, and I ain't about to change now."

"Just thought I'd ask," said John Morgan.

The old man nodded. He reached with his staff and got underway, stabbing and stepping. "May God bless you on your journey, son, bless you as He surely has me."

He rode the sun down that day and did not stop save to water his horse and relieve himself. The just-past-full moon his guiding light, he left the tracks at Kenansville, setting a course for the land he'd come to think of as his own, the land where his Sarah lay waiting, where the two people he cared most for patiently awaited his return. Home is where he was going and it was only now that he realized his sad song was far from over, that his Sarah and his mother and father and sisters were all watching him, depending on him to carry on. With this thought he rode as he had always ridden, as a man driven by purpose, the world dark and very still, not a whisper of wind, and above the ancient night sky's stellar beauty there for all to see and beneath him the heat of a good horse and him riding tall with eyes fixed straight ahead. He rode thusly into a future known only to God. He rode and he did not look back.